Without another word Amaranth walked into the slow, dark water eddying beneath the limbs of a twisted, low-hanging tree. After a minute, Amaranth's head broke the surface. "I heard them!" she cried wildly. "I heard angels! Singing!"

"Magic," snorted Gydrik derisively. "Come on, you'll catch your death. Dry off and get dressed, and then we'll go back to the cabin."

She emerged from the river like a young goddess or a princess of the sea nymphs. The rank odor of the close and tenacious ointment thickened the air, but Gydrik hardly noticed. He felt a hot flush rip through his body as he saw Amaranth as if for the first time. She was more than pretty, more than lovely—she was the absolute, divine embodiment of beauty. She was the perfect model of everything the human soul aspired to. She was—irresistible.

"Amaranth," he whispered hoarsely.

"What is it? This damned stuff doesn't want to wash off. I'm going to have to smell it until it *wears* off. I don't know if I can stand it."

"Amaranth, I love you."

She looked up at him, pleased. "Oh, Gydrik, I feel the same way about—" Then her face fell. "Ah, I see: the magic. The spell's made you want me."

Magic In Ithkar 2

Edited By
André Norton
And
Robert Adams

A TOM DOHERTY ASSOCIATES BOOK

MAGIC IN ITHKAR 2

Copyright © 1985 by André Norton and Robert Adams

First printing: December 1985

A TOR Book

Published by Tom Doherty Associates
49 West 24 Street
New York, N.Y. 10010

Cover art by Walter Velez

ISBN: 0-812-54745-4
CAN. ED.: 0-812-54746-2

Printed in the United States of America

Acknowledgments

"Prologue" copyright © 1985 by Robert Adams

"Flux of Fortune" copyright © 1985 by Mildred Downey Broxon

"Geydelle's Protective" copyright © 1985 by Lin Carter

"If There Be Magic" copyright © 1985 by Marylois Dunn

"Babes on Bawd Way" copyright © 1985 by George Alec Effinger

"Sardofa's Horseshoes" copyright © 1985 by Gregory Frost

"The Ruby Wand of Asrazel" copyright © 1985 by Joseph Green

"Bird of Paradise" copyright © 1985 by Linda Haldeman

"Flaming-Arrow" copyright © 1985 by R. A. Lafferty

"The Shaman Flute" copyright © 1985 by Shariann Lewitt

"Shadow Quest" copyright © 1985 by Brad Linaweaver

"Kissmeowt and the Healing Friar" copyright © 1985 by A. R. Major

"The Cards of Eldrianza" copyright © 1985 by Mary H. Schaub

"The Marbled Horn" copyright © 1985 by Lynn Ward

Table of Contents

Prologue by Robert Adams   1

Flux of Fortune by Mildred Downey Broxon   10

Geydelle's Protective by Lin Carter   35

If There Be Magic by Marylois Dunn   42

Babes on Bawd Way by George Alec Effinger   71

Sardofa's Horseshoes by Gregory Frost   97

The Ruby Wand of Asrazel by Joseph Green   120

Bird of Paradise by Linda Haldeman   144

Flaming-Arrow by R. A. Lafferty   169

The Shaman Flute by Shariann Lewitt   190

Shadow Quest by Brad Linaweaver   212

Kissmeowt and the Healing Friar by A. R. Major   235

The Cards of Eldrianza by Mary H. Schaub   253

The Marbled Horn by Lynn Ward   280

Biographical Notes   303

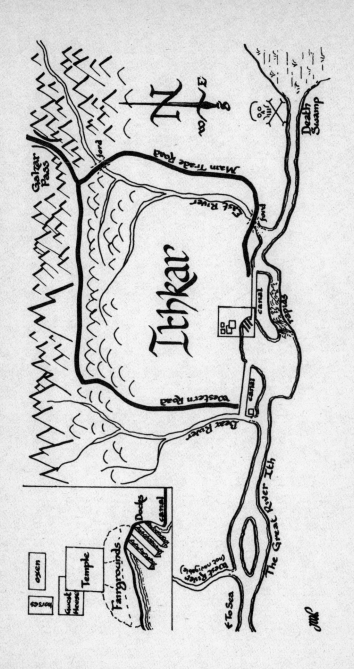

PROLOGUE

Robert Adams

The Three Lordly Ones are said to have descended in their sun-bright Egg and come to rest on a spot near to the bank of the river Ith. The priests of their temple reckon this event to have occurred four hundred, two score, and eight years ago (and who should better know?). Though the Three never made any claim to godhead, they now are adored as such, and for at least four centuries, many pilgrims have come on the anniversary of the day of their coming to render their worship and to importune the Three to return.

The Three are said to have remained on the spot of their descent for almost a generation—twenty-one years and seven months—though they journeyed often in smaller Eggs that, it is told, could move far faster than even a shooting star and so bore them in only a bare day across snowy and impassable mountains, across stormy and monster-infested seas, to lands that most folk know only in fable.

Since not even the learned priests can fine down the exact date of their coming closer than a ten-day, pilgrims came and still come all during this period, and centuries ago, the Ithkar Temple and its denizens lived out the rest of each year on the donations of the pilgrims, the produce of the temple's ploughlands, orchards, and herds, plus whatever edible fish they could catch in the Ith.

But wheresoever numbers of folk do gather for almost any purpose, other folk will come to sell them necessaries and luxuries. Pilgrimage Ten-day at Ithkar Temple was no different. Each year succeeding, more and more peddlers and hawkers gathered around the temple, the more astute arriving before the start of Holy Ten-day, so as to be well set up for business upon the influx of even the first-day pilgrims. Of course, other sellers, noting that these merchants always appropriated the best locations, began to plan their arrivals even earlier to claim these spots for their own. Within a few more years, most of the merchants were in place a full ten-day before the beginning of Holy Ten-day and many of the pilgrims then began to come earlier, in search of the bargains and rare merchandise often to be found at Ithkar Fair, as it was coming to be called far and wide.

Now, in modern times, the Fair at Ithkar has lengthened to three full ten-days in duration and still is extending in time even as it increases in size.

Nearly seventeen score years ago, the then high priest of Ithkar Temple, one Yuub, realized that the priests and priestesses of the shrine were mostly missing out on a marvelous source of easy, laborless income. He it was who first sacrificed the nearer gardens—betwixt the temple enclave and the river-lake—and made of them three (later, four) campgrounds for the merchants and tradesmen, so that they no longer surround the temple on all sides as in the past. He it was, also, who first hired on temporary fair-wards—local bullies and old soldiers—to maintain order with their bronze-shod staves, enforce the will of the priests, and collect the monies due for the marked-off shop-spaces during the fair.

As the Temple at Ithkar waxed richer, successors to old Yuub continued to improve the temple and its environs. A guest house was built onto the northwestern corner of the temple's main building in order to house the wealthier and nobler pilgrims in a greater degree of comfort (for which, of course, they were charged a more substantial figure than those who bode in tents, pavilions, or wagons or who simply rolled in a blanket on a bit of ground under the stars). A guest stable followed shortly, then a partially roofed pen for draft oxen. The next project was a canal to bypass the terrible rapids that lay between the East River's confluence with the river Ith and the Harbor of Ithkar.

Two centuries ago, a high priest arranged to have huge logs of a very hard, dense, long-lasting wood rafted down from the northern mountains, then paid the hire of workmen to sink them as footings for the three long docks below the lower fair precincts, these to replace the old floating-docks which had for long received water-borne pilgrims, fairgoers, traders, merchants, and the like. Now these docking facilities are utilized year-round by users of the main trade road that wends from the steppes up the northern slopes of the mountains, through demon-haunted Galzar Pass, then down the south slopes and the foothills and the plain to the Valley of the Ith. Southbound users of the main trade road had, before the building of the docks and the digging of the canal, been obliged to either ford the East River well to the northeast, prior to its being joined by tributaries and thus widened, then to follow a road that led down to a ford not far above the Ith, or to raft down the East River, then portage around the rapids and falls.

With the great success of the temple or eastern canal there clear for all to see, the great noble whose lands lay just to the west of the lands of the temple in the Ith Valley had dug a longer, somewhat wider canal connecting Bear River to the harbor and its fine docks, charging fees for the use of his canal and, through arrangement, sharing in the commerce-taxes that the temple derived from year-round use of its docks by the transmontane traders, hunters, trappers, and steppe nomads who tended to use the Bear River route rather than the main trade road.

Before Bear River was rendered navigable by an earthquake that eliminated the worst of its rapids, the folk who used it had come down into Ith Valley via the longer, harder western road rather than the eastern through well-founded fear of wide-ranging denizens of the Death Swamp.

Many long centuries before the blessed arrival of the Three, it is related, a huge and prosperous city lay on the banks of the Ith somewhere within what now is deadly swamp but then were pleasant, fertile lands and pastures, vineyards, and orchards. But the people of this city were not content with the richness of the life they enjoyed, so they and other cities made war upon another coalition of lands and cities, using not only swords and spears and iron maces and bows, but terrible weapons that bore death from afar—death not only for warriors, but for entire cities and lands and all of their people and beasts. It was one such weapon as these that destroyed the city, rendered all living things within it dead in one terrible day and night, left all of the wrecked homes and empty buildings not destroyed outright clustered about a new lake created by the weapon, a long and wide and shallow lake with a bottom composed of green glass.

In those long-ago days it was that lands surrounding the destroyed and lifeless city earned the name of Death Swamp, for many of the most fertile of the former city's lands had lain well below the usual level of the river Ith and had been protected from riverine encroachments by miles of earthern levees, but with no care or maintenance of those levees, spring floods first weakened them, then breached them and inundated field and farm, pasture and vineyard and orchard. Within a very short time, reeds waved high over expanses that once had produced grain-crops, while monstrous, sinuous shapes wriggled through the muck that had so lately been verdant pasturelands filled with sleek kine.

Monstrous beasts, kin of the mountain dragons, dwelt in many swamplands and in as many near swamp wastes— this was a fact known to all—but the denizens of Death Swamp were not as these more normal beasts, it was said, being deformed in sundry ways, larger ofttimes, and more deadly. It also was said that the Death Swamp monsters were of preternatural sentience.

Descriptions of the Death Swamp monsters were almost all ancient ones, for precious few ever deliberately penetrated the dim, overgrown, terrible place that even the Three had warned should be avoided, adding that there were other places akin to it in lurking deadliness hither and yon in the world, sites rendered by the forgotten weapons of that long-ago war inimical to all forms of natural life.

Of the few who do brave the Death Swamp, fewer still

come out at all, and many of those are mad or have changed drastically in manners of thinking, acting, and speech, and seldom for the better. The sole reason that any still venture within the lands and waters surrounding that blasted city is the extraordinarily high prices that wizards will pay for artifacts of that ancient place, many of which have proven to be of great and abiding power. And magic is as much a part of this world as the air and the water, the fire and the very earth itself.

The fair precincts are surrounded by palings of peeled logs sunk into the earth some foot or so apart, and those entering the gates must surrender all weapons other than eating-knives. Be they merchants or traders, they and the wares they would purvey must undergo questioning, weighing, and scrutiny by the fair-wards and the wizard-of-the-gate, lest spells be used to enhance the appearance of shoddy goods. Some magic is allowed, but it must be clearly advertised as such in advance and it must be magic of only the right-hand path.

Those apprehended within fair or temple precincts practicing unauthorized magic, harmful magic, or black magic can be haled before the fair-court. The high priest or those from the temple he appoints then hears the case and decides punishment, which punishment can range from a mere fine or warning up to and including being stripped of all possessions, declared outlaw (and thus fair game for any cheated customer or other enemy), and whipped from out the precincts, naked and unarmed.

The Ithkar Fair is devided into three main sections, each of which is laid out around a nucleus of permanent shops and booths; however, the vast majority of stalls are erected afresh each year, then demolished after the fair. Most distant from the temple precincts lies the section wherein operate dealers in live animals and in animal products—horses and other beasts of burden, hounds and coursing-cats, hawks, cormorants and other trained or trainable birds, domestic beasts, and wild rarities, many of these last captured afar and brought for sale to the wealthier for their private menageries.

In this fourth section, too, are sold such mundane things as bales of wool, hides, rich furs, supplies for the hunter and the trapper. Here, also, are places wherein performing animals can be shown and put through their paces, offered for sale or for hire to entertain private gatherings and parties of the well born or the well to do. Of recent years, quite a number of all-human performing acts have taken to auditioning here for prospective patrons.

The westernmost section of the main three houses craftsmen and dealers in base metals—armor, tools, and smaller hardware of all sorts and descriptions. Once the folk dealing in the sundries of wizardry were to be found here as well, but no more. Farrier/horseleeches are here, as are wheelwrights, saddlers, yoke-makers, and the like.

The middle section of the main three holds dealers in foods, clothing, and footwear. Here are weavers, tailors, embroiderers, bottiers, felters, spinners of thread, dealers in needles and pins, booths that sell feathers and plumes, metalcaster booths with brooches, torques, and arm- or finger- or ear-rings of red copper or bronze or brass or iron. Cookshops abound here, some of them with tasting-booths from which tidbits can be bought, some of them offering cooks and servers for hire to cater private parties or feasts. Also to be found here are the dealers in beers, ales, wines, meads, and certain more potent decoctions, with the result that there are almost always more fair-wards—proud in their tooled-leathern buffcoats and etched, crested brazen helmets, all bearing their lead-filled, bronze-shod quarterstaves—in evidence about the middlemost section.

The easternmost of the three main sections houses the workers in wood and stone—cabinetmakers, woodcarvers, master carpenters; statuette-carvers to master masons. Dealers in glassware are here to be found, candlemakers, purveyors of medicinal herbs, decoctions, scented oils, incense, and perfumeries, potters of every description and class, and lampmakers as well.

In this section one may purchase an alabaster chess set and, a little distance farther along, an inlaid table to accommodate it. Here to be seen and examined are miniature models of the works of the master masons and carpenters, with whom contracts for future work may be arranged; likewise, custom furniture may be ordered from the cabinetmakers.

Within the outskirts of the temple complex itself is a newer, much smaller subsection, centered around the temple's main gate. Here, where the ever-greedy priests' agents can keep close watch on them and on their customers, are the money-changers, dealers in letters of credit, public scribes, artisans in fine metals and jewelry, image-makers, a few who deal in odd manuscripts, pictures, small art treasures, and oddities found or dug out of strange ruins or distant places. Here, also, are those who deal in items enhanced by magic.

There are a few scattered priests, priestesses, mendicants, and cultists from overseas or far distant lands who worship other gods and are allowed to beg in the streets of the fair. They are, however, strictly forbidden to proselytize and are kept always under strictest surveillance by the men and women of the temple. One such alien god is called Thotharn, and about him and his rites of worship some rather odd and sinister stories have been bruited over the years; a committee of the priests of the Three is conducting secret studies of this god and his servants, while considering banning them from the fair.

Since all who legally enter the fair or the temple must surrender their weapons at the gates and swear themselves and their servants or employees to be bound by fair-law and fair-court for the duration of their stay, the well-trained, disciplined, and often quick-tempered fair-wards, armed with their weighted staves, seldom experience trouble in maintaining order.

The bulk of their work takes them to the middle section, with its array of pot-shops, or to the outer fringes of the enclave, where gather the inevitable collection of rogues, sturdy beggars, bravos, petty wizards, potion-makers and witches, would-be entertainers, snake-charmers, whores, and, it is rumored, more than a few assassins-for-hire.

And now, to all who have paid their gate-offering, welcome to the Fair at Ithkar.

FLUX OF FORTUNE

Mildred Downey Broxon

As the *Wavewitch* rounded the last bend on the river Ith, Anvadlim caught his first glimpse of commerce-sacred Ithkar. A few permanent dwellings huddled around the temple, but most of the flatland was taken over by the walled fair enclosure.

What struck him next was sewage stench. He stood at the rail and watched yelling urchins grab for lines. The captain tossed them a handful of coins. His grin showed rotten teeth. "Well, here you are, safe and sound, as promised." Anvadlim wiped spittle from his beard and stepped back.

"Indeed, and at a scant three times the going rate." He'd found this out at an intermediate port of call.

The captain shrugged. "So, it's business. And I *did* hold off the pirates. Fairgoing spells are expensive."

Privately, Anvadlim thought the starved and scurvy-ridden pirates had been little menace, but then the captain's store of pallid thunderbolts and wispy waterwalkers would have been depleted by any stronger threat. He shouldered his packsack and tucked his medicine chest under his arm. No need to mention to the captain, in parting, that his special hangover cure—a good percentage of the fare—would soon expire, retroactively and with force. Whistling, he stepped down the gangplank.

Humanity jostled about him. "Special love-charms," one whispered, "guaranteed." "Gold jewelry, real gold, with starstones, cheap, special for you!" "Pity on a cripple!" (Whose sores were artful fakes.) "Souvenir of Ithkar, nice price." "Filthy pictures—"

Anvadlim spared a glance. Some of the positions doubtless required costly antigravity spells. He pressed on through the dockside crowd, uphill to the fair's gate.

Peeled logs, topped by flickering lights, set off the fair area. He queued up, then realized he had the wrong line: this was for reentrants. He sighed and moved to his proper place.

Here, again, hucksters teemed. The young woman in front of him—a professional wrestler, from her costume—bought an ever-blooming flower for her hair. Anvadlim resisted self-adjusting sandals and a soilproof tunic.

At last his turn came. He stepped forward to face the gate fair-ward, who assumed the bored-yet-sinister aspect common to customs officials everywhere. Huge, leather-coated, and brass-helmed, he carried a bronze-shod staff. Behind him, at an inlaid table, a slight, black-robed figure scratched a stylus over a wax tablet. A junior priest from the temple, no doubt, on Watch duty along with a bored wizard.

The fair-ward shifted his bulk. "Name?" His voice would have flattened a bull blithern.

"Anvadlim. Of Tsobbet," he added, forestalling the next bellow.

"Wares or trade?"

"Physician."

The pale, black-clad wizard glanced up sharply for the first time. "You are surely aware that sorcery is not permitted here."

Anvadlim shrugged. "I can manage without." In truth, he was not as skilled in mystic incantations as were many of his colleagues. Perhaps that was why he had never prospered.

The watcher signed to the fair-ward.

"Open your luggage." It was not a request. Anvadlim shrugged out of his packsack. The fair-ward upended it: out tumbled a patched pair of trews, a mended tunic, worn but clean breechclout, thin socks, and soft shoes. A leather pouch landed with a muffled clink. Opened, it poured out a handful of coppers, three silvers, and one tiny gold coin. The official grinned. "Now for the chest." Anvadlim hesitated. "Come on, hand it over."

"It's got special—"

"We're not to allow uninspected magic in here." Clumsy fingers fumbled with the clasp.

Anvadlim capitulated. "Here, let me do it." Open, the chest breathed spicy scents of drugs.

"Zat all? Hmf." The fair-ward peered down, then beckoned the watcher. "What d'you make of that? Anything forbidden?"

The wizard rose in one fluid motion from beside the priest, picked up a packet, read the label, sniffed, and nodded. "Standard preparations." The voice was musical.

He pointed to another packet, larger, bound with tapes. "Open that." The fair-ward tore at the fastenings.

"No, don't—" Anvadlim was too late. Gleaming knives tumbled onto the table. The watcher cocked his head.

"Weapons? Surely you know they are forbidden."

"These aren't weapons. Scalpels, lancets, tools of my trade."

"Why did you not wish the package opened, if so?" Indeed, the blades were too small to do harm. The watcher fingered them.

Anvadlim sighed. "I'd set a small stasis spell, nothing to harm or beguile, only to ward off burning sickness. The magic is broken if any but I unwrap them." Now he'd have to boil everything again, wrap it in freshly steamed cloths; he choked back his irritation. The fair-ward pawed through the rest of the implements, clearly disappointed at not finding contraband.

"Very well, you are cleared. Now make your offering." He jerked his thumb toward a farther table, under an awning, where sat another black-clad figure, this one older and wearing jewels. He was surrounded by stacks of coins, flasks of wine, bolts of silk, and bundles of furs. "Keep it moving."

Anvadlim moved to the table, proffered his pass, and dropped two copper coins in a bowl. The functionary shook his head. So, a physician is supposed to be worth more. If I were skilled in magic . . . As it was, more cash would leave him without food or lodging. Fortunately it seemed they accepted tribute in kind. With grave gestures he opened his medicine chest, extracted a packet, and counted five pills into a vial, which he stoppered with a fluff of wool. "These will give a man strength," he said, winking. "They are very potent indeed." The priest palmed the vial and motioned Anvadlim to enter the grounds.

"Keep it moving," he heard the fair-ward say, "keep it moving."

Anvadlim stifled a grin. The powerful physic he'd handed the tax collector would be sure to do just that.

In the distance, the temple bulked huge and black. Between Anvadlim and its mass thronged fairgoers by the thousands: animal trainers, drink-sellers, women who sold their favors; conjurers, clothiers, antique-fakers and god-speakers; dancers, herdsmen, and tourists. Save for the fair-wards, all went unarmed, a strange sight in so motley a crowd. Ahead, Anvadlim saw the female wrestler, her "ever-blooming" flower of a sudden shriveled. She cursed and tossed it under the hooves of a beer-wagon horse.

Farther on stood a neat corral, where horned ponies, knee-deep in straw, switched flies with their catlike tails. Beside the fence, on a brightly painted wagon, a young man did sleight-of-hand. He was quite good: Anvadlim was a connoisseur. His own stage experience often helped him with doctoring. The fellow's disappearance into a billowing smoke cloud was particularly impressive. Have to try that on warts some time.

A gong sounded, and three young men—Anvadlim recognized one as the "magician" without his robes—leaped into a cleared space. They introduced themselves as brothers and, joking, began to toss objects at each other: balls at first, then fruit, and, soon, flaming torches and a full wine bottle. Anvadlim set down his chest. They were *good*.

They poured the wine—uncorking it as it spun in midair— drank, tossed the goblets over their shoulders, and picked up nine scythes. These must have been imported under dispensation, for the edges glittered deadly. They arced and spun, while the crowd stood mesmerized.

A hoot shattered the reverent hush, a stone *thwack*ed, and a juggler winced. Blood flowed from his nose, he faltered, and the rhythm broke. His companions stepped in to recover—one, two, three, four scythes were transferred and kept up their dance, then another four—and a second stone struck. Where were the fair-wards? He watched in horror as the ninth scythe reached apogee and descended. The juggler shielded his face with his forearm. Blood spurted over Anvadlim.

That's arterial! Heedless of shouts and shrieks, he pushed toward the stricken entertainer, who, left-handed, gripped his right arm. Crimson gushed between his fingers and pooled in the dirt. Pale, he sank to his knees. His two companions stood helpless.

All my equipment is contaminated. Those interfering bastards at the gate broke my stasis spells. Well, the patient might survive a later burning sickness, but not his present loss of blood. Act now, then worry. He rummaged in his pack for his clean tunic, pushed the man flat, and held it over the wound. Almost immediately the cloth was soaked through. Left-handed, he sought again in his pack and found a belt. With one hand and his teeth he wound it 'round the arm and pulled.

The bleeding slowed. The young man lay waxy pale in the dirt. A curious crowd watched, ready to turn on the physician if the case went sour. He heard muttering. Weary, he closed his eyes.

"Excuse me, sir." The voice belonged to the troupe's stage magician. "Can I help?"

The lad meant well. Anvadlim tried to keep bitterness from his tone. "I doubt it. I need someplace clean and quiet, lots of boiling water, and an assistant who won't faint. And I need all this *yesterday*."

To his surprise, orders were given and followed. He could hear, in the background, a fair-ward bellowing. And, on an improvised stretcher, the patient—pale as death—was borne across the sector line to the nearest tavern.

Anvadlim rinsed the blood from his hands and surveyed the scene: it looked as if every container in the tavern brimmed with water. When he'd yelled for boiling water, *fast*, his helpers had taken him at his word. Well, he'd been able to renew the stasis spells before surgery. He muttered a short prayer to Scarn of the Talons.

The juggler was resting now on a cot amid the kegs and jeroboams, where no one would disturb him but Anvadlim or the landlady of the Bibulous Bullock. This last—Mim was her name—spilled her breasts across a goblet-strewn table and sighed. "Now what do I do with all this water?"

"Drink it?"

She brayed. "*Drink* it? Ah, off with ye!" She hitched up her bodice. "It's not drinking *water* has kept me so healthy through a wicked life."

Anvadlim sipped sour beer and glanced down. The liquid was scummy. "Think I'll switch to wine."

Mim grimaced. "Th' beer goes sour every year, about the second ten-day of the fair. They've ruled against stay-fresh spells: call them 'illegal enhancement,' if ye please."

The harsh purple wine was small improvement, but that might be blamed on the vintage: early last week. Anvadlim considered his luck. The landlady, awed by his skill and worried over her pregnant daughter, had offered him lodging. The grateful juggling troupe had promised to set up a small tent tomorrow where he could see patients. He might earn a few coppers. He'd long since given up any thought of growing rich.

In the far corner a pitcher shattered on the packed-dirt floor. Mim reached beneath her apron, pulled out a horn, and blew. Tent-flaps flew open and two huge fair-wards burst in. She pointed, and the guardians of the peace hoisted one miscreant each and flung them outside.

Conversation resumed. Mim shrugged. "There's advantages in Ithkar after all. Back home I'd have waded in there meself—can't keep a decent bouncer. My poor man took his gravesickness with a brawlish knock on the head, black bile to whoever did it. But the fair-wards, now, we don't even have to pay extry—comes out of everybody's taxes; and no wettin' their whistles fer free, either, 'cause they don't drink on duty." She paused, amazed by such virtue.

Anvadlim sipped his wine. It might drown the dubious dinner—alcohol supposedly killed noxious growths. . . . He yawned. "Time for bed."

She lit him to his cot in the community tent, where several men already snored, and left the candle. Anvadlim set in on a crate. Bedbugs. Lice. Villainous vermin. He sighed, opened his medicine chest, and removed a packet.

A conical pile of powder, lit with the candle flame, *whoosh*ed and billowed smoke. He pulled back the gray bedclothes and sprinkled the contents of another packet, chanting:

"Bloodsip, firebite, tiny-teeth needles,
Fleas and can't conjure 'ems, blundering beetles,
Long-legged legions, leap lightly away.
Death smite all who bite me, ere dawning of day."

He made a pillow of his clothing and blew out the light. In the morning Anvadlim checked on the juggler.

Awake he was, though still very pale and drowsy from numbing drugs. His skin was cool—no burning sickness—and he was pathetically grateful.

"Ah, well"—Anvadlim brushed off the stammered thanks—"you're too fine an entertainer to lose." Vats of boiled water yet stood about. Anvadlim poured some into a jug and left it by the bed. "Drink a lot of this," he said. "The wine here will likely kill you." His own mouth tasted like iron filings.

Fairgoers rose early: outside, though the shadows stretched blue and cool, commerce throve. Nearby, in an empty area, he saw the jugglers setting up a small tent.

"Will this assigned place be all right for location, sir? The way is well traveled, and the pump's not too far."

"Thank you, thank you," Anvadlim said, "I'm sure it will be fine." Their gratitude was embarrassing, even if he *had* performed a miracle of surgery. He strolled on, eager to see the fair before starting work.

Food and drink booths were interspersed with clothing vendors and sellers of jewelry. He admired the bright weaves and extreme patterns of high fashion, but such were suitable neither to his age nor his purse. He did pause before a stall where a string of bright red soft leather boots bobbed in the breeze. They must still be dyeing some of the leather: he watched a crimson trickle stain the mud. His own boots were shabby and brown with travel dust. He sighed and moved on, to watch a tailor try to fit a very portly customer. Back in Tsobbet—or, indeed, in many other places—the craftsman would simply have used a fitting charm. How long it lasted was proportional to the cost of the garment.

Anvadlim crossed into the next sector, where hammers rang on metal and saws rasped wood. Good strong armor, he noticed: he hated battlefield injuries.

Nearer the temple lurked money-changers and dealers in antiquities. Anvadlim checked the exchange rates, found them favorable, and converted some of his cash to local currency. He paused, also, at a booth selling ancient amulets. The greenstone charm of Synkalos, god of head colds, tempted: the traditional swollen face and agonized expression were movingly rendered.

He was struck by a flying figure, and heard shouts of "Stop, thief!" Tables tumbled and shopkeepers shrieked: all was chaos for several minutes until the fair-wards appeared, red-faced and puffing.

"What's the matter here? Where's the local man? We had to come all the way from section three."

Anvadlim wondered why they were short-handed, and realized he'd seen only one or two of the leather-coated giants all morning. He checked his money pouch. Unarmed, amid all these strangers—he'd always heard the fair was safe, but not so. He hastened back to his lodgings.

His tent was finally erected. Anvadlim took out the painted canvas banner with the traditional flower-and-scythe of the physician. Below, for those who could read, were hieroglyphs. He took one sniff at the cooking smells from the Bibulous Bullock, shuddered, and walked down the road to a fried-lizard stand. Never mind if it cost more. Coins did no good in the afterlife.

Back at his tent, he waited for his first client. Word had spread: folk arrived with boils, obscure skin rashes, and head colds. He longed again for the Synkalos charm. On a severe grease burn, after washing it in boiled water, he applied one of his special stasis dressings. He'd just finished muttering a prayer to the protector of the inept when he heard shouting in the street. A well-dressed youth flung open the tent-flaps. "Quickly! Kri—my friend—is hurt."

Anvadlim looked out. A young man lay cursing on a stretcher, covered only with a sheet. His right shoulder was distorted. His slightly drunken companions set down the litter. The patient swore an oath that made even Anvadlim blink: the deity mentioned was old and nasty. "What happened?"

The young man winced. "Fell—out—of—bed." Alcohol was heavy on his breath. "Well—more like—off the—trapeze."

"That's all right," Anvadlim hastened. "I understand." Fool stunt. Broke an elbow trying that once. Lucky it was the left one or I couldn't have done surgery. "This might hurt a bit." He grasped the arm above the wrist and positioned his right foot in the armpit. A slow steady pull brought a click and another oath. Anvadlim bound the shoulder, advised a week of rest, and suggested that next time perhaps the *lady* might prefer to try the trapeze.

This last brought a weak smile and a look of embarrassment. The young man made as if to reach for his pouch, then realized he wore none. He held out his left hand to a companion. The other youth removed his ring and handed it over. "I haven't any money with me," the patient explained.

Anvadlim examined the ornament: twisted gold, with a silver tracing of vines and snakes. He'd seen its like before. "Very well. Thank you." He dropped the ring into his belt-pouch.

Ambulatory now, sheet draped in a dashing style, the youth left with his companions. Anvadlim smiled a moment and summoned his next patient.

When he saw her his smile vanished.

"I am Lirli, Mim's daughter." She panted a little, as well she might. She was heavily pregnant, not so great in belly but rather swollen all over. Her breath came shallow and from high in the chest. A noise from the street made her twitch.

He bade her sit and examined her puffy ankles. This was bad, very bad. He was about to ask questions when beyond the canvas tent-wall he heard cries. If those young louts had come back . . . He thrust aside the flaps and saw a slim black-robed figure prone in the dirt. Anvadlim rolled it over with his foot and gazed, dubious, on the thin face and soiled garment. A spasm brought pink vomit and the stench of feces.

His immediate impulse was to draw away, yell, "Plague!" and run.

He'd seen plague: physicians fallen beside their patients, dead-carts rumbling through the streets, the stench of funeral pyres. He choked back panic and dragged the figure into the tent.

The pregnant woman drew back in horror. He cursed himself for endangering her. "Go back and stay with your mother. Touch nothing. I'll see you later."

He turned his attention to the new patient. One of the watchers from the temple, that much he could tell from the black robe. The lack of ornament proclaimed him a novice.

The slight figure tossed his head and moaned. The breathing was quick and shallow; at the wrist, the life-beat was weak, and the skin felt dry and hot. Whatever ailed him was serious. Puzzled, Anvadlim sat back on his haunches. Unless all temple acolytes looked the same, was this not the very watcher who had kept the entrance gate? But he had grown so wasted in little more than one day's time.

As he watched, the breathing slowed. One last rattle and the figure lay still. Shaken, he reached again for the wrist, then for the side of the throat: the life-beat had stopped. He sat in silence, as always when he witnessed the great change, then rinsed his hands in some of the boiled water and set out to summon a fair-ward.

Locating one took time. They were scarcer, it seemed, than yesterday. He told a fair-ward he finally found what had happened and promised to testify to the circumstances.

He walked back through streets that seemed rowdier than usual: minor scuffles, shouting, the occasional yell of rage. Evidently Ithkar was not as closely governed as he had thought.

When he returned to the Bibulous Bullock he found Mim sitting with her daughter. The girl's limbs were jerking, and her eyes rolled back in her head. Even though he, as a man, was considered unfit to deal with childbirth, Anvadlim had traveled far. Once he'd managed to disguise himself and slip into the birthing chamber with the wise-women, at a time when the mother was not expected to survive. What he'd witnessed still troubled his dreams. He'd seen cases like this: they usually ended in convulsions, early labor, a dead mother and child. Mim's daughter was very near to fits. He administered a strong sedative and sent her to lie in a quiet place.

Mim passed him a glass in silence, poured herself one, and drew figures in spilled wine. He looked away: such signs were not for men. "I wouldn't have brought her along," she said, low, "but she's still two months from her time, I thought it safe. Alone, she'd have fretted. Her man's out fishing, and late coming back. There's no one else to leave her with; his folk didn't like his wedding a tavern-keeper's daughter." Her face held real pain. "She's bad, isn't she?"

Anvadlim nodded.

"Me sister went that way. Wise-women tried everything—even burned a rabbit alive, to stop her pain. The squeals, I think it was, set her off. I shouldn't even speak of this." A long wait, then: "They tried to pull the child early, so she wouldn't die abirthin' an' haunt them evermore. Horrid, it was, their dirty hands tearin' an' all for naught, she died, child died, too, a dread cursin' on the place." She shivered. "Heard 'em in the night, I did; had to move far away. Some of the birthin' women never was the same, they say that's what happens, a judgment on 'em, like, an' the land goes bad from the blood—"

Talk had ceased in the tavern. The customers, almost all male, listened. Whispers may have reached them of dark and secret things, wrongness and wild night walkings. One by one they crept away.

Mim drank more wine, spilling a little. She was shaken, he saw, and she was not a woman easily cowed. She'd helped him in surgery with calm competence. "Couldn't go through that again. Thought maybe—if I took her with me—maybe Ithkar would bring luck. But she's doing bad, isn't she? You'd never know how pretty she used to be, swollen up now like a drowned one." She gulped. "Old woman in the village, when I wouldn't have her muckin' about, said Lirli's husband was drowned and so she caught the drownin', too, off his baby." The big woman took up one corner of her apron and wiped her eyes.

"I'll see what I can do," Anvadlim said. "Right now, keep her quiet, let her rest, make her lie down." He looked in on Lirli before returning to his own tent: drugged, she slept like death.

That evening he furled his sign and went toward the temple. Fewer folk walked the street now. At the pump, he watched them draw water for drinking and cooking and washing. There weren't many pumps in the fairgrounds. The temple had its own water supply, and supplied the nobles' guest houses. He climbed the hill and watched liveried servants dump slop jars in the gutters. One, in particular, seemed disgusted by his task. Anvadlim paused beside him. "Lovely evening." The man grunted. He tried again: "Must be easy work, serving the nobility: good food, soft place to sleep—"

"Hah!" He'd struck a nerve. "Some might think so. Easy work indeed, down the hill these twenty times since yesterday, no sooner get up there and turn around—" His face contorted. "Two days in all, it's been going on: never a free moment since we got to the fair. If I'd known I was hiring out to haul—" He gestured at his elegant clothing: rose brocade, silver trim, and soft shining boots, spattered now by mud and offal. "Might as well have stayed on the farm. Some stinks are clean."

Anvadlim commiserated and made his way through the temple courtyard, where he announced himself to the door guard. This, he saw, was a novice, rather than a fair-ward.

The doctor was expected: he'd been summoned to an inquest on the death of the temple watcher. He followed a guide through twisting stone corridors and was shown into a cozy room where three black-clad men sat behind a table. He looked closely: yes, the middle-aged one was the tax gatherer from the fair gate. The man glared in recognition. On his left sat an elderly man Anvadlim had never seen, and on his right a young priest, noteboard and stylus ready.

The room's tapestries held stars, line-connected and labeled in curious script. Anvadlim recognized none of the constellations. He would have liked to examine them more closely, especially by the room's clear flameless light, but he must attend to the proceedings. The middle-aged priest, evidently the one in authority, asked Anvadlim's name, occupation, and place of business at the fair. In his own words, Anvadlim related what had happened to the young watcher at his doorstep.

The three men sat, hands folded, in silence. Finally the leader spoke: "So far you have stated what occurred. We have no reason to doubt you. But you, a *physician*"—he stressed the word, and Anvadlim remembered the "potency pills"—"a trained man, you must have some idea of the cause of death."

Anvadlim shrugged. "I have traveled widely, and have seen much. I thought I recognized the symptoms. Usually, though, there are more victims, with plague."

"What?" The older man half rose. "No, Father Glikso, let him answer."

"We called it the plague. Or *a* plague. There are several sorts, and this looks like one of them. As it spreads, many sicken, some die. The old, and the very young, and the weak are easiest for anything to kill. Save for there being only one case, yes, I would think it a form of plague."

The young priest spoke up: "Well, there *have*—" Glikso frowned.

The older one said, "Perhaps we should . . ." but trailed off as well.

"Have you any recommendations?" asked Glikso.

Anvadlim shrugged again. "It spreads, I know not how. In such crowded conditions it could get very bad. If there are more cases, I would advise closing the fair." Glikso's gasp sounded in the silence. He rose.

"Thank you. We will take this under advisement. There have been, of course, no other cases, but thank you for your help." He handed over a small pouch of coins. *Hush money?* Anvadlim took it.

Leaving, he turned and said, "Odd, how few fair-wards I've seen about. This must be a more than usually prosperous year."

"Ah, yes," said Glikso, "folk come from all over. We find ourselves somewhat short-handed."

Anvadlim nodded. "Nobles, too; they make a splendid showing. It is a great credit to the fair that so many folk of quality attend. The rose-and-silver livery, I seem to remember—that's from Ginorfu, that smelly little fish-salting town up north, isn't it?"

The young priest swelled with pride. "Oh, no, those are the colors of House Krimar. The Bek of Krimar himself is visiting."

"What an honor." Anvadlim bowed himself out. In the courtyard he kicked the stone wall. *Pestilence and putrefaction.* He turned his steps toward the guest house.

House Krimar's rose-and-silver banners fluttered from the windows. Uniformed guards flanked the doorway and, when he approached, barred Anvadlim's entry.

"Lord Krimar sent for me," he lied. When they hesitated, he looked about furtively and gave the heart-sign of the physician, then set a finger to his lips. That much admitted him to the private quarters, where he was detained by an elderly manservant.

"I was not informed that Lord Krimar was expecting you," he said, "and the family are not receiving."

"In their worry, they may have forgotten to convey the message." He fumbled in his pouch and produced the ring he'd been given. "The young master sent this." The majordomo's eyes widened slightly. With a bow, he took it. "I shall see."

It was a gamble; Anvadlim thought he'd recognized southern workmanship, but even drunk, the noble youth had not been foolish enough to reveal his identity. In a moment the servant returned. "Young master will see you."

The figure who sat in a cushioned chamber was not the half-drunken lad of the morning: he was fully clothed and sober now, his arm supported by a silken sling. And he was angry. "What do you mean?" he said as soon as the servant left them. "I paid you. Have you come, perhaps, to tell my father where I was?" The handsome face twisted. "Go ahead, tell the old fool, for all the good it will do."

Anvadlim stepped closer. "Your father is very ill."

The youth stiffened. "How did you know?"

"He must have become ill on the journey; he was ailing when he arrived, and has worsened. He is a large man, is he not, and strong?"

The son nodded. "Do you know him, then?"

Anvadlim shook his head. "I knew he must be strong. The weak ones die soon. Even the fair-wards are stricken." Silence lengthened. "He brought the plague."

The youth shrugged, then winced: his shoulder still hurt. "A small indisposition on the journey, nothing serious, some wrong water, perhaps. He drinks only water, for his health. You can't drink water when traveling, the spells don't carry over from place to place, you take a chance—but he's here now, and everyone knows the temple water is safe. And yet—"

"He grows weaker," Anvadlim said, "and the sickness spreads to the fair, where folk are dying." He was very tired. "You must take him away."

The young man laughed. "No chance! He is too ill to move; they would say I killed him to inherit."

"Let me see him, then. I might make him more comfortable."

The youth poured himself more wine. "No."

"Then," Anvadlim said, "we must close down the fair." He turned to go. Laughter followed him. No one would believe him. There was something, he knew, about waste, and crowding, and water supply. He'd seen it before. He was a traveled man.

Walking back down the hill he noticed, once again, how the gutters ran down toward the level of the communal pump in the tavern section. Somehow, he was glad he'd not been drinking that water unboiled. It was dark, now, and torches had been extinguished at many stalls—perhaps the owners were too ill to tend them. Roving bands of toughs prowled the streets, without a fair-ward in sight. Of course. They're among the first to fall ill—they, who bear the heat of the day in heavy leather armor, and who are forbidden to drink on duty—anything but water.

He hurried on. Suddenly the fair was no longer a safe place, and not only because of whatever illness stalked it. His tent stood empty. Inside, a few jars had been smashed, their contents scattered and mingled: barks and powders and salts, fish scales and dried insects. Senseless vandalism, or a search for drugs?

He stepped inside the larger tavern tent. Fewer customers slouched therein—only the regulars, who had scarcely moved since he'd arrived. Red of nose, bleary of eye, loud and slurred of speech—but alive, and no worse off than they'd been yesterday. Water doubtless never passed their lips.

Mim came in from the storage area, saw him, and hurried over. Her face was pale. "Lirli's awake," the landlady said, "and any little sound—I think she's starting, too soon—"

"I'll go see." He stepped into the storage area. There, on the cot, Lirli lay. Her face was even puffier, and she tossed like a woman in early labor. Perhaps it had not started yet. Perhaps he could calm her, stave it off. He prepared another draught, urged her to lie quiet, and blew out the candle. He sat in the dark until her breathing slowed to a soft snore. *Two months short of her time. I can't keep her drugged. But she's near fits, and starting birth pains. We'll lose the baby, too. And lose* her *in childbed.* He was not superstitious, but the thought grasped cold around his heart.

And the fair. Contagion was spreading; those who kept the peace were sick or dead: it would end like the fall of Tsobbet and he never, ever wanted to see that again.

At first he could not identify the noise: *whoosh*, crackling, breakage. Then he saw, through the canvas wall, flickering light. Fire! Not in the Bullock, though, but next door. A tent city could flare up in moments. He heard screams, now, and more shouting. He should go help, organize a bucket brigade from that accursed pump, do something—

On the bed the woman moaned. The noise had wakened
her, not to full consciousness, but enough to trigger the
birth rhythm. It could not be denied. Others could damn
well fight the fire.

Oddly, it was not a difficult labor; of course, the child
was small. Even more oddly, the tiny girl was pink and
squalled, even though her frame looked wizened. Anvadlim
watched in wonder as the grandmother swaddled it. She
grinned. "With all the excitement outside, they never
knew what happened in here, did they?" She shrugged.
"The condition Lirli was in, they'd have been more feared
of her than of fire, any day. Fire you can put out with
water. Childbed ghosts you can't put out, lacking spells,
and mayhap not even then."

More frightened of Lirli than of fire. And not, in any
way, frightened of the plague—or of what is spreading it.
He thought for a while, looking at the new mother, pale
and motionless. At first glance she might be dead. "Mim,
how are you at playacting?"

The woman shrugged. "Ye works where I has, ye gets
pretty good at lotsa things. Maybe playactin' most of all."

"All right," Anvadlim said, leaning forward. "I have a
plan. I'll tell you what, and I'll tell you why, and I'll tell
you fast. We must be ready by first light."

Dawn's glow showed few astir in an oddly quiet fair.
Next door, the ashes of a tent smoldered. Anvadlim had
sent two of the jugglers up the hill toward the temple,
bearing a sedated Lirli in a curtained litter. Mim, heavily
veiled and carrying the tiny infant, walked alongside.

They waited until servants emerged from guest houses
and rich pavilions, bearing away the leavings of the night.

The jugglers, black clad, stood holding their burden. Folk stepped around them. When the crowd was large enough, Mim set up a wail: "My daughter, my daughter! Curses on this land, curses on this fair, on all herein. My daughter will walk now and rend you, her teeth in your throat, her claws at your eyes. My daughter, my daughter!"

Curious, the servants drew closer. A few nobles yawned from their pavilions. Mim wailed louder. "Dead in giving birth, oh, horror! Now she will walk. The ground is foul with blood!" The baby whimpered. Folk shuffled, uncomfortable. Why would a woman near term travel to the fair? And without protective sorcery—

With a shriek Mim drew back the curtains of the litter, where Lirli lay still as death. "*You* killed her, rioters, fire-setters, peace-breakers! She lay in labor, far from any wise-women to help her—alone, dying among strangers, dying to give birth!" With a dramatic gesture she lifted a bowl and flung the contents on the ground, amid the other refuse in the drainage ditch. "See! Her life's blood stains the land!" She jerked the curtains closed, gestured to the jugglers, and the procession moved off downhill.

Below, in the flat area near the communal pump, Anvadlim watched until folk came to draw water, then stepped forth himself. He filled his bucket and drew back in horror. "Blood! The water has turned to blood!" As indeed it seemed: the pump gushed crimson. "A curse," he intoned, "a dreadful curse. What could have brought it?"

On cue, the somber procession approached, Mim lamenting her daughter's tragic death. Anvadlim stared at his reddened hands and tried to wipe them clean. It'll take weeks for the dye to wear off. Others looked at the water, tried the pump, and stood stricken as it gushed redder still.

"Woman," Anvadlim said. Mim paused. "What has happened? How did your daughter meet death? Can it have aught to do with—with *this*?" His gesture included the pump.

Mim stood magnificent in grief. "My daughter, rest her—though she'll not rest now, not never—died in child-bed, brought there before her time, unguarded, none to aid her, to let go. She died here among strangers at the fair, and she'll haunt this cursed ground!"

"The birthing spirits from your land are strong, then?" Anvadlim said.

"Strong, and hard to banish. Naught slays them but burning and boiling and poisons. I flee this place, I and my poor daughter—though her ghost remains." With that, Mim strode on.

Folk glanced at each other. The water *did* run red, and word had come about the blood, up on the hill. One by one they crept away.

Anvadlim sat in the chamber somewhere in the bowels of the temple. Once more his eyes strayed to the starry tapestries, and he wondered—but he was, again, here on business. Only Glikso and the old priest sat with him today. The tax gatherer found words difficult. "You realize what you have done?"

"I?" Anvadlim was all innocence. "I've done nothing. There is a curse on the land, which must be removed. Childbed death is very dangerous, you know. The pollution lingers, and the ghost is insatiable."

"You have closed the fair." Glikso's face was flushed; Anvadlim wondered if he were prone to apoplexy. His fist slammed the table. *"You! Have! Closed! The! Fair!"*

"That's enough, Father Glikso." The old man held out

a bony hand in admonition and looked directly at Anvadlim.
"You were certain?"

Anvadlim nodded. "I have, as I've said, traveled widely.
The sickness was in the water." Anger took him. "It's
been awaiting you all these years, fair after fair, it's only
divine mercy you've been spared this long! Look at your
sewage arrangements! Look at your *water supply!* All you
needed was a plague bringer and, by blithernsballs, you
finally got one!" More gently, "I suppose the poor fellow
is dead."

The elderly priest nodded. "A pity. The Bek of Krimar
was a good man. His son . . ." He shrugged.

Anvadlim persisted. "How many others did he take
with him, fair-wards and visitors? Would you really have
let the fair go on, while folk fell in the streets?"

"We—" Glikso began, but the old priest interrupted.

"Quiet, Glikso." Then, to Anvadlim, "We've lost so
much knowledge. You say you have a spell, a method,
against the burning sickness and, perhaps, against plague.
You boil things. Why does this work?"

Anvadlim shrugged.

"Our old records have moldered. And if we do not run
the fair, even more knowledge will be lost, scattered over
the world in bits, never shared. Oh, I know, Father Glikso,
the fair brings money into the treasury. But it brings a
greater treasure than that." For a moment he leaned his
head on his hands. "So many died, so many. . . . You,
physician, *you* closed down the fair. You sent folk away.
You sit there red-handed." He grinned and pointed at
Anvadlim's crimson palms. "Leather dye from the boot-
seller, was it not?"

Anvadlim started to speak. The priest waved him silent.
"You are a brave man, Anvadlim of Tsobbet. You have

knowledge and we''—he gestured at the tapestries, where stars winked in strange patterns—''we also have knowledge, and questions, and a sacred duty to run the fair. Would you consent, for a time, to be known as Anvadlim of Ithkar, to work with us and see to the people's safety?''

Anvadlim considered. He was not, by any means, done with traveling. But here was a need, and— His gaze stole to the star pictures. ''I'll work with you,'' he said. ''First, we must purify the fairgrounds and the water.''

When Glikso left, muttering, Anvadlim and the old priest were already concocting a ritual. Anvadlim felt it required powdered lime; he and the priest could work up a proper chant later.

GEYDELLE'S PROTECTIVE

Lin Carter

Syrion arrived early in the morning on the first day of the famous Fair at Ithkar; the spirits bound to his will by talismanry deposited him on the crest of a nearby hill. From this prospect he obtained a clear view of the grounds: the lanes were choked with drays and wagons, the brisk morning rang with the pounding of hammers and creak of pulleys as booths were erected and tents were raised.

Youngest, most gay and handsome of the sorcerers for many lands about, Syrion would normally have attended the fair attired in the height of current fashion—perchance in a pleated linen jupon alternately striped with cerise and lavender, olive leggings, with bunches of rose-pink ribbons aflutter from throat and shoulder tabs.

However, he was overmuch given to malicious jibes, pranks, and tricks, and his mischievous and irreverent ways had earned him many enemies among his fellow

sorcerers. So, on this occasion, he had adopted a moderate
disguise and went robed from throat to wrist and heel in
the somber gray of a novice magician of the Second
Circle.

Descending the hillslope, Syrion entered the gate and
wandered about the grounds, eventually locating the area
given over to the purveyors of supplies, artifacts, and
manuscripts appertaining to the arts sorcerous. Here he
strolled with modest mien among booths where merchants
were already setting out trays of amulets and scaraboids,
formulae and antique grimoires, plaques, miniature idols,
and suchlike. These trays displayed more than a few articles that the young sorcerer found desiresome, but he
resolved to shop at length and peruse every item on sale
before deciding which to purchase.

At the end of the lane he found a booth erected in front
of a tent draped in funereal purples, before which a plump
and placid wizard of uncertain age sat tailor fashion on a
silk carpet, fat hands folded upon his paunch. He nodded
amiably as Syrion neared the booth.

"Pray examine my offerings at your leisure, young sir:
should there be any piece that attracts your interest, please
inquire and I will tell you what I know concerning it. I, by
the way, am Vovomé, a wizard from the southlands."

"Pleased to make your acquaintance, sir," murmured
Syrion politely. "I am hight Tuur, a mere student of the
Second." He ran his eyes along the rows of items; there
were some excellent periapts cunningly carven from jade,
amber, malachite, and other stones; a matched set of the
planetary kameas cut into tablets of their corresponding
metals; and a folio of demonic portraits through which he
leafed absently. The one article that most seized his inter-

est he pretended to ignore, finally examining it after having scrutinized each and every one of Vovomé's wares.

It was a talisman of purple faience which reposed under a glass bell jar upon a small cushion of yellow velvet. He recognized it at once, and his heart beat faster. He wet his lips, striving to dissemble his intense interest.

"This is interesting," he remarked with a pretense of casualness. "May I examine it?"

"Certainly, young sir," Vovomé replied, a slight smile making folds in his plump cheeks. "But even a student such as yourself should recognize the piece as Geydelle's Protective, one of the most fabulous talismans of recent cycles. I assure you that it is a veritable Geydelle, and of incredible rarity."

Syrion removed the talisman and fingered it: the surface was sharply incised with potent charactry, and he could feel the power with which it was charged go tingling through his fingertips. There was no doubting its authenticity.

Geydelle had been a celebrated magician of a former epoch, famous for his mastery of the talismanic art. The piece in question was virtually priceless: it rendered its wearer invulnerable to any malign spell or enchantment, and his manse impregnable to magical assault, even by one of the princes of demonry. With the protective upon his person, never again should Syrion have cause to fear the wrath of those whom his mischiefs had mortally offended.

Afire with cupidity to own the treasure, Syrion inquired as to the price of the "bauble" (as he depreciated it); Vovomé named a sum that all but wrung a gasp from Syrion. It was many times the amount of funds he had borne with him or could possibly raise. He attempted to haggle, but Vovomé waved his words away, maintaining that smug smile which Syrion had begun to find annoying.

He offered to exchange some of his own rarities and implements, even the talismanic rings worn upon his fingers, but Vovomé displayed the rings upon his own pudgy fingers.

"The price is even as I have stated it, young sir. Good day."

Syrion sauntered away in seeming nonchalance, inwardly seething with frustrated desire. Geydelle's Protective *must* be his; it was the answer to every dilemma that irked him.

At the booth of a sausage-seller he procured steaming tubes of spiced meat, but downed them without even tasting the succulent stuffing. He gulped down a goblet of golden wine of very decent vintage at another booth, obtaining therefrom neither inebriation nor even pleasure.

Later in the afternoon, he returned to the tent of Vovomé. The protective still reposed on its yellow cushion unpurchased.

"It would seem, honored sir, that no one wishes to meet the value you have set upon this bauble," he said. "Perchance you have overpriced it?"

"Not so; the talisman is worth every coin of the sum," replied the wizard sleepily.

"You are certain of its genuineness? I had understood that no examples of the protective were known to be extant."

"Nine such were fashioned by Geydelle and charged with power," Vovomé said with a yawn. "Only two are believed currently in existence."

"If it is as authentic as you claim, it puzzles me that a wizard of your seniority is willing to part with such a curio, even at the rather overinflated price you have placed upon it."

The wizard shrugged. "For some decades I have been absorbed in the creation of synthetic life," he murmured. "My vat creatures require constant attention and, being hybrids of man, insect, and crustacean, rare and expensive nutrients. Rather than beggar myself to continue my experiments, I am forced to offer some pieces from my collection for sale."

They discussed the matter for a time; when Vovomé blandly remained obdurate, Syrion shrugged in exasperation and walked away. But he was resolved that the protective would be his, if not by one means, then by another. . . .

Night fell over the great fair, its purple wings gemmed with stars. Booth after booth, tent after tent, were closed as their proprietors ate the evening meal and retired. Syrion lurked in the shadows, remaining as unobtrusive as possible, a desperate resolve eating at his heart.

During the long day he had spied many of the mages whose ire he had aroused with his mischievous pranks and mockeries, but none of these had recognized, in the sober student clad in gray, with modestly downcast eyes, the merry, foppish jester, Syrion.

He had lingered in the vicinity of Vovomé's tent, remaining out of sight. If the plump wizard noticed his lingerings, he paid them no heed. In the course of time, Vovomé, too, closed down his booth and bore his wares within the tent. Just before the flap was shut, Syrion contrived to hasten by and glance within: by the luminosity of a lamp crystal he saw that the protective, still unpurchased, now reposed under its glass atop a low wooden pedestal.

Hours crawled by; Syrion kept his eyes on the tent-flap. Eventually the light dimmed, and he crept from his place of concealment. Giving the wizard time enough to compose himself for slumber, the young magician approached the rear of Vovomé's tent, whereupon he uttered the most potent syllables of Orome's Spell of Slumber. Three times did Syrion vocalize this enchantment, which thus became powerful enough to cast every man, woman, child, and beast in all of the great fair into the deepest of unbreakable slumbers.

With the razor-edge of an adamantine blade, which he had smuggled into the fair, he then slit the rear of the tent and glided soundlessly within. The faint glimmer of the lamp crystal disclosed the plump wizard seated in his chair, head bowed in somnolence. The glimmer sparkled on the glass bell jar that covered Geydelle's Protective.

Noiseless as a breath of breeze, Syrion approached, one hand extended to uncover the talisman and make it his own. He would be far away, at home in his manse of rose marble among the Urdrium Hills, before the spell broke with sunrise and the wizard awoke. Vovomé would be exceedingly wrathful but, ignorant of the identity of the "young student," could work no vengeance upon the thief. And wearing the precious talisman, the combined wizards of the world were powerless to do injury to Syrion.

His hand reached out.

A voice spoke softly, musingly, from behind him.

"For a youth of your low degree of initiation, young sir, I must admit your mastery of Orome's Spell of Slumber was faultless. My congratulations!"

Syrion gasped, faltered, turned: Vovomé sat, smiling blandly, hands folded in his lap. He was wide awake!

"But why aren't you—I mean, how did you—" whispered Syrion through dry lips. The wizard smiled sleepily.

"I said there were only two of Geydelle's Protectives

now extant. I am willing, in my need, to sell the one . . .
but I wear the other.''

And, lifting one hand in a lazy gesture, he reduced the
unfortunate Syrion to a small heap of ash.

IF THERE BE MAGIC

Marylois Dunn

Tendrils of light mist rose from the river in a soft canopy at treetop level. In a small clearing beside the Ith, a great fire cast its glow upward, throwing the golden reflection back upon the people and beasts belonging to five wagons camped there.

Within the shifting aura there was peace and laughter. Without, in the forest, was darkness, but those who traveled to the Fair at Ithkar were protected, some said, by the gods. In any case, no traveler to the fair was molested.

It was no surprise, then, to the encampment when the slender figure of a woman stepped from darkness into the light. She stopped a moment to allow her eyes to adjust and then moved forward. She was followed closely by a tall gray horse and an even taller, grayer wagon.

Around the fire, music and laughter died until the young man named Topoli recognized her and cried out, "Ferrol.

Welcome. We waited for you at the crossroads this afternoon until we dared wait no longer. When you did not
come, we thought you were not coming this year.''

She lifted her left hand in greeting. ''Ho, friends. Make
a little space for me by your fire to brew a cup of tea. It is
the fault of the butterflies that we are late. They led us to
fresh fennel blossoms. I could not pass them by. I had to
have some for my customers.

''Old Alexi and I are weary beyond words, but a bit of
tea will refresh me enough to put the old fellow out to feed
and rest.''

Several of the women gathered her in, gave her tea
already brewed and food from their own pans.

Topoli came over. ''Allow me to take care of your
horse, Ferrol,'' he offered.

She looked at him, then looked away quickly lest he
take her glance for a bold invitation. How handsome he
had become in this year past. How strong he looked. She
clenched her right hand in her pocket and smiled at him.
''Thanks, no, Topoli. Being blind, he knows my touch.
Any other makes him uneasy.'' Ferrol looked through the
leaping flames. ''Tell me, Almark, have you already told
the story about your dragon?''

An older man lifted his head. ''Not yet, Ferrol.''

''Good,'' she said as she rose to tend the horse. ''Then I
am not too late to hear some of the good stories. Wait for
me.''

After Alexi ate, Ferrol took him to water and finished
brushing his dark gray coat while he drank. ''You are still
beautiful, my old battle charger, my only love,'' she murmured where only the two of them could hear. ''No longer
young, but still beautiful.''

As she led him back to the picket ground, he nuzzled her with velvet lips, but what he thought, he could not say.

The storytelling and singing finished around the fire, which burned low. Children were taken to their beds by parents as tired as they. Jolinda, basketmaker and mother of Topoli, came to sit beside Ferrol, taking Ferrol's right hand into her lap, holding it loosely without looking at it. "Tell me, child. Have you done any more work with your loom?"

"You see, little mother. It is a hand unfit for the loom. That is a dream I have had to forgo."

"I have heard there will be a magician at the fair from one of the southern continents. He is a black man but his magic is white. He is supposed to be a heal-all, among other things."

"Little mother, every season there is a heal-all or magician at the fair, and every year I have gone with a heart full of hope, a mind full of dreams. Each time the hopes are shattered and the dreams blown away like the smoke the magicians make. Have you not learned, as I have, there is no magic? There is illusion, but that is quite a different thing. It will not restore fingers to a hand which has lost two of its important parts." She held up the clawlike hand with its thumb and two remaining fingers. The index and middle fingers were gone as if they had never been. "The wound healed without a scar because my mother was skilled in the use of herbs. I have worked the hand myself until it is flexible and useful. But it cannot do the intricate knotting that good weaving requires. I can catch the shuttle, though I am slow to return it. I weave the cloth I use." She lifted her shoulders expressively. "The beautiful spiderlike patterns in my head must remain there, in my head."

"But are you happy?"

"Is any one of us ever really happy? I am not unhappy, Jolinda. I will never be the artist I wanted to be. I am useful. I learned the yeoman chores of my mother's art. She was an herbalist. I am not. I merely gather herbs to sell to the herbalists at the fair. I gather the finest specimens of their kind, and I do not destroy the field for one flower."

"Does what you sell keep you through the winter?"

"And more. We require little, Alexi and I."

"But you have no husband."

Ferrol looked at her imperfect hand. "With this? What man wants a wife to caress him with her claw? Oh, there are those who pity me. I do not want pity or need it. Should I find love, I would not reject it, but I will not be disappointed if it does not come."

"And if I know one who does not pity you?"

Ferrol smiled. "Are you matchmaking?"

"A mother hopes. You could do worse." Jolinda laughed. "You truly do not believe in magic, do you, Ferrol? Perhaps you are to be pitied for that far more than for the loss of two fingers. When magic goes, life has little joy."

"You're wrong, little mother. If there be magic, it is in the joy of a good day's gathering, the joy of a crop brought in, the joy of a new kid, the joy of a pie well baked. When you cannot have magic, you must do with the small joys."

"But no magic!" Jolinda shook her head sadly.

"No magic!" Ferrol's voice was firm. She stood and helped the older woman to her feet. "It is late and the fire falls low. If we do not get to bed, we will not be fast up in the morning."

*   *   *

The small caravan joined other caravans until there was only one steady stream of travelers moving toward a single goal, Ithkar. They arrived at noon on the eighth day of Ferrol's journey, and she found the spot where her wagon had stood for as long as she remembered. Once the wagon was in place, Alexi unhitched and put with the other horses, Ferrol did not open her wagon or set up her wares immediately. First, she took a cloth-wrapped bundle from the box under the front seat and made her way down the lane toward the Temple of the Three Lordly Ones. She admired the booths, which became more opulent as she neared the temple. Most of the permanent booths had held the same tenants always. Like herself, the children took over when the parents could no longer come. The fair was more than a diversion in the year; it was a way of life.

Ferrol entered the gates of the temple with some trepidation. She had been inside the walls of few stone structures. Those castles that existed in her north country homeland were not the kind a single maiden, even a damaged one, would wish to enter alone.

The personal tribute she carried was made of the finest herbs she had gathered during the year. Since Jolinda taught Ferrol the simpler arts of weaving reeds and grasses into shapes and baskets, she always wove something and attached the herbs to it. This offering was a wreath covered with the best of the dried herbs, and interspersed among the dried leaves were dried blossoms. The yarrow, both gold and white, had retained its colors particularly well. Great clumps of borage had yielded enough blue stars to replace those in the skies, had she been so disposed. Ferrol had dried them carefully in sifted sand to retain their shape and color. When she unwrapped the wreath she was not ashamed of her tribute. Its colors were bright and its odor fragrant.

The priestess at the table of tributes was unknown to her, and Ferrol greeted her respectfully. "Madam, to honor the Three Lordly Ones, I have brought this small gift."

"It is worthy," the priestess said. "Such lovely colors are unusual in dried flowers. Did you use magic?"

"No magic, madam. I have no magic. I work with my mind and my hands. I have no need of magic."

The priestess raised her eyebrows slightly. "You do not believe in magic . . . ?" She left a long empty space at the end of the sentence and Ferrol supplied her name.

The priestess smiled. "Ferrol. A lovely name, like the flowers. You are of an age to have children, Ferrol. Have you any?"

"None, madam, nor husband. I have lived alone in the north country since my parents died. I have chickens and goats for food, kittens, and an old battle charger for companionship."

"A spare life!"

"Not unpleasant. When flowers bloom in the upper valleys, I am free to go about my picking while other women work in the fields. I work as hard as they, but on my own schedule. It is a freedom I enjoy."

"Aye," the priestess said sadly. "I remember freedom. To go with the wind. It is a sorrow in my life to be so confined, and I feel a sorrow in your life as well."

Ferrol held up her crippled hand. "Not so much as it once was."

The priestess, accustomed to perfection, reached out but did not quite touch the hand. "Ah, this is not a flaw of birth. How did it happen?"

"Here. Some ten fairs back. I was playing with some of

the other children while my mother and father tended their wagon and Mother mixed herbs and made potions. A wagon unlike any we knew was in the lane, a wagon with iron-rimmed wheels. One of my playmates, meaning no harm, pushed me into the wagon. I lost my balance and fell. I still remember the sound as the wheel rolled over those two fingers. There was nothing left to heal, of course.

"Some of the priests came, other heal-alls came, but all their magics, benevolent and otherwise, did nothing to restore those poor pulverized bones. They had to be cut away. Some said magic made the scar smooth. That may be, though I hold it was my mother's skill as a healer and her love."

The priestess nodded. "Count yourself fortunate. This is a hard land. It is a fortunate female child who has both mother and father and who is loved. I cannot say the same for myself." The priestess hesitated, then continued: "Ferrol, I cannot recommend him. He is not of our belief, but here at the temple we have heard tales of a magician from across the seas who does great miracles of healing. His tent is in the outer circle, I believe. The fair-wards have been told to see that he does no great magics, but small illusions and healings will not be condemned. It seems a shame that you must go with a hand that is surely a hindrance. I feel you were ordained for other things than gathering herbs, however well you do it."

"Perhaps. The hand is not useless, but it is awkward and without skill. Do you speak of the black magician?"

"You have already heard of him?"

"On the road here, I was told he would be at the fair."

"Good. It is not seemly that I recommend one outside these gates. Should anyone ask, you can say truthfully 'on the road.' '' She smiled an unpriestly smile. A mischievous smile. "If he is a true heal-all, let me know."

"I will, madam. I always bring a portion of my earnings to the temple before I go. I will ask for you. Is it proper that I ask your name?"

"I am called Lyerlith, and that is the name you must use. My name at birth was Sigurd. I should not speak it. Somehow, I want you to know."

Ferrol looked at her, past the priestess, to the girl younger than herself decked out in the facial paint and the clothing of a priestess. A novice priestess. "You have made insightful observations of me and my work, Madam Lyerlith. I wish we could talk where you have not the duties of the temple about you. Is that possible?"

"I doubt it," Lyerlith said. "Lyerlith never leaves the temple."

"Perhaps of a dark evening, Sigurd may?"

"Perhaps." She smiled.

"You never see the fair?"

"Oh, I have seen it many times in the past. When my father sold me to the temple, I was chosen to bear the duties of Lyerlith. I may send one of the servants to your wagon to purchase a fragrant pillow full of your herbs. I would like to rest my head again in the sweet fields of the North."

Without the words being spoken, Ferrol knew the servant would be Sigurd if it could be arranged. She described her wagon and Alexi.

"I know the location well." Lyerlith clapped her hands. "It is near the wagon where they fry those delicious thin strips of meat, and across the way is the best bread wagon at the fair. Sometimes I pass those stone ovens out of fair season just to smell the ash. Even that makes my mouth water. I shall also send for some of the meat and bread.''

Ferrol could not contain her laughter. She had the feeling that the fare of a lesser priestess was somewhat dull. ''I will see that they send you the best of whatever is on the fire when your servant comes,'' she promised, ''and you shall have a pillow of the herbs of your choice. I can do no less for a priestess of the Three Lordly Ones.''

As she returned, a fair-ward stepped from between two booths holding his stave before Ferrol to halt her progress.

''Ho, Ferrol. Greetings. Remember you Horscht of Umberia?''

''Ho, Horscht. I do remember that you did me favors last fair by keeping those pilfering children away from my wagon.''

''And I have already done you favors this year. Two wagons have I sent away from your preferred spot. It is not easy to hold a place from reassiment when you are so late coming.''

''I know. I know. The fennel bloomed late this year, and without fennel I might as well not come. Thank you for saving my space for me. What favor can I do for you in return?''

His young-old face dropped its stern fair-ward's expression and became that of a young boy. ''An evening beside your fire. Some of your good food and good company. I am bespoken now to the most beautiful girl ever to come from Ithkar. I would like you to meet my beloved Azra.''

''Horscht!'' She touched his hand in genuine delight. ''I am so pleased. I would like to meet your beloved. I know how fortunate she is to have you, and I imagine you would only choose someone special in both looks and skills. Come any night. I will be here or nearby.''

He touched his cap in salute and stepped around her, quickly melting into the crowd.

The fair was good for Ferrol. Days passed quickly. Her rich stock dwindled to a few dried leaves and petals for pillows, which she fashioned from cloth of her own weaving. The atmosphere was such that she, like almost everyone else, would stay until the very last day, taking from strangers and friends the companionship she would be without for the rest of the year.

Ferrol's fireside was a popular place. Her teakettle was always hot, her cakes tasty. Her conversation was humorous, and she had a rare quality, that of the listener. It is a world truth that while not everyone enjoys a talker, everyone loves a listener.

Not a night passed that someone did not bring up the black magician with tales of his marvelous healings. Most were too kind to urge her openly to seek him out. Others said bluntly, ''Go. See if he will heal your hand.''

Ferrol passed each reference off politely but made no effort to see the magician. Magic, like religion, only works for those who believe, and for Ferrol, there was no magic.

''I think you should go,'' Topoli said on one of those nights. ''I don't care about your hand being crippled, but I know you care. He may be able to do something.''

Ferrol smiled as she refilled his cup. She had gained a new appreciation for Topoli at this fair. He was good to her in many ways, caring for her wagon as he did for his mother's, bringing her firewood and hay for Alexi. Jolinda was fortunate that her son, of an age to go awandering, chose to stay and care for her. Ferrol spoke in a kind but firm voice. ''I do not wish to go, Topoli. You know my reasons. We are good friends. Let us not speak of this again."

He subsided ungraciously.

Aarfari the breadmaker came, bringing two loaves. "Your fire looks so cheerful. My husband is wandering, looking at the sights in the outer ring. Here, I have brought loaves to share. Have you butter?"

Ferrol brought out goat butter laced with sweet herbs and a knife for slicing and spreading. She also brought Aarfari a cup for tea.

"Tell me, Ferrol," Aarfari said. "Has that priestess sent for any more bread? If she did, I wasn't aware of it. I don't get many temple folk at my wagon. I'm always glad to send something to the temple. Perhaps it will come to the attention of someone of authority and I will be chosen to bake for the temple next year."

Jolinda said, "If you would send these loaves to the tribute table, I think they would have to ask you to be their permanent baker. I would hire you if it were up to me."

Their laughter was interrupted as a fair-ward stepped into the firelight. "Ho! What is this raucous laughter? Are you making fun of the temple folk or fomenting a revolution against the meisters of the fair?"

Ferrol threw back her head and laughed. "You rascal. Horscht, you are a true villain to scare us out of our wits."

Horscht laughed and drew forward the girl standing behind him. "I promised to bring my lady to meet you, Ferrol. May we join your circle?"

As they made space, Ferrol thought she had never seen such beauty in the ranks of ordinary people. The fire showed Azra to have a great mane of hair as black as the moonless night. Her eyes were pale blue, too pale. There seemed to be no iris, only a dark pupil. That could have been a trick of firelight, but it was no trick of light that her features were arranged in such symmetrical and lovely fashion. When she laughed, her teeth were small and perfect. Even her clothing could have been woven on fairy looms. Ferrol liked Horscht and knew him to be a good man, but she did not understand how he could have won this beauty or how he would be able to keep her.

As she was introduced, Azra had the art of turning her full attention on each person as if they were the only two around the fire. Even steady, sturdy Topoli blushed under her attention. She won them all quickly and Horscht glowed with pride at their easy acceptance of his treasure.

Ferrol, watching and listening as Azra's sweet voice rose and fell in the fireside chatter, found she had her imperfect hand hidden in a fold of her skirt. It surprised her that her fingers clenched when Topoli reached out to touch Azra to draw her attention. Horscht did not seem to mind. Why should she?

Loud voices sounded in the lane. Horscht shrugged and stood. "I'll be back," he said.

"That sounds like a fight close to our wagon. I'd better go see." With a nod to Ferrol and Azra, Topoli accompanied him.

Azra did not look after either of them as they left. "Have any of you seen the black magician?" she asked. "I want to go, but my uncle will not permit me to go alone and Horscht will not go with me. Tell me, what is he like? What kind of magic does he do? Is it just tricks and illusions, or is it real?"

"I have not seen him," Ferrol said. "I am told by many sources that he is very good. A true magician."

Azra stretched her hands to the fire. "You'd think the

men were afraid to talk about the magician. I certainly do not fear him.''

"Or anything else," Ferrol murmured.

Azra's eyes flashed, then she threw back her head and laughed. "Very little else. You are observant, Ferrol. I think there is little you fear yourself.''

"Oh, I have fears," Ferrol said. "Both those which can be named and those which cannot.''

"How strange that you would make yourself ordinary. I sense that you are far from ordinary. The quality of your herbs is famous. My uncle says you must use magic to find such high-grade plants and store them in such fine condition.''

Jolinda and Aarfari laughed. "No magic. Not Ferrol. She loves the plants and works hard at her trade. Magic is not involved.''

"There are many kinds of magic," Azra said with a mysterious nod.

"Come, Jolinda," Aarfari said. "I have a loaf of bread for your and Topoli's breakfast." They bade Ferrol good night and left her to entertain her beautiful guest.

Ferrol watched Azra's lips tighten and her eyes narrow as they left.

"They have worked hard since daybreak. It grows late and they are weary.''

"Have you worked hard since daybreak also?''

"No. My work is done during the year. While I am at the fair, I have the easiest days of my year. I have only to serve those who come to the wagon. I rise early, attend my beast, clean the area, and have the rest of the day to do as I will.

"Tell me about yourself, Azra. What are your interests? Have you a craft or art?''

Azra was astonished. "I am a lady. I have no need of skill or tradesman's craft. Do I look like one of those craftswomen?"

Ferrol laughed. "Indeed you do not. Even less do you look like Horscht's wife. How came you to be bespoken to him?"

"Oh, I do like Horscht. He is kind and very dear. But my father was a lord who married below his station. When my parents died, I was sent to live with my mother's brother. He is good to me, but he fears my interest in the ancient art. When Horscht came calling, my uncle thought it a good thing. He would get me safely married in a peasant's cottage, I would have a dozen babies and be too busy to concentrate on learning the true magician's arts."

Ferrol did not like to hear Horscht called a peasant in such a disparaging tone. By definition, she was also a peasant. She had found something about Azra she did not like, but her annoyance was not in her face or voice. "And that is why your uncle keeps you away from the black magician. He fears what you might add to your store of knowledge. Where did you learn the magic you have?"

"From a servant of my father's. He taught me a few tricks, a few illusions. I want to be able to cast spells, change structure, alter time. I want to know true magic. I would give anything to know. It is like an unquenchable desert thirst."

There was fire in Azra's eyes for the first time.

Poor Horscht, Ferrol thought. She is so beautiful and he loves her. She only uses him to appease her uncle.

"Come with me, Ferrol. Surely you want to see the magician, too. He can mend your crippled hand."

How did she know? Ferrol clenched the hand she had kept hidden. "He cannot mend what is not there to mend.

Even a magician cannot grow new fingers. However, since you want to go so much, I will go with you. But not tonight. Were Horscht to find us gone, he would set the entire fair upside down. Instead, let us meet somewhere tomorrow at set of sun. I will go with you.''

Since the magician was in the outer section of the fair, they agreed to meet at the watchtower near the entrance of the fairgrounds.

Ferrol lay awake for a long time asking herself what madness could have come over her to make her agree to see the magician. She had no desire to go, and she certainly was not inclined to do Azra favors. The more she thought about the girl, the less she liked her.

In her dreams Ferrol saw a raven-haired beauty being pursued by a wizened harridan with stringy hair of indeterminate color and pale, pale eyes. She woke cold and sweating and lay the rest of the night rethinking their conversation and their plans.

Shortly before noon a servant wearing the garb of the temple came to Ferrol's wagon. "The Lady Lyerlith desires you buy bread and meat for her.''

It was not the first time, and Ferrol took his change to make the purchases Lyerlith desired. As she wrapped the food she told the servant, "Tell the Lady Lyerlith that I am going to see the black magician as she wished. I meet another lady at the temple at set of sun. She may wish to send her servant Sigurd with us.''

"I do not know a servant named Sigurd," the man said.

"Do you know all the personal servants of all the priestesses?''

"I thought I did," he muttered. "I'll tell her." He was still muttering as he disappeared into the crowd.

Ferrol had looked for Sigurd every night since their meeting, but the girl had not come. For one so young, she was insightful. Ferrol wanted her perceptions when she met the black magician with Azra.

Taking a basket she had made from the sacred birch withes she gathered at the headwaters of the Ith, she filled it with a carefully selected portion of herbs from her remaining stock. She lined the bottom of the basket with cloves of garlic, covering that layer with sweet basil leaves. Dried peony blossoms and mugwort, foxglove and fennel, centaury and angelica; group by group she layered them, topping them over with bay leaves and dried yarrow. Sprigs of rosemary were laid around the outer edge of the top, and in the center she placed some small white flowers with six thick-fleshed petals and a fragrance that could overcome almost any odor. It was a mixture she thought would overcome any witchcraft the magician could call on them. Ferrol did not know how efficacious it was against foreign magic, but she felt better for having some of her familiar friends clutched in her basket while the magician worked his spells. She knew there was magic in these things of the earth. As for the other kind, they would see.

Ferrol arrived as the sun disappeared behind the western hills. Azra was only a few moments later.

"Let us hurry," she said with a tug at Ferrol's sleeve. "I don't want to miss anything."

"Hold back a bit, Azra. There is another who may come. Let us wait a few moments longer."

Azra looked at her sharply. "You asked someone else? All right. Since she is coming, I suppose we must wait. I presume it is a woman?"

"A girl. Like yourself," Ferrol said. "Young, curious

about the magician. She does not have the same interest in him that you do.''

Azra searched her face again. ''I wish magic could tell me what is behind those dark eyes of yours.'' She turned away and waited beside Ferrol with much foot shifting and many sighs.

A slender figure moved out of the shadows. When she threw back the hood of her light cloak, the torches cast gleams of light upon the dark gold braids coiled around Sigurd's head. ''Thank you for waiting. I'm sorry to be so late. I had duties.''

Ferrol introduced the two and thought the greeting between them less than gracious.

''Do you know the way?'' Azra asked when the amenities were done.

They shook their heads. ''No.''

''Then follow me.'' She swirled away and was gone down the midlane. Sigurd looked at Ferrol strangely but set out with her to follow Azra as best they could through the quickening darkness.

As Ferrol's section of the fair became quiet at night, this outer area seemed to attract more traffic than in the daytime. Torches burned everywhere outside the booths and tents, and lamps and candles brightened their interiors where the business of the shopkeepers was to beguile and entertain as well as to present their exotic merchandise.

Azra stood at the marquee of the largest tent, whose colors in the torchlight seemed to be a flowing together of green and gold as oil flows on water. She fanned herself impatiently, looking back for her slower companions.

''Come! Come! He is already at work inside. Hurry! We don't want to miss anything.''

Sigurd chuckled softly, whispering to Ferrol, ''Where

did you find that pathetic child? It is like you to befriend such a one."

Pathetic child! Ferrol was astonished. That was the last appellation she would have laid on the lovely Azra. "She is the bespoken of a good friend. She hasn't much in the way of personality, but there are obvious compensations. You know men. Most seldom look below the surface."

Sigurd gave her another strange look. "Your friend must be an unusual man."

"I can arrange for you to meet him."

"Do not bother. Lyerlith is a virgin priestess."

Ferrol, embarrassed, turned and led the way into the tent.

The tent was larger than it seemed from the outside. Favored patrons sat around an inner circle on flowered fields of the finest rugs. Two, sometimes three layers of patrons shifted and struggled for a good place to stand behind those rugs. Ferrol and Sigurd moved around, their shoulders sometimes brushing the walls of the tent, until they reached Azra. She had quickly charmed a merchant into providing space for her on his carpet. When Ferrol and Sigurd moved near, he graciously made room for them as well.

Ferrol had heard the magician was black and tall; other than that she did not know what to expect. He was as black as the shadow of a rock inside an unlit cave, but the man was no shadow. He was solid, seven feet tall, neither heavy nor thin, but his bones were well covered and he was totally bald.

He wore a robe of fine wool, dyed pale blue and embroidered with fantastic creatures, animals never seen by eye of mortal man, legendary creatures that, as he moved, seemed alive and moving with him. The work was so fine

Ferrol wondered if it was the embroidery of the famous Esmene, who she had heard was at the fair, working again after three years' absence.

The crowd settled. The magician smiled widely, showing a snowfield of teeth in his dark face as he began performing his tricks and small illusions. After many small entertainments, he sent a rope coiling toward the roof of the tent. When it almost reached the shadowed ceiling, it stopped, straightened, whereupon a small attendant climbed it and disappeared in a puff of smoke. That seemed to be the major trick of the evening, for, like the attendant, the magician disappeared in a puff of fire and smoke.

Nothing happened for a while. The people standing around the outer ring became restive and began to move away, seeking more exciting entertainment elsewhere.

"Is this what he calls magic?" Azra said bitterly. "I came here to see spells and magic, not children's tricks."

"Magic is forbidden on the fairgrounds," Sigurd said, "except for these small magics."

"Do not hurry away with the crowd, ladies," the merchant whose rug they shared said, leaning forward to speak in a whisper. "The show has not begun. The tricks are for the casual viewers. Now they are satisfied and have gone their ways, there will be another performance, one we have all paid dearly to see." He indicated his fellows around on their rugs.

"I must go soon," Sigurd whispered in Ferrol's ear. "I think you'd better stay with Azra. I have a strange feeling about this place."

"Can you find your way back to the temple?"

"Of course," Sigurd said.

Before she could rise to go, there was a stir in the tent and the magician stepped from behind a silken panel. This time he was dressed in a dark red robe embroidered with glittering stars and heavenly configurations that moved as he moved and sometimes when he was still. The magician turned slowly, spreading his wide smile around the room. "For those of you who are concerned about the time," he said in his lightly accented voice, "do not be. When you have seen all you wish to see, though it last for many years, you may return to this place and this time if you wish to." His strange honey-colored eyes stopped briefly on Sigurd, flicked over Azra, and seemed, to Ferrol, to search out her very soul.

She clutched the little basket in her lap and the magician smiled more widely. He moved over to her, bent forward, and with his hand wafted air from above the basket toward his nostrils. His eyebrows raised and for a moment the smile became thoughtful. Then he turned again, revealing the full sweep of the wide robe. The swirling robe, the warmth of the tent, the smoke that seemed to be filling the room, his laughter, were all stifling Ferrol. She thought if she did not leave the tent, she would be sick. She must have air. Fresh air.

Fresh air was blowing on Ferrol's face. More than that, she was shivering, standing on a plain of deep snow with a sweep of wild, cold wind driving needles of ice through her summer garment.

Sigurd, standing behind her, put her arms around Ferrol for warmth. "I'm freezing," she said. "He has transported us to this place. Why? Where is Azra?"

They found her on the ground already covered with a thin drift of icy particles over her gossamer gown. They took her between them, trying to keep her thin body warm.

"What are you doing?" she murmured after a while. "Where are we?"

"I suspect that we are still in the magician's tent and this is one of his better illusions," Ferrol said.

"It is better than I care to experience," Sigurd said.

Ferrol still clutched the basket of herbs in her claw hand. She plunged her left hand into the basket, bringing out a mixture of the herbs, which she sprinkled on all of them. There was no change in either their position or in the chill wind, which was rapidly sucking away their body heat.

They heard a sound behind them. Sigurd turned, whirling away from her companions, crouched in a fighting stance, a small dirk in her hand.

"You must forgive me, ladies. I had to have some place to put you while I attended to my other patrons," the magician said. "I did not realize a storm was blowing here. You must have covering."

He lifted his hand to the sky and swept it down. As his fingers pointed toward Azra, they held a cloak of dark sable, which he wrapped around her. He swept down a cloak of red fox for Ferrol and another of a spotted golden fur for Sigurd. As the ice was real, the cloaks were warm.

Azra shrank back into her cloak. "I did not come to you for wild adventure."

"But life is adventure." The magician smiled enigmatically. "I assure you, young ladies, this is no illusion. Were I to leave you here, you would live out your lives in this place. You could travel forever on this planet and not find a compatible place. I have brought you here to convince you that all is not illusion.

"Azra, show me yourself without your spell."

"No," she whispered. "I dare not. If I lose the illusion, I may not be able to restore it."

"*I* can restore it and more, but I must have your trust. How can you learn from one you do not trust?"

She looked at him, pale eyes brimming with tears. When she looked at her companions, Azra dropped her gaze.

Ferrol sucked in breath as she watched the slender, beautiful form of Azra draw in on itself, become gray and withered. The great mane of hair became limp, brownish wisps. It was the creature of her dreams. Sigurd did not seem surprised. "You never saw the illusion, did you?" Ferrol asked.

Sigurd shook her head. "No. Perhaps it is my training in the temple. I wondered what you saw in this poor creature."

The magician held out his hands to Azra. "Come. I will tell you a secret."

She put her withered hands into his smooth black ones and he drew her near, bending ever to whisper long into her ear. After a time she stepped back, raising her arms over her head. She whirled around so rapidly that the cloak wrapped around her completely, hiding her from view. When she stopped and the cloak was still, the beautiful Azra stood before them, if anything more breathtaking than before.

This time Sigurd gasped. The illusion was complete.

"You see why I wanted to meet the magician?" Azra said.

"I had no idea. Does Horscht know?" Ferrol asked.

"No. And my uncle, who has never seen the illusion, thinks he is besotted to take me with so little dowry."

"Will you show him the real Azra?"

"No. He loves the illusion."

"And you love the illusion," Sigurd said.

"Are you simple?" Azra snapped. "Of course I love it. Would you be as the real Azra is?"

"If you do not marry your young man, what *do* you want for your life?" the magician asked.

"I don't know," she cried. "I don't know."

"I know she wishes to learn real magic. She seems to have a talent for illusion. Will you teach her?" Sigurd asked.

"I believe I can." He smiled at Azra. "How would you like to travel with me as one of my attendants? Perhaps, some day, you may even become my assistant."

"Master, would you?" Azra prostrated herself, her forehead touching his silk-clad feet. "Would you take me with you, teach me?"

He lifted her to her feet. "Would you ever look back?"

Azra held out her arms to him. "Never!"

"What of your uncle? What of Horscht?"

She waved her hand toward Ferrol and Sigurd without taking her eyes from his. "They will tell them something. I was kidnapped by bandits. Anything. Take me with you now."

The magician held his hands over her head, weaving a complicated pattern around her, and before their eyes she was erased from the scene as if she had never been.

"I have sent her to my home. She will be cared for and attended like a princess until I return. In time, I may create a real person as lovely as the illusionary one."

"Until now I have never believed in magic," Ferrol said. "It has never worked for me."

"Never, Mistress Ferrol? Ah, yes, I know you as I

knew your parents long ago. You have a sweet heritage, mistress, and a sad life. Let me see your hand.''

Silently she held it out to him. He took the claw, holding it loosely, then tightly, stretching it out and compressing it to test its flexibility.

"No magic has worked before, nor will mine," he said. "The wound was made by iron, was it not?"

She nodded.

"Ah. In some lands, iron has no power. Here, it is a dire weapon. But you already know that, eh?"

She nodded again.

"You know, of course, the difference between real magic and illusion, as poor Azra did not?"

"Yes," she said softly. "Until this moment, I thought it was all illusion."

"Much is." He smiled gently. "I can give you an illusion as strong as Azra's. It will be so strong you will feel your fingers move, see them bleed when they are cut. Others will see the hand as whole as you will yourself. If that is what you want, I will teach you. But I cannot restore your fingers. No man can."

"I had hoped you could," Sigurd said. "I have been in the temple long enough to know that our healing magic, as fine as it is, does not extend to the creation of new fingers."

"Your Three cannot?"

"I suppose they could if they could be bothered. My experience thus far is that the Lordly Ones are greatly distant from the business of the temple. Most of the mysteries are what you call illusions."

"And are you happy creating these illusions for the peasantry?"

"Peasantry is not an ill profession," she said. "I am of

peasant stock myself, sold to the temple when it appeared I would be somewhat comely and reasonably bright.''

"A modest assessment on both counts," the magician murmured. "I entertain the thought that you are not happy in your role as virgin priestess. Your blood is too warm. Your feet and your heart cry out for adventure.''

"You are discerning," Sigurd said, "but my fate is sealed. I do not see how I can escape the bonds my father placed on me. There is honor involved here.''

"And you would honor your father's commitment? An honorable lady? And what would you do with your life?''

"Oh, I have all sorts of wild dreams," she said lightly. "To be a warrior woman searching the land for miscreants, righting wrongs. To be a simple housewife with many children tumbling around my doorstep. To sail the seas at the helm of a great ship. Dreams, all.''

"Not entirely impossible. I will weave you a simple spell and we will allow it to work out as it will. Anything is better than what you have, yes?''

"Almost anything, yes," she said.

He wove again with his hands, but Sigurd did not disappear nor change in any way. She merely snuggled deeper into her spotted cape as he turned back to Ferrol.

"And what have you decided for yourself? Shall I teach you the illusion?''

"I wanted to be a weaver. With the illusionary hand could I weave?''

"As if it were real." He waited for her answer.

"I always wanted to weave beautiful tapestries, rugs, things of great importance. In the coldest winter, I work slowly at the loom making simple cloth for my own use. I think those hours are the most boring hours of my life. It might be different with a facile hand, but I doubt it. I would rather be outside seeking my friends the herbs, picking them at their peak of power, curing them with love so those who are true herbalists can use them to work their healing magics. Earth magics. When I think of an entire year spent at the loom, I shudder. My shoulders ache. I have grown beyond that dream. My life is not unhappy. I have friends. I have Alexi. My needs are simple.''

"Do you not wish also for a congenial husband and a tumble of children? Is that not every maiden's dream?''

"And mine. But the claw has aways stood in the way. I fear the reaction of a man when I touch him with that hand.''

"I know of one young man who wants to be touched by your hand.''

Ferrol shook her head and laughed sadly. "You jest. There is no one.''

"There is Topoli.''

"He is a boy.''

"He is two years older than you. He loves the fields and forests. He knows the mountain paths and swamp ways. Why have you not allowed him to show you what he can do? To show you that he cares for you?''

"I don't know,'' Ferrol said thoughtfully. "I never thought of him as more than a friend.''

"I will make you no magic. You need none. Herbalists come to you for their supply who could easily pick for themselves at home. You are a magician of sorts yourself, an earth magician. I will weave you no spells, just give you some things to think about.''

"If my herbs are so good, why didn't they work on you?'' Ferrol held up her small basket.

He smiled. "As you said, you are an herb gatherer, not

an herbalist. What you have chosen are of the best, but they are against witchcraft. I work no witchcraft.''

Ferrol threw back her head laughing, and Sigurd and the magician joined her. They were still laughing when the three of them reappeared in the magician's tent. It was empty save for them. The patrons, even the rugs and furnishings, were gone.

''I leave soon,'' he said. ''I trust all will be well with you.''

''Take care of Azra,'' Ferrol said.

He smiled and stepped through the curtains at the rear of the tent.

''If I don't get back to the temple at once, I'll be in serious trouble,'' Sigurd said.

''I think we already are.'' Ferrol turned as a troupe of fair-wards led by Horscht pushed into the tent.

''Ferrol! What are you doing here? Have you seen Azra? She is missing, also a priestess from the temple.''

The fox cape, still about her shoulders, was much too warm. Ferrol slipped it off and folded it over her arm as Sigurd had already done.

''We came with Azra to see the magician.''

Horscht's face paled. ''He is gone! He, his wagons, his horses, his people, all gone. Has she gone with him? She has talked of nothing else since he came.''

He looked so forlorn that Sigurd stepped forward. ''Horscht! You are a man. You must know what it is to have a desire so strong that it consumes you day and night. It never leaves your mind.''

He nodded.

''So did your Azra. She wanted to go with the magician. She begged him to take her, to teach her the secrets only magicians know. It is for the best that she goes with him.''

"No!" he said angrily.

"Sigurd tells you true, Horscht. We were with her when the magician took her. She wanted to go." Ferrol made her voice as gentle as she could.

"But I loved her," he said.

"Do you love her enough to let her have what she most desires, the magician's secrets?"

"Perhaps she will come back."

"I would not wait for her, were I you," Ferrol said.

"I knew she did not love me in the same way I loved her. I thought she had some feeling for me."

"She did have some good feeling for you. Magic was something she wanted above all else."

Horscht straightened his shoulders and lifted his head, suddenly embarrassed that he had so revealed himself. "I will survive," he said. "It is time I moved on, anyway. I have lived in Ithkar all my life. It is time I saw some of the rest of the world."

Sigurd stepped forward and linked her arm in his. "Then, sir, perhaps you will escort me to the temple. It seems I have business there." She hefted the cloak so Ferrol could see the weight of it. "There are pockets in this cloak which seem to be filled with gold. Escort me to the temple that I may purchase the freedom of another lady, a lady who would like to see some of the rest of the world."

Horscht looked at her sharply. "I have seen you before. You are the priestess Lyerlith."

"No," she said. "I am Sigurd. Someone else will have to be Lyerlith, for I cannot."

Horscht seemed dazed when he turned to Ferrol. "Will

you be all right if I send some of my men to take you back
to your wagon?''

"I will be glad of their company," she said.

Ferrol chuckled all the way back to her wagon as she
remembered how they had looked together, both tall blonds,
both adventurers at heart. If it worked out that way, she
thought they could be happy together.

A small fire burned in the circle behind her wagon.
When she stepped into its light, Topoli came to his feet.

"Ferrol! Where have you been? I've been looking for
you for hours."

"Another friend and I took Azra to see the magician.
It's much too long a story for tonight. I must attend Alexi.
Poor fellow. Probably thinks he is going to starve."

"I tended him hours ago. He's fine. Are you?"

"Alexi allowed you to tend him?"

"Alexi and I are old friends."

She nodded. "Alexi is not the only one blind. I think
there are a good many things I have not seen with my eyes
open."

Topoli smiled at her. "You do not mind that I made
friends with Alexi behind your back?"

"You may be sorry when you find yourself doing most
of the tending," she said. "Come. I see there is tea made.
Let us have a cup together and talk."

The small fire flitted and flickered, cast its light over
them, danced in their eyes so they could see things in each
other they had not seen before. It cracked and chortled,
setting their soft words to its own tune. Once or twice
Ferrol looked up, thinking she heard the magician laugh,
but there was no one there. Only Topoli and the fire. In
her mind she sent a swift "Thank you" to the magician. If
there be magic, she said to herself, I have found it.

BABES ON BAWD WAY

George Alec Effinger

Gydrik—that was the name he'd picked for himself; back on the farm, his folks called him Smoon. He hated that name. It had been chosen to please a rich uncle who nevertheless gave away his entire fortune to a pretty romp who worked in a betting-shop, whose enigmatic smile turned out to be less the result of some mysterious charm than her simple vacancy of mind—anyway, Gydrik took a seat at a planked table by the whitewashed back wall of the inn. It was a large, dimly lighted, smoky place, a permanent establishment open the year 'round, unlike the scores of similar though smaller taverns and wineshops housed nearby in tents and hastily thrown up flat-roofed shacks. This nameless inn was a favorite gathering place of mercenary soldiers, outlaws, and assassins. They were a dangerous crew; Gydrik had been well warned away from here, and of course it was the first place he sought out when he arrived in Ithkar. He longed to take a rich man's gold and bind himself and his sword arm into service. Back on the farm, they talked about such ruffians as these with awe and fear. That's the way Gydrik wanted them to talk about him. The laughing, drinking, cursing, fighting men in the inn were just as he had imagined them, and he felt his heart pounding loudly in his chest. He prayed that none of them would speak to him, yet he recklessly hoped that one might. He suspected that he looked just like what he was, a boy fresh from the country, and he wanted desperately to be taken for one of these swaggering louts. Every one of them seemed able to ruin Gydrik's health with bare hands alone, so he tried to look inconspicuous; if anyone offered him the slightest insult, he knew he'd have to fight, and he'd never really done much of that before. Not with men like these, anyway.

A huge, balding man with a wild, tufted beard, wearing a wine-soaked, greasy apron came over to the table. "So?" he growled.

"What?" asked Gydrik. His mouth was suddenly very dry.

"Buy something or get out." The man glared at him.

"Oh, yes, sure. I want some ale, and I want some of whatever those fellows are eating."

"Are you going to take it away from them? Or do you want me to do it for you?"

Gydrik felt himself blushing. "No," he said, "I mean, I don't want *theirs*. I mean, if you have any more of it, I'd like a plate."

"Right off the farm, aren't you, kid?" The bearded man turned away shaking his head and went to fetch Gydrik's ale.

It had taken Gydrik almost four full days to make his

way from his family's farm southward to the Fair at Ithkar. It was almost summer's end, and although his parents and his brothers and his aunts and uncles were unanimous in their feeling that he was making a bad mistake, Gydrik had slung his great-grandfather's long two-handed sword on his back and put the rising sun on his left hand. He told himself that he would march resolutely away to make his fortune, without regret and without sentiment; but he turned to look back at the farm again and again until a long, dusty turn in the road hid it from view. At last, for the first time in his life, he was on his own.

And now he was here in Ithkar, in a riotous mughouse filled with rowdies and ronyons. He felt like a fool, an ignorant, naked, and very vulnerable fool. He had had to leave the great sword at the entrance to the fair; that had given him a moment of serious doubt. Weaponless, he would have to rely on either great wit or physical prowess. He had never had occasion to test either quality in himself. He shrugged; such a test might never come, and he concerned himself with his meal instead. He had just realized that he'd burned the roof of his mouth on a hot chunk of meat when someone rested a hand on the table beside his plate.

It was a young woman's hand, slim and graceful, yet callused and strong-looking. Gydrik looked up. She was slender and of medium height, and very pretty. She had very long black hair that she let fall untrammeled where it would. Everything else about her was as careless, as if no one had ever told her how lovely she was; and if she knew it, it was of no very great importance to her. She had pale green eyes that reminded Gydrik of the first tender shoots in his father's spring fields. Her features were fine, yet she did not appear in the least frail or delicate; on the contrary, her determined expression and her poised, rather assertive posture spoke of some inner reserve of strength. Her skin was an even, unblemished amber color—she had not lived an indoor life—and it set off the remarkable whiteness of her teeth and the surprising redness of her full lips. Gydrik had never seen a woman like her, not back on the farm. He was not aware that he was staring at her; he was conscious of only two things: the misty brightness of her beautiful eyes, and the annoying pain of his burned mouth. He swallowed a gulp of ale while he thought about what he ought to say to her.

"Would you mind some company?" she asked. She gave him a quick, warm smile.

Damn it, he thought, she's a harlot. Back on the farm, they had told him quite a lot about this sort of woman. Even among his neighbors there had been women of dubious virtue. They, however, were not harlots, not by his mother's lights; they were just fornicatrices. A harlot was a special and perilous case. To become a harlot (according to the hazy explanation Gydrik's mother provided) a woman had to make some sort of pact with demonic powers, although Gydrik had difficulty understanding this. It seemed to him that a woman could go ahead and realize such an ambition without diabolic sponsorship. But then, he told himself, his folks knew lots more about life than he did. There were, no doubt, all sorts of things about harlotry that he couldn't even imagine.

And now, not two feet away, there stood the prettiest girl he'd ever met, and she was quite evidently a harlot, knowledgeable in all those secret, tantalizing, evil, exquisite things that his mother wouldn't even talk about.

"Well?" she said, raising an eyebrow.

"Oh, sure, sit down. Would you like something to

drink?'' The innkeeper was already waiting to take her order.

"Some lamb's-wool would be nice,'' she said. "That's a drink we liked back on the . . . I mean, where I come from. You make it by mixing the pulp of roasted apples with a pint of—''

"This ain't no fancy city tavern, miss,'' said the bald-headed proprietor. "You can have a mug of ale or a glass of wine, and that's as good as it gets.''

"Some wine, then.''

Gydrik was afraid to say anything that might reveal his ignorance. He had not, after all, intended to seek the company of such a woman; but now, struck by this particular girl's particular loveliness, he decided that perhaps it would be a good thing. To be sure, it would introduce him quickly to the more illicit side of life, a side wholly unknown to him back on the farm. This was the world in which he intended to make his way and his fame. The expense—and he did not have much money to spare— could be considered an investment. What lord or wealthy merchant would hire a trooper or a bodyguard who had in truth never been in a brawl or with a woman? Whatever Gydrik's personal feelings were in the matter (and they were, at the moment, chaotically mixed), he was absolutely certain that some sort of transaction was called for. He hoped that the girl would take charge of the formalities, because he didn't have the faintest idea of what came next.

The ill-mannered chuff brought the wine, and Gydrik paid. "Thank you,'' said the girl.

"You're very welcome,'' said Gydrik. "Do you come here often?''

"No," she said. "To tell the truth, this is the first time I've been in this place."

"It's an interesting place. Noisy, though." Here the conversation lagged again for a moment.

"Listen to them," she said, indicating the drunkards and picaroons at a nearby table. "Blatant as calves, bellowing like a roe in rutting time. What's your name?"

"I'm Gydrik."

"My name is . . ." She hesitated, then smiled in a self-conscious way. "You can call me Amaranth."

"That's not your real name?"

"No, it's not."

"Well, Gydrik's not my real name, either."

"Fine," said Amaranth. "We won't bother with real names, then. You don't tell me yours, and I won't tell you mine." They both smiled.

Gydrik realized that he liked her very much. He wondered if he was allowed to like her; he hadn't paid her a brass dodkin yet.

Amaranth took a sip of the wine and winced a little. "Now, I hope you won't think me bold," she said, "but I came over here to ask you a question."

"I thought so," said Gydrik. He recalled his mother's warning: There are two sorts of harlot, the first being those who seduce with brazen wantonness, and the second being those who seduce with feigned innocence and simplicity.

She looked at him curiously. "A girl like me is out of place in a tavern like this." She glanced over her shoulder at the ruffians engaged in a boisterous game of treytrip and shuddered. "You don't seem nearly so brutish as they. Why, you're big and sturdy and thick-ribbed, but there's something nice in your face that I don't see in theirs. If there were some trouble, I'm sure you could protect me, but I don't think you'd start the fight. You're manly enough, but you're no common cutthroat."

Gydrik smiled, unable to think of anything to say. He wondered how much of her complimentary speech was honest admiration, and how much mere professional patter.

"That's why I wanted to speak to you," Amaranth continued. She glanced down at her fingers, which were nervously playing with the stem of the wineglass. "I've come to the fair only today. I intend to live my own life, on my own terms, so I thought . . . I mean, I plan to . . . that is, in the morning I'm going to start working on Bawd Way." She looked up at Gydrik to gauge his reaction.

"Then you're not a . . . harlot?" he said, surprised.

Her face reddened. "Not exactly yet, no," she murmured.

"Well, how much experience have you had, then? With men, I mean?"

She looked away. "Not any to speak of," she said.

"You mean you're a virgin?" He was incredulous.

She jerked her head around and glared at him furiously. "Yes, I am!" she cried. "And you can save your astonishment. The condition, I'm told, is curable. It isn't permanent or fatal, like being a fool, which is the case with some other people around here."

"I'm sorry, Amaranth," said Gydrik softly. "I only thought—"

Her expression changed again; she smiled, and the atmosphere brightened considerably. "You thought I *was* a harlot, didn't you? That's wonderful! If you believed I was a harlot, then other men will, too. I was so worried that I looked too . . . you know, *pure* or something."

Gydrik was about to tell her that she did, indeed, look sort of pure, but he stopped himself. He wasn't sure that was what she wanted to hear.

"If I'm going to be a harlot," she said, "then I'll need someone to protect me. You understand."

Gydrik scratched his head. "But aren't the harlots under the protection of the fair-court, the same as the other craftsmen and traders?"

"Of course they are. But the fair-wards can't be everywhere, and can't help a poor harlot alone with a patron suddenly turned black-hearted caitiff. And the fair-wards don't concern themselves with the fierce fights between the harlots. A girl needs someone to make certain that everyone respects her and allows her a small bit of the street to attract her business. I want to be left in peace. I need a strong man to do that for me."

"A procurer, you mean."

Amaranth looked as if she had just tasted something bitter. "I have no need for a procurer," she said. "My comeliness speaks for itself. I need a protector only. You seem a likely young man, wise in the ways in the world and more knowing than I, familiar with all the ins and outs of the fair and the city of Ithkar. I'm offering you a simple business proposition, one that may well be very profitable."

"I am a fighting man, a warrior," said Gydrik. "I never had any ambition to become a . . . a pander."

"Will you kindly stop saying that? You'll be my champion, my shield. Let me take care of the commerce. All you must do is sort of hover about ominously in the background."

"I can do that," said Gydrik.

"Of course you can."

He paused to consider telling her that she was a bit mistaken in her judgment of him; he really didn't know a blessed thing about the city of Ithkar or the fair. He couldn't even find his way to Bawd Way, the alley be-

tween the collection of cookshops and alehouses leading to
the outer precinct of the fair, where the beggars, pickpock-
ets, and false wizards camped.

"Then it's settled," decided Amaranth. "Let's find a
place to stay, and in the morning we'll choose a location to
set up shop."

"Set up shop," echoed Gydrik wonderingly.

Finding a room during the fair was more difficult than
either of them expected. If Amaranth had been a seamstress or Gydrik a smith, they might have slept in their
wagon; but both had arrived in Ithkar on foot. There were
rooms available at outrageous fees within the temple and
here and there throughout the fair. The variety of damp
and foul-smelling tents for rent were likewise obnoxious in
nature and extortionate in price. They considered walking
into the city, thinking that prices there must be lower than
in the fair proper, but both were by that hour tired, and
neither relished the long walk. At last, Gydrik opened his
purse and bought a rough, ragged, woollen blanket, far
from new, for Amaranth. They found an open place some
distance east of the carpenters' booths, voiced their hopes
that it would not rain that night, and settled themselves to
seek sleep, Amaranth wrapped in the insufficient blanket,
Gydrik with no blanket at all, sitting with his back against
a stout, black, shag-barked tree. It was, as they had prophe-
sied back on the farm, an inauspicious start to his new life
of danger and daring.

Morning came quickly, and with it the realization that
neither had found much rest, but both had discovered
unpleasant aches and sore muscles. Gydrik looked at her in
the morning light: her face was prettier than ever, though
her expression was weary and her frown forbidding. Her
hair was bedraggled, with twigs and leaves stuck in it, and

her plain brown lockram dress now mud-stained. Her slender bare arms were streaked with grime. She was still a lovely girl, but she was not Gydrik's idea of an enticing courtesan. What she lacked in kohl and lip rouge she would need to make up in personality. Gydrik shrugged; she had been so assured the night before, perhaps she knew what she—what *they* were getting into. Gydrik hoped so.

Their entrance into Bawd Way was a portent of what was to come. For perhaps a hundred yards there was a narrow, twisting lane bordered by gaudy canvas pavilions and shabby booths and sheds, all leaning together, their weathered and aging boards painted thickly with a bewildering muddle of eye-catching colors. A curious stench permeated the air. A woman stood outside each tent or shanty; these queans, too, were aging and weathered, and they, too, were covered from head to toe with color and paint, from their wildly tinted hair and encarmined cheeks to their tawdry, clinquant finery. The harlots stared at Amaranth and Gydrik; she turned to him and opened her mouth, but she did not speak. He felt embarrassed for her. He saw her falter, and then he saw her pluck up her courage. She tried to rub away a smudge of dirt on her chin. "I wish I had a comb," she murmured.

"What do you want to do?" asked Gydrik. "Do you want to leave?"

Her eyes opened wider. "Oh, no, I can't do that." She walked over to one of the riggish women, who was regarding her with rude amusement. "Excuse me," said Amaranth, "how can I . . . who do I see about getting a place here to work?"

The harlot laughed, a harsh, braying sound. "La, you!" she cried to her associates. "Look at this one!" She laughed again. "You're going to have to wash off the stink of the stables before any man is going to look twice at you." She turned her attention to Gydrik. "And I suppose this is your fine belswagger. Don't you two know that we in the city aren't wearing straw in our hair this season?" Then the other women began mocking and laughing, and Gydrik wished that he had never met this Amaranth, had never even wanted to come to Ithkar and its blessed fair.

The withered, grossly prinked harlot grinned, showing two gold teeth and empty spaces for three more. She reached out and felt the coarse cloth of Amaranth's dress. "Oh, this is a pleasure!" she cried. "Oh, this is nice stuff! You're lucky to have such a generous gallant, to give you a gown like this!"

Amaranth jerked away, then slapped the harlot so hard across the face that the smack echoed in the alleyway, and the woman tottered back against the decrepit shack, a red handprint emblazoned on her cheek. There were tears in her eyes, and she was furious. She took a threatening step toward Amaranth, but the young woman just swung her hand smartly and hit the woman again. This time the fat-faced woman sat down heavily in the dust and made no attempt to rise. She held her hand against her stinging cheek.

"Ridicule me, if you want," said Amaranth in a low, chilling voice, "but don't say a word against Gydrik. He's my friend, and he's been good to me. Understand?" The harlot on the ground nodded slowly. The other women were silent.

Amaranth turned around proudly and walked up the narrow lane. Gydrik hurried after her. "Now, see," she remonstrated, "*you're* supposed to do that kind of thing for me."

Gydrik stammered, "I—I suppose I just wasn't getting as mad as fast as you were. I would have slapped her myself in a little while."

Amaranth smiled at him. "I know you would have," she said sweetly. "Now, there has to be some official within the fair here to tax these women. I saw none such at the gate. Mayhap I did not ask rightly. He'll find me a place." Gydrik was astonished by her good sense; that idea would never have occurred to him. He had never known any girl like her back on the farm.

The temple's factor was plump, short, red-faced, always smiling, happy to be of service, and glad to welcome new taxpayers to the street. He collected a licensing fee from Gydrik, wrote out an official receipt that Amaranth must keep with her at all times (he called her, in his ingratiating yet sniggering voice, a "demimondaine"), and wished them both great success in their enterprise. The taxman assigned Amaranth to an unused location midway down Bawd Way. The thing was little more than a dilapidated shack made of warped and broken boards, fronted by a frayed curtain of red stammel that could be thrown back over the roof to air the place out. Airing the place out didn't accomplish much in the way of making it more pleasant. Amaranth sighed. "This will have to do for now," she said. "As we become richer, no doubt we'll be able to afford a better place."

Gydrik turned up his nose. "You'll want a fresher mattress, at least. This bag of straw has probably been here since the days of the Three Lordly Ones."

Amaranth gave him a sharp glance. "Gydrik," she said, "you shouldn't mention them in such a place as this."

He was taken aback. "No? Why not?"

"Just for my sake, don't. Well, I suppose we'll have to make the best of this, dirt floor, ancient mattress, musty air, and all. Now, you go do your job and let me attend to mine."

"Good," said Gydrik. He still didn't know precisely what she expected him to do. "You'll be all right?"

"I'll be fine. You're my protector; if I need you, I'll shout."

Gydrik nodded. That meant that she expected him to stay nearby—but where? The other harlots must have had men watching over them in a similar capacity; he had to find out where they loitered. He glanced around the small shack one more time, thought of nothing pertinent to say, and ducked gratefully back into the fresh air. He ambled up the board-paved lane, and the trulls called to him as he passed, making little chirping sounds and low whistles. He smiled at them and tried to seem casual, but he felt an odd disquiet. His cheeks reddened as he walked by the wanton, mobled women. Perhaps ten or twelve shacks west of Amaranth's, there was a large tent set up with tables and benches and several great kegs. Here was where he was supposed to sit and pass the time with the other men—what had that strumpet called him? A belswagger? It had a nice ring to it and left no bad taste, as pander or whore-monger did.

He sat himself down and ordered a pot of ale, noticing that his supply of coins was beginning to run rather low. Of course, tonight he would receive his wages from Amaranth. They had never actually settled on how they would split the income, but Gydrik was not a greedy young man: half sounded reasonable enough to him. Then they would find the most elaborate and succulent dinner anywhere in the fairgrounds, and they'd eat and drink and celebrate their new lives and independence. Until evening, however, it was Gydrik's duty to stay here in the canvas alehouse, and come to Amaranth's rescue if need be. He swallowed some of the foaming brew and promised himself that he would put in a full and resolute day's work. When Amaranth paid him his brocage, he'd be able to take it with a clear conscience.

The afternoon passed rather quickly. Gydrik made the acquaintance of many of the fellows who spent their days drinking and telling immoderate tales of their own cleverness and accomplishments. He was quickly welcomed into their society, and was pleased to learn that there seemed to be little professional jealousy among them, or, if there was, it was well hidden from the watchful eyes of the fair-wards. The harlot who had accosted Amaranth, whose name was Bathykolpia but whom everyone called Dearie, was represented by a barrel-chested cullion named Lorph. Lorph was already mugged up before noon, when Gydrik met him, yet he continued to down measure after measure of a liquor called snowbroth, which was served very cold. He laughed uproariously when Gydrik recited the story of Amaranth's battle with Dearie. "She's got it coming," cried Lorph. "She's always got it coming."

Toward cockshut, as the cool sun slipped away to its rendezvous with night, Gydrik staggered back up Bawd Way to see how Amaranth had fared this first day in her new career. He was himself a trifle buoyed by ale and good fellowship, so he was dismayed to hear the girl weeping from within the shack. Gydrik drew himself up and took a deep breath, then threw aside the fabric curtain. He expected to see some foul blackguard attempting to exploit her helplessness, but she was alone in the darkness.

She sat upon the old mattress and cried into her trembling hands.

"What's wrong?" asked Gydrik.

Amaranth looked up. "Oh," she said tearfully, "it's you."

"Of course it is. Why are you crying? Has someone hurt you? Why didn't you call?"

Amaranth shook her head. "No, it isn't that." Her eyes sought his, pleading. "Gydrik, what's wrong with me? Am I repellent to you? Am I some kind of hideous witch?"

He went to her and took her hand. "Of course not," he said. "Back on the farm, I never even hoped to meet anyone as pretty as you."

"Then why—" She began to sniffle again.

"Why what?"

Her shoulders slumped. "Then why didn't a single man approach me today? Not one! All the others had their share of admirers. There were certainly enough blissom idlers passing up and down the alley. Not one even deigned to speak to me. Why?"

Gydrik was astonished. He had no answer for her. "You mean, you didn't make any money?" he asked.

She gave him an angry look. "Money! That's all you men think about! What about me? What am I supposed to think?"

The image of the magnificent feast faded sadly from Gydrik's mind. He began to see what Amaranth was worried about. Why *hadn't* anyone spent time with her? He chewed his lip as he thought. They sat in silence for many minutes, but neither could solve the riddle. Amaranth was as good-looking as any of the other women—better than most, if the truth be told. She was young and fair of face, with a form that would please even the most exacting critic of feminine grace and figure. Yet, quite clearly, she had failed.

"There is certainly nothing wrong with you, Amaranth," said Gydrik after a while. "There is no defect in your charms. If that be true, then the defect must be in their presentation."

Her face lit up. "It's true that I did not look like the others," she admitted.

"No," said Gydrik, "perhaps you seemed too wholesome. Perhaps the sort of gentleman or knave who passes through this way is seeking the very spangled, gilded, lacquered, rigged-out kind of trollop you and I both despise."

She shrugged. "I suppose that if I'm to be a success in this industry, I will have to adopt its standards. I cannot hope to reform the tastes of so many people. I am only one powerless girl."

"Let us get some rest," he suggested, "and tomorrow I will consult a wizard."

"Can you afford a wizard?"

Gydrik frowned in the darkness. "I can afford a *small* wizard, but we need only a *small* miracle." Amaranth, her empty stomach complaining, stretched out upon the mattress, and Gydrik covered her with her blanket. He curled up nearby on the dirt floor. He had only three silver coins and a spill of coppers. Before he fell asleep, he wondered what he would be prepared to do when they had been spent.

The next day, Gydrik moved away about fifty yards and watched what happened after Amaranth went to work. Men began strolling up and down Bawd Way not long after midday, stopping to talk with this harlot or that, negotiating fees or just perusing the wares. By midafternoon, some of the harlots had earned the first money of the day, and all had been approached at least once. All but Amaranth, that is. She stood defiantly, her eyes red with weeping and her cheeks red with shame. "I must do something to change this," Gydrik told himself. "She is being humiliated, and it is my fault. It is because I have no head for business. I should have taken a job as a mercenary soldier, but I have got myself into this, and I owe it to Amaranth to make the best of it." He turned and hurried away from Bawd Way, toward the even meaner district where the petty wizards and quacksalvers had their stands.

Little more than three pieces of silver, that was all that Gydrik had in his purse. He knew he couldn't afford a great and renowned magician. He had to settle for one who was lesser-skilled, hoping that the necessary charm was inexpensive, and that the wizard himself was not a charlatan or worse.

There were dozens of minor wizards to choose from, all operating out of booths or tents, the same as the pie-makers and the needlewomen. Back on the farm, they called these unsavory and ill-famed magicians "tresclatiú," or "three-handed ones," as opposed to the more reputable wizards whose magics derived from some firmer connection with the temple. The epithet came from an old saying that a tresclaton had one hand to take your silver, one hand to blind your eyes to his actions, and a third hand to perform some witchery for which you would no doubt soon be sorry. There was no way to know which of these conjurers had, in fact, any real power and, if so, could control it. Gydrik felt a great uneasiness steal over him, but, with a sudden determination, he stepped up to the booth of the tresclaton who appeared to be the least mad.

A hand-lettered board said his name was Schechanale the Ordained. He was humming idly to himself and grooming his long bridled beard. "Help you with something, son?" he asked.

Gydrik was reassured by the tresclaton's friendly and wholly sane tone of voice. "I need a spell or something," he said.

"You have come, as they say, to the right place. You're a stout lad, deep-chested, with powerful arms. You're pledged to service, aren't you? And you want something to protect you in battle. I have a wide range of simple—"

"Not quite. I need something that will give me good business sense."

Schechanale raised his eyebrows. "Interesting, most interesting, and a pleasant change, I might add. Now, you must understand that business sense isn't something like strength or keen eyesight that I could take care of with a single draught or incantation. 'Business sense' is an abstract and complex idea. I must know more. Do you plan to employ yourself here at the fair?" Gydrik nodded. "And in which section?"

"On Bawd Way," said Gydrik. "Maybe you have something that would make someone irresistible to men."

There was a startled silence from the wizard. "I try not to make judgments about other people's lives," he said. "Still, I just can't understand why a promising young man like yourself would resort to selling himself to strangers. Surely you could find more rewarding— Never mind, it's not my place to say such things." He turned to rummage through his collection of talismans and preparations.

Gydrik found himself blushing again. "You don't understand. It isn't for me, it's for a girl. All the men seem to want the more vulgar and uncouth harlots. Amaranth is pretty and very amiable, but she can't compete with those other blowsy strumpets."

Schechanale laughed. He made a row of five identical earthenware pots on his counter. "These will work like a charm, as they say."

"What are they?" asked Gydrik.

"Your magic to make the sweet Amaranth irresistible to men. It comes in five different forms."

"What are the differences between them?"

"Only price. For a thousand pieces of silver, you get this one." The tresclaton opened the lid of the first jar and removed a small piece of parchment. "She need only recite this charm under certain particular conditions, and she will be irresistible. For five hundred pieces of silver, you get the second jar." Under the lid was a little cloth bag on a leather cord. "When she wears this, no man can choose to leave her. For one hundred pieces of silver, this third jar contains a pleasant-tasting liquor. When she drinks it, she will control the will of any man, if that man has partaken of some alcoholic beverage during the preceding day. For ten pieces of silver, the fourth jar will provide a sort of periapt that she must keep beneath her bed. Any man who comes near will be held by its charm and she will be irresistible to him, but only in that place."

"What about the fifth jar?" asked Gydrik.

"Well, that costs three pieces of silver, and is just as effective as any of the rest."

"I'll take that, then."

"I have to warn you," said Schechanale. "The reason it's so cheap is that it is rather unpleasant. You might say disgusting. It is an ointment—I'll ask you not to lift the lid until you take the pot away—which your young lady must smear over her entire body. She must then slip naked into the river Ith at precisely midnight, and remain beneath the surface of the water until she begins to hear angelic voices singing. When she emerges, the unguent will have had its effect. She will find, however, that the substance itself is unusually difficult to remove, and while it remains it will surround her with a particularly unpleasant fragrance. It may last upwards of a year. Her swains, nevertheless, will flock to her side despite it.''

Gydrik had only a single moment of hesitation; then he took his last three pieces of silver, gave them to the wizard, and took the small unglazed pot. He felt a peculiar mixture of excitement and misgiving.

That night, about a mile from the fair and beyond the gates of Ithkar, Gydrik sat upon the bank of the river and watched as Amaranth shrugged out of her dress and her unflattering line smicket. Although he was a good twenty yards away when she opened the pot of ointment, the stench made him gag. Amaranth fell to her knees, nearly overcome. She looked up at him dubiously. "Go ahead," he urged, "put it on."

Still she hesitated. "I don't want to," she said.

"What have you got to lose?"

"My stomach," she replied. She took a deep breath and held it, then dipped three fingers into the pot and began spreading the thick, reeking stuff over her skin. "All over?" she asked.

"All over."

"My hair, too?"

"I suppose so."

She was weak with nausea when she finished, and she hurried to the edge of the river. "This water doesn't smell so sweet, either," she complained.

"You've gone this far," said Gydrik. "Let's get it

finished." Even back on the farm, where there was always
an assortment of terrible odors, he'd never smelled anything so bad.

Without another word Amaranth walked into the slow,
dark water eddying beneath the limbs of a twisted, low-
hanging tree. The stars were hard and fast in the sky, not
twinkling but staring down coldly. There was no sound but
the gentle lapping of the water. Gydrik nervously tossed
pebbles into the river and waited. After a minute, Amaranth's head broke the surface. "I heard them!" she cried
wildly. "I heard angels! Singing!"

"Magic," snorted Gydrik derisively. "Come on, you'll
catch your death. Dry off and get dressed, and then we'll
go back to the cabin."

She emerged from the river like a young goddess or a
princess of the sea nymphs. The rank odor of the close and
tenacious ointment thickened the air, but Gydrik hardly
noticed. He felt a hot flush rip through his body as he saw
Amaranth as if for the first time. She was more than
pretty, more than lovely—she was the absolute, divine
embodiment of beauty. She was the perfect model of
everything the human soul aspired to. She was—irresistible.

"Amaranth," he whispered hoarsely.

"What is it? This damned stuff doesn't want to wash
off. I'm going to have to smell it until it *wears* off. I don't
know if I can stand it."

"Amaranth, I love you."

She looked up at him, pleased. "Oh, Gydrik, I feel the
same way about—" Then her face fell. "Ah, I see: the
magic. The spell's made you want me. Well, forget about
it. This is for business only. I don't need you mooning
over me. You won't be helpful to me that way. I'm sorry
it's affected you, too, but you'll just have to learn to live

with it." She turned away from him and drew on her coarse clothing.

He felt a burning desire and, at the same time, a cold, heavy sickness. He knew that she was right. She would never yield to him. She knew that his passion was induced by that bawbling wizard's sorcery, and so it meant nothing to her. What torture he had purchased for himself, for only three pieces of silver!

He discovered that he couldn't bear to stay in the same shack with her so long as she spurned his artificially induced love. He couldn't sleep, he couldn't even hope to rest. While she lay on the mattress and dreamed, he wandered through the fair, muttering and cursing himself for a wantwit. Even after midnight, many tents and shops were still entertaining customers, but Gydrik had little money now, just a few coppers, not enough to buy a spoiled sausage. He was hungry and he was tired; even worse, however, was the trouble in his soul.

He didn't return to Bawd Way until long after sunrise. He was surprised and heartsick to see a cluster of brabbling men already around their shack. There were gentlemen in silk shirts and high leather boots; yellow-bearded savage mercenaries with their long hair bound in braids; portly, well-to-do merchants and curious springalds; rich men and servants; graybeards and striplings. The sight made an odd, stark, cold rage grow in him. Gydrik pushed through the crowd of enchanted admirers. Amaranth was at the center of the circle, entertaining bids from the more affluent. "One hundred pieces of gold!" cried one. "Two hundred!" shouted another. Still the bidding went higher. Gydrik elbowed them aside and grabbed Amaranth by the wrist, dragging her away.

"Let me go!" she said angrily. "They're offering yellowboys now! Gold!"

"No," he said grimly. He pulled her along the street. The men watched in astonishment, the harlots pointed and jeered.

"I can earn a fortune today," said Amaranth. "I already have a thousand pieces of silver."

"I don't care." He ignored her protests and the blows she struck on his head and back. She screamed for help, but it was obvious that she was merely being disciplined by her gallant, so no one paid attention. At last, after a wearying contest of wills, they arrived at the booth of Schechanale the Ordained.

The wizard smiled. "Some problem?" he asked.

"Isn't it illegal here at the fair to beauty merchandise by magic?" demanded Gydrik.

"It is."

"Then you should have warned me. You've nimmed me out of my money. I want you to remove the spell and refund my silver."

The tresclaton shook his head. "The spell enhances nothing. What the customer buys is still the same as ever. Remember, my foolish lad, that the harlot does not truly sell herself, only her time and her forbearance. My magic has changed only our perception of the fair Amaranth. If you paint a figure upon an urn, it does not change the function of the urn. The unguent has the same effect as the gaudy cosmetics used by her competitors, but to a greater degree. And the other harlots all employ the same spell themselves; that is why Amaranth attracted no patrons before. The ointment is legal. The fair-court ruled upon it many years ago."

Gydrik wanted to seize the old man by the throat, but he

did not dare. He felt himself seething. "How much does it cost to remove the spell?" he asked.

"No, you airling!" cried Amaranth. "My fortune!"

"How much!"

Schechanale clucked his tongue. "It's very rare that anyone desires the spell removed. I don't know if anyone even keeps such a thing in stock. It's been a long time, I wonder if I still have— Yes, here we are. An alexipharmick. Five hundred pieces of silver."

The high price startled Gydrik, but he recovered quickly. "We'll take it," he said.

"You nidget, I'll be damned first!" shouted Amaranth.

"You'll be black-eyed if you don't give me that money," said Gydrik. Such behavior and speech was quite out of character for the young man, but of course he was in the grip of a powerful and not entirely holy compulsion. He wrested Amaranth's purse away from her and paid the tresclaton. He received in return a small vial of clear liquid that smelled of violets. "She drinks this?" he asked.

"Yes, that's all," said Schechanale.

"Drink it," Gydrik ordered.

"No," she said firmly.

"Drink it!" He shut her nostrils with one hand, resisting her struggles and scratches. When she opened her mouth at last to gasp a breath, he poured in the potion. Almost immediately, she relaxed. So did Gydrik; the resistless passion receded.

"I heard the angels sing again," said Amaranth softly.

"Now go away," said the tresclaton. "She still smells terrible."

Gydrik took Amaranth's hand gently and led her toward the alehouses and cookshops. As they walked along silently, he made a very surprising discovery. "Amaranth," he said wonderingly.

"I'm angry with you. Worse than that: I'm livid. I'm furious, indignant, wrathful—"

"Amaranth, I still love you."

She stopped in her tracks. "Go to! You couldn't. That wizard removed the charm. These men aren't flocking around me anymore. Maybe you're just weak from hunger."

"No, listen to me. I don't feel that overpowering desire, the false feeling the magic caused; but I still feel . . . something. I still . . . love you."

She gazed at him, a little smile on her face. "That's nice," she said. She took his hand and they walked on, not caring where they were headed. That first moment, that first realization of bliss, is usually so bewildering that hunger, thirst, and weariness are overwhelmed.

Gydrik was overjoyed to learn that Amaranth had not needed to sell her honor to earn the thousand pieces of silver. A wealthy old landowner had paid the fee, and then had been too overcome by the magic to defile her with his touch. He had merely sat at her feet and adored her until she'd grown bored and restless and chased him away. The landlord had left happy and filled with ensorcelled joy. That was when Gydrik had arrived to end Amaranth's promising career.

The two of them passed the remainder of that day wandering, delighted merely to be in each other's company. They took no notice of where they went or what they did. Afterward, they could never recall anything else that happened to them at the fair.

And does this lead to a happy ending? Well, sadly, no. And yes, too. The afterclap was that they decided to take the remaining silver pieces and buy a farm near Gydrik's folks. After all, farming was what he knew best and what he was best suited for. And so, as it developed, was she. Holgenna—for that was her real name—had run away from her parents' farm on the same day as Smoon. The two were soon married. They suffered hard times, celebrated the births of three sons and two daughters, grew older, and came eventually to despair of their lives. On occasion, each resented the other, because each blamed the other for the common, colorless, laborious life they led, rather than the life of adventure and excitement they had sought at the fair. Then, as is the way with life, things changed once more. As they grew still older, and their children grew up, both Smoon and Holgenna made a vital discovery, a kind of magic in its own right: yes, it was true that they had been transformed into the image of their own parents, a fate they had despised in their youth; but the secret they learned at last was that, in the same way, their children would be transformed into them. This, in the wisdom of the Three Lordly Ones, guaranteed them a kind of immortality, which was just what the gods had intended. So it was, at the last, a happy ending. The strapping Smoon and the lovely Holgenna fell deeply in love once again, and passed the remainder of their lives in peace and contentment.

SARDOFA'S HORSESHOES

Gregory Frost

A sparse crowd lined the great square gallery of the Lordly Ones' temple. At the crowd's edge, alone within the colonnade, the foreigner stood. The splendor of his green silk robe set him apart from others in the crowd as much as did his attitude, his pose. He had one foot propped upon the base of the nearest column, one arm across his knee. Indifferently, he took a crunching bite of the juicy, bittersweet *krushe* purchased from a fruit vendor outside the temple. He scratched at his nostrils, sniffed, then patted one shiny sleeve to his mouth.

Behind him, the crowd strolled along the gallery in clusters. Most of them studied the carvings that lined the walls of the gallery: there, a father showed his young son the landing of the Three; there, a family stood back, the better to view a wide bas-relief from the Great Creation Tales, in this instance a depiction of the Three Lordly

Ones hovering in the void around a central point that they were compressing with their hands into the world.

Other visitors, like the foreigner in resplendent green, stared transfixed out at the mountainous shrine in the center of the temple complex. Their eyes beheld the shrine with awe. But in the eyes of Vasu, the foreigner, something darker than admiration lurked.

Across the bright, open square, separate from the numerous other buildings that comprised the temple at Ithkar, the Shrine of the Three Lordly Ones rose up in layered peaks and plateaus—each level a mass of sculpted heads and dancing asparas—that architecturally led the eye to a large central pinnacle. This, like a manmade volcanic cone, was open at the top to allow sunlight to reach deep inside the shrine. Directly below it lay the wide stone platform on which the Sky Lords had first appeared—the platform around which priests and priestesses gathered for prayer and divine guidance, where the words of the Sky Lords whispered in their ears.

The platform that he, Vasu, had come to destroy.

He tossed away the core of the *krushe* and wiped his hand on his silk robe in the neglectful manner of one who has a thousand more such robes. Turning, he spat out a seed and went through the crowd, pausing momentarily as he saw on the wall behind him the carved aspect of his lord, his god—Thotharn. The aspect of a squat hourglass-shaped cloud he knew very well. It surprised him that outcast Thotharn's image should still be here for people to view. Well, he thought, they would have a better view of it soon enough.

Proud as a god himself, Vasu passed the carved panel and strode beneath a long surbased arch. Outside the gallery, he entered another world.

Beyond the temple walls, the Fair at Ithkar was at a midday high. The narrow street churned, a human sea, waves of bobbing heads. Wealthy merchants ignored hobbling beggars who pursued them; dour priests watched over the stalls where their usurers doled out and took in money; nimble-fingered thieves, knowing the stalls to be dangerous territory, worked the crowd while their mates looked out for a flash of sun off a brass helmet or the shiny tip of a quarterstaff above the sea of heads, which signaled the arrival of fair-wards.

Vasu watched the thieves at work. He considered, and as quickly dismissed, the advisability of contacting them. The skills of a common cutpurse could not aid him in his task. He saw again in his mind's eye the hot, treeless square between the gallery and the shrine. No thief, no matter how crafty, could make the journey. The answer would have to be sought elsewhere. And, he was certain, it must be sorcerous to be successful. He stepped into the crowd.

The search took him half an hour but could easily have taken four times as long. He was lucky. Other worshipers of Thotharn were here, he knew. However, recognition in this mass of humanity was no easy thing. Their sigil was that evilly smiling mask—usually no larger than the signet of a ring so as not to draw attention from the opposition.

In a street within the tavern and restaurant district, a group of dancers performed, repeating the same two numbers over and over while a hawker invited the crowd to view their full show that night. Off to one side, watching the dancers with a heavy, incurious gaze, a bedizened woman stood. The revealing clothing she wore was of a foreign cut. This at first caught Vasu's eye and drew him to her. Her brown hair was cropped short, revealing to him the lobe of one ear and the charm piercing it—a silver face agrin. She must have sensed his unwavering stare, and she turned her head to meet it.

Vasu made his way through the crowd to her. "Have you ever seen a night without stars?" he asked softly.

She returned to watching the dancers. "A night without stars is still not as dark as Thotharn."

"So true. I have a mission to exile the three usurpers. To succeed I must reach the top of their shrine."

"You'll need 'high' magic, then." When he failed to acknowledge her pun in any way, she went on flatly, "Only a man invisible could walk the courtyard from the gallery to the shrine. And priests are everywhere, watching."

"I know—I've spent my entire morning observing them. I've studied the shrine from every side. There is no obvious access."

"Have you spoken to any magicians?" she asked.

"Not as yet."

"Good. Don't. Most visible magic is scrutinized by the priests and fair-wards. And many of the magic users are connected to the temple."

"Are they as strict as that?"

She laughed, though it seemed at the dancers. "If they weren't, would your mission pose such a problem? Or be necessary at all? Thotharn might enter here himself if magic wasn't limited." The dance ended. The crowd applauded lightly.

"I suppose," he answered glumly. "Now that you've told me what I mustn't do, can you recommend what I should?" There was a hint of arrogance in his voice. He disliked her assertiveness. It stung his pride.

"Perhaps. There is a blacksmith who's come here for years. His name is Sardofa. He makes the usual implements, wagon wheels and such, but specializes in more elaborate workings in gold and silver. It's claimed he has alchemical knowledge and has discovered a way to alloy his gold with iron—a process that also imbues the metal with magical properties. For instance, his sword blades, made for armorers to fashion, can cut through ordinary iron. Whereas the same metal made into armor wards—"

"This is all very wondrous," he interrupted, "but I have no intention of fighting my way across that friendless courtyard. And no armor of this world can withstand a Priest's Song."

"Of course, this is so," she agreed, rankled by his tone. "His horseshoes, though, can raise a horse from the ground, up."

Vasu said nothing, although his mouth moved as if reciting vowels. He envisioned himself on a horse with wings, high up in the clouds, the city laid out in flat perspective below him. But of course that was absurd—in daylight he would be a spectacle. He altered his fantasy to a night scene. Flying, that was high sorcery indeed.

"Where is he, this Sardofa?"

"I'll show you," she answered, and set off into the throng so that he had to quickly shove his way through in order not to lose her.

The dancers began again.

The stall lay on the north side of the fair. A great blue-and-yellow-striped canopy had been tied over it with a hole in the center for the chimney of a forge. Two empty pens for animals, drapes concealing private chambers in the rear, and the large black forge itself filled the enclosure. From under the canopy, one could look out and see a segment of the harbor and boats that navigated it, and beyond that a wide plain stretching back to mountains, which were vague like mirages against the sky. Vasu smelled the tang of dead fish in the air.

His guide led him to the striped canopy. Inside, a young man sat beside the forge, polishing a lantern.

"You there," the woman called to the lantern polisher. "This man needs your services. Be good with him—he's *rich*." She laughed and turned away, and had vanished into the crowd before Vasu could as much as react.

Flustered by the attention she had drawn to him, he hurried into the tent to escape the crowd, but then halted just inside, having not yet threaded a lie for the occasion.

The young man came over to him, still carrying the lantern and cloth. "What is it you seek?" he asked.

"I . . . ah"—Vasu smoothed down his robe—"I wish to speak with your master."

The young man looked perplexed. "Who would you be referring to?"

"Sardofa the blacksmith."

Grinning as if he had heard this misapprehension many times before, the young man answered, "That's me."

Vasu regarded him anew. This young Sardofa had muscle, but hardly as much as he expected. Blacksmiths he had always thought of as great human bulls who could heft a keg of nails without travail. And also he imagined them as older men. This one was young enough to be an apprentice . . . or was he being deceived? She had said that Sardofa was an alchemist, and who knew that *they* knew? They sought gold and youth, of that he was sure. What if Sardofa had found both?

Vasu realized abruptly that Sardofa awaited his reply. "I was told . . . I was told you could make special shoes for my horse," he said.

"What, special? Is one leg shorter than the rest?"

"No." Did everyone find it diverting to twit him? "What I meant was, shoes with special properties. Your name commands a great deal of respect, you know." As he spoke, the words became fluid, the story he would tell jelled. "You are the chief among your peers and all of them speak fondly—if a little jealously—of your abilities."

The young man's smile broadened as these testimonials were recited. "Your tongue is sand," he replied, "because the wind of a desert blows off it."

"No, truly not," wheedled Vasu. "We asked all around and all I heard was 'Sardofa.' "

"What is it you want, then?"

"I've told you—magical horseshoes."

"I think not."

"Look, I can pay you extraordinarily well. You wouldn't need to work for years."

"If they exist at all, why should you desire such shoes?"

"Back home, you see, I have a wife. She's extremely beautiful but, frankly, only on the surface. Beneath her perfection lies a spirit twisted with greed. I give her presents to feed this spirit, to keep her faithful to me. I know you will say, 'Then do away with her, stupid man,' but you see . . . ah, I love that exterior too much. I thought that a gift such as a horse that can fly would appease her for a long time. It would be worth any price to me."

The young blacksmith began rubbing the lantern again. "I think you would find the properties in these supposed horseshoes limited. A horse so equipped would only be able to fly for the briefest while, no more than two succes-

sive nights during any cycle of the moon, the 'when' of it
determined by the time of shoeing. Such are the limits of
the magic. What I'm saying—''

"Yes, yes," interrupted Vasu. "I—she can only ride
the horse twice a month."

"Just so." He kept his head lowered but raised his eyes
to the foreigner. "You still want them?"

"Absolutely. The, um, monthly rejuvenation of your
magic will monthly refresh my marriage."

Sardofa laughed quietly. "Where's this horse of yours,
then, glib man?"

The corner of Vasu's mouth twitched. "I'll just go and
get him. Shall I?"

Sardofa nodded absently. Vasu hurried off, triumphant.

Immediately, the young man set down his lamp and rag
and went to the forge, where he called out toward the rear
of the tent. A moment later, a short man came out. He had
massive arms, a barrel chest, and white hair hanging to his
shoulders. The young lantern polisher reached into his
tunic, then held his hand up. On his open palm lay a group
of shiny, iridescent black nails. "We've little time now.
What of these?" he asked.

The old man sidled over to him and looked askance into
his palm, then whistled appreciatively, softly, between his
teeth.

The narrow street lay deep in shadow when Vasu led his
new stallion back to Sardofa. It had taken him hours to
barter the price of that horse down to a level that satisfied
him. The tall, thin horse-trader had been a worthy opponent, had fought Vasu's bids with the awareness of a man
assured of victory in the end. Though it had cost him

valuable time, Vasu admitted now that he had found the
interchange more invigorating than tedious and the powerful sorrel stallion a great prize.

Sardofa stood at the forge. Smoke billowed up its chimney and the odor of fish had vanished beneath the smell of
burning coal. The young blacksmith held a cherry-red-hot
nail in tongs over the fire, turning it, then working it
lightly with a small hammer. Seeing Vasu there at the
entrance to the stall, he set down his hammer. From beside
the anvil he gathered up a handful of yellow powder,
which he sprinkled over the nail as he turned it, until it had
a solid smoking coat of powder. Then he plunged the nail
into his slake trough. The water hissed and fulvous smoke
rose up. Wiping his hands on his apron, Sardofa came
forward.

"Your horse was far away—I thought perhaps you had
sent home for it." He continued past Vasu, began mur-
muring to the horse and rubbed its throat. "Worth the
delay, however. What a fine stallion. Has he serviced
many mares?"

Vasu blinked. "I—no . . . not as yet."

"There should be more like him." He walked around to
the rear of the horse. "Lead him in, straight."

Obeying, Vasu took the stallion under the canopy.

"Now, bring him back to me." With a sigh, Vasu did
as ordered. "Good." Sardofa took a thin cord out of a bag
tied at his belt. The cord had a weight attached. He went
'round the horse, holding the cord up at various points and
noting where the weight hung. Each time, he muttered in
satisfaction. Then he spoke gently to the horse and began
rubbing down its left foreleg. Vasu did not see him nudge
the stallion, but it shifted its stance as if pushed, and the

smith lifted its leg and bent over to study the exposed
hoof. This he repeated for all four legs. Afterward, with
obvious admiration, he told Vasu, "His legs are clean—as
close to perfect as any animal I've ever seen." He strode
off into the enclosed rear of the tent, returning with tools,
brushes, and a bucket.

Vasu had never paid any attention to such procedures
before. Now he stood rooted, captivated by Sardofa's
craft.

The old shoes must first be removed. Sardofa used
pincers and wedges to draw each shoe off as cautiously as
if the horse were made of crystal. He cleansed each hoof
next with liquid from the bucket, then using pliers, pried
away the old nail stubs. With files he rasped, flattened,
and smoothed the hooves.

By the time he had finished, sweat coated him. Vasu
realized with surprise that night had fallen outside. Hours
had passed and he, so engrossed, had not noticed at all.
All the light now came from half a dozen lanterns of the
sort Sardofa had earlier been polishing. Vasu wondered
when they had been lighted, and by whom. Perhaps they
had been burning when he'd arrived and he simply had not
noticed. But his suspicions were that the blacksmith's
magic had in some way been responsible.

Sardofa was gone behind the draperies again for a few
minutes. Upon his return, he carried with him the four
shoes. But before Vasu had a good look at them, Sardofa
set them aside and took his place before the forge. Reaching up, he grabbed hold of a bellows lever and began to
pump. The nearly dead coals glowed to life once more.
New coals were heaped upon them.

Vasu realized his legs were tired and he sat down against
a tent-post to rest. A cold spot pressed against his middle.

He reached into his green robe, fingers closing over the small ceramic phial he carried, wrapped in rags, in a hidden sash. Even through the rags and material, when pressed against him the cold potency of Thotharn's magic leaked out.

The sounds of hammering began soon. Sardofa's work rang out a steady beat that would stop abruptly but begin again within a minute. Vasu listened to it and dozed. Outside, a scanty evening crowd drifted past, glancing in, then moving on into the darkness. Fair-wards looked in only to make sure all was well. Farther back from the light an occasional priest went silently past like a corpse wrapped in cerements. Somewhere not far away a live animal show was taking place—the sounds of a cheering audience echoed through the streets, slithering into Vasu's light sleep in the form of a vision: a crowd fleeing, a hundred wide mouths screaming in terror, from the rising black cloud of Thotharn in the temple.

The hammering and heating continued late into the night.

He awoke to someone laughing riotously. The sound came from outside the tent—two drunken figures stumbling past. The dark street was otherwise deserted, silent.

Vasu rubbed his eyes and got to his feet.

The blacksmith stood at his forge still. The light of his fire gleamed in his sweat. He tapped lightly along the length of a hot nail, turning it with tongs, shaping it with care as before. Seeing that Vasu had awakened, Sardofa nodded to him and gestured behind himself with his hammer. "They're done—see what you think." He returned to work. Vasu walked around him.

The shoes lay in a heap of gold and oiled leather. He picked one up and looked it over. The shoe itself had an

even sheen, duller somewhat than pure gold, unlike anything he had ever seen. Six holes had been punched into it,
three on a side. Vasu marveled at its simple beauty. Yet
even more striking was the leather boot attached to it. He
had seen similar boots on horses before—certain foreign
armies had used such things—but never had any been
decorated like this. The leather was as soft as cloth. Gold
studwork adorned it in perfect trumpets and spirals. The
boot fitted against the side of the shoe perfectly, the studs
securing it welded in place. He took up another and compared them. The details in the studwork, the texture of the
leather—truly these were more amazing than anything he
had ever seen. He found that he was holding his breath.
His pulse drummed in his head.

Sardofa plunged a finished nail into the water trough. A
small pile of them lay beside him. Long, black, and
shimmering in the glow from the coals, they were shaped
like slender, lopsided cones. He glanced at Vasu. "You
like them, the shoes?"

"Beyond description. I tell you, I can *feel* the magic in
them." He added, "My wife will be overwhelmed."

"Then I shall finish."

Vasu followed him across the tent and watched, with an
expanding sense of rapture, while Sardofa selected each
nail and hammered it in slowly, steadily, so as not to
injure the horse. When a shoe had been attached, he bent
off the nail tips and rasped them smooth. Then, before
lacing up the boots, he applied a salve to each hoof. The
horse, to which all of this was routine, responded with
eternal patience. When the last boot had been laced up,
Sardofa stood and wiped his hands on a cloth. Turning to
Vasu, he found a large purse held out to him. "It's slightly

more than we agreed upon," explained Vasu, "but your craftsmanship has dazzled me."

The blacksmith gave him an odd smile, as if that praise contained a subtle joke, but he bowed to the praise all the same. He said, "Remember, only tonight and tomorrow night will your horse fly this month, for the magic has taken with the shoeing as I said. After tomorrow you must wait until the scythe moon has come round again."

Vasu nodded gravely. "I won't forget." He took the reins of his horse and walked out from beneath the canopy. The sky was full of stars. The crescent moon hung now above the temple, the central spire like a snow-covered mountain below it.

A whisper of a voice wreathed the night breeze: *The time is come.* Thotharn knew that the magic was ready. Away in the north a tiny sparkle of light indicated the mountains. A fire on a slope. He thought of the brigands who dwelled there to prey on travelers and stragglers. In the shadows thrown off by their fire, Thotharn would be lurking, and Vasu wondered if such men as those thieves could sense the insatiable hunger so near. Behind him the lanterns in Sardofa's tent were extinguished all at once. He looked back, but only the glow of hot coals remained visible within, like the eyes of heaped rats. Vasu led his horse away.

They left the fair and walked out onto the plain. Not far away, the river rolled silently past. No one else was there, and the empty plain offered no place for someone to hide. He adjusted the cool, wrapped phial again in his robe, then pulled himself up on the horse. For a moment he did not move, concentrated on summoning up the will to fly. He urged the horse forward. Nothing happened—the horse

simply walked along. He kicked in his heels and the horse
sped its pace. It trotted, then broke into a canter, and in
the instant its front hooves hit the ground, the ground
began to fall away. There was no sense of motion, of
lifting or flying. The weightless silence suffused Vasu with
vertigo. He clung perilously to the horse's back, eyes
closed, teeth clenched against a rising urge to vomit. The
nausea dissipated gradually. Vasu dared to open his eyes.
Below, in nearly complete darkness, the fair district was
laid out like a map. Occasional lights twinkled here and
there, most of them in the tavern district where late night
revelry continued unabated. Vasu found himself chuckling. He pulled on the reins and the stallion turned, bank-
ing smoothly. He leaned around its neck to look at it. The
stallion's dark eye seemed glazed. Its front legs pumped as
if cantering along an invisible road.

For a while he worked with the horse until satisfied that
he could maneuver in any direction. He tugged on one rein
then and headed for the shrine.

In the light of the moon, the massive carved heads
loomed up like the faces of real gods out of the void, their
mouths open as if in the midst of a silent chant. As he
floated near, Vasu became uneasy within their empty gaze.
The divine dancers, too, bothered him. When he glanced
away they seemed to move, to assume different poses. But
for him to stare at them was to come under the scrutiny of
the towering heads. He cursed himself for such superstitious behavior. *His* god would protect him from such
things. He ignored his own awareness that here his god
could not come.

The central spire became a cone. He drifted toward it
like a ship in still water, smoothly, silently. Soon he could

see the opening at the top. Again he thought of volcanoes.
The horse nickered uneasily.

The heads of the temple surrounded him. He avoided
looking at them as he reached into his robe for the phial.
To unwrap it he had to let go of the reins; he dared not
drop it, although (he thought giddily) he could certainly
get another from Thotharn with his magnificent flying
steed to carry him to the unknown East.

The ceramic phial came free of its cloth wrappings.
Vasu took the reins once more and gripped the phial
tightly. One long strip of cloth floated down and draped
over the arm of an aspara.

The opening in the spire lay directly beneath him now.

To his right something groaned like an ancient door
drawing back. He glanced, wide-eyed, away from the
spire.

One of the enormous heads turned by degrees to stare at
him. Moonlight caught more movement and he looked past
the heads like a man who knows there is no longer anything that can frighten him, and he found dancers stepping
across the roof toward him. Other heads came to bear upon
him. The night shuddered with their creaking. Sightless
eyes pierced him from every direction.

The stallion sprang to life suddenly, jerked up, and
whinnied. Vasu grabbed the reins in his cold, numb fingers and the phial slipped from his grasp. He tried to catch
it and nearly tumbled off the horse. Hopelessly, he watched
the phial fall wide of its mark and shatter on the roof. A
thin blue flame erupted where it struck. In the sudden light
he saw the figures drawing nearer, saw them clearly for
what they were: priests and fair-wards, more of the former
appearing from within the gaping mouths of the great
heads. They had been waiting for him.

"Sardofa," he said aloud. The name seemed to release him from a spell. He kicked the horse, tugged hard on the reins, ascending as the nearest fair-wards tried to strike him with their staves.

A weird howl started up then. For a moment Vasu thought someone had caught fire from the blue flame. But the sound changed, becoming louder, developing a pattern. He knew what it was then and his heart froze.

They had sent a Priest's Song after him.

Desperately he tried to go higher still, but too late. The song had penetrated him. The night began to swirl as if a storm were gathering from every direction. The swirls took on shape and color—nightmarish phantoms emerged, tried to grab his robes and pull him from his perch. Cold, clutching fingers reached for him. Demons dove down at him. Even knowing they were false, he could not keep from smothering in panic. He covered his eyes, but the demons lived on his palms and behind his eyelids, in his brain. Briefly, he came to his senses and realized he had dropped the reins.

The fantastic swirl parted. Vasu saw open plain rushing up at him as if an incipient mountain were erupting into the sky. He yanked frantically at the reins. The horse did not respond; some concomitant nightmare had taken control of it, too. The view of the world below sealed up. Demons swirled and howled around him again. Fingers of ice brushed his cheek. Then the sky exploded for an instant into brighter color, a shudder of sound.

Vasu felt himself flung free of the horse. Through the wail of demons, some animal split open the night with its agony and just as abruptly stopped.

The colors bled into darkness. The demons dissipated on the wind.

Vasu lay on his back, stars stretched out in a black blanket. He smelled the rot of fish, much stronger than in the blacksmith's tent. With great care he sat up. His body ached as though the demons had dislocated every joint. Holding himself upright made him tremble, but he appeared to be intact. He lay, he discovered, in a dry ravine along with garbage from the fair, fish heads and vegetables. His temples pounded blindingly for a minute, then subsided. He reached up, grabbed hold of a patch of grass at the edge of the ravine, and pulled himself up to where he could see out.

The nearest building lay some three hundred yards off. Everything was dark and silent. No one appeared to be looking for him. Nevertheless, he knew he would have little time if what he believed were true, if the blacksmith had, at some point, warned the priests. But how could the man have known his intent? Perhaps the priests were simply guarding the temple more carefully during the fair. No, because there had been fair-wards with them. No, his instincts were right—those people had known. Soon they would come for him. His one escape lay with the stallion. He must fly to Thotharn, acquire another phial, then drop straight down out of the sky and fling it into the depths of that accursed temple. Let them come out—the moving heads wouldn't deter him this time. He would attack and be gone before any priest could gather the wits to send a song into the night.

First, however, he had to find his horse.

It lay not far away in the ravine. Upon seeing it, he knew the horse was dead. He knelt beside it, mind racing, thoughts tumbling into chaos. He fought down the urge to flee on foot. When the sun came up, he would die out there.

There seemed to be no choice but one. He must remove the shoes from this horse and put them on another, and he must do it now, tonight. Then he could fly off and return for revenge tomorrow night. He had watched Sardofa well enough to shoe a horse himself. It need not be perfect—the animal only had to take a few steps. Tools, he would need proper tools. Getting to his feet, Vasu decided on a plan: He would return to Sardofa's tent, kill him, and steal the tools. Who, after all, would search for him there? With any luck, they would all believe he had made good his escape.

He entered the outer district of the fair, sneaking between a wagon and a covered cage. Some large bird within the cage heard him passing and squawked loudly. Vasu thought his heart would rupture.

After that he kept to the side of streets but away from cages, pausing for breath behind bales of wool or beside feed troughs. Fair-wards passed by, but they neither saw nor appeared to be looking for him. He went farther into the fair, to the man who had sold him the stallion.

The horse-dealer's wagon was silent and dark. Vasu began concocting the story he would use. In the end it did him no good. The lanky horse-dealer knew a man on the run when he saw one. He offered Vasu an old plow horse with protruding ribs and a swayed back. The price he named was the same as he had originally demanded for the stallion. When Vasu tried to protest, the dealer suggested he go elsewhere with his lies. Defeated, Vasu gave in and paid the price.

He led off the withered, plodding horse in the direction of Sardofa's forge.

The sounds of light hammering reached him before he had even stepped into the road. Dim light spilled out from

under the canopy. Vasu silently tied the horse beside the
stall and then edged into the light, intending to grab the
nearest hammer or iron and strike the blacksmith.

But the young smith was not in sight. Instead, a short,
stocky, white-haired man stood at the forge, looking like
the grandfather of all blacksmiths. Before Vasu could
reevaluate the situation, the old seamed face swung 'round
toward him.

"Proper folk don't creep up on a blind side," said the
smith indignantly, and Vasu could see that he was wall-
eyed and probably blind in his right eye.

"Forgive me. I was looking for the one called Sardofa."

"You can stop your sneaking, then. I'm he."

Vasu responded as if he were a bellows and the old man
had stepped on his handle. He gathered the wits enough to
ask, "Your son, then?"

The old man shook his head. "Haven't one. Nor a wife.
Never. Never had the time. I 'prenticed days to the smith
and nights to the alchemist. When do you suppose I slept?"
He guffawed and went back to work.

Vasu came beside him. Choking back the urge to become hysterical, he asked, "You have an apprentice, then?"

Old Sardofa continued working as he answered. "Yes,
in his second year. But he can do most of the basics."

"Shoeing a horse?" Vasu clasped his hands as though
in prayer.

"Oh, yes. Good at that. I shouldn't think he'll have
trouble while I'm here, either—provided all the barrels in
Flerga don't burst their hoops at once." He laughed uproariously and did not notice how ashen his foreign visitor
had become. "He has the knack, you know," he went on
blithely, "which is mostly in the back and shoulders. If it
were a knack of the head, well, he wouldn't have had

much chance, I have to say." He set down his hammer.
"Now, what is it you need with all these questions?"

Vasu was staring in the dirt. The younger man had not
been Sardofa at all, had tricked him. Where had this old
one been, then, that he knew nothing of what had occurred? Somewhere, seeing the sights no doubt. The exact
explanation would just have to wait.

Looking up and trying to determine which eye to make
contact with, he said, "I've a horse needs shoeing. I have
the shoes, too, as well as the skill to put them on. What I
lack here is the tools and nails. I want to buy tools from
you."

"Why?"

"No one else is awake."

Sardofa nodded. "Still don't know when I sleep," he
said to himself. "I will sell you some finished nails and
loan you the tools if you insist on doing the hard part
yourself. You a smith?"

"Ahm, yes, yes I am," Vasu replied swiftly.

"Why all the questions about apprentices, then?"

Why, indeed. "Oh, well, to be frank with you, I was—
am—looking for an apprentice for my shop. In the place I
come from there is no one else interested."

Sardofa handed him various tools, which Vasu held
uncomfortably the way anyone who had never used them
would. The old man asked, "Are you sure you need no
help?"

"No, I've done plenty of . . . shoeings." He tried to
smile but felt as transparent as a seductress's veil.

Sardofa shook his head as if to say, "It's your horse."
He counted out two dozen black nails. Having no time in
his plan for returning the tools and no urge to thieve from

the old man, Vasu overpaid for the nails with the last of his money. Then he ran from the tent.

Soft chuckling from the blacksmith followed him into the night.

A cloudy dawn inched over the horizon. Its wan light revealed a group of four riders heading out of the fair toward a single, animated figure in dirty green robes, seated atop what might have been a lumpish mound of sand. A similar mound lay not far from this at the edge of a ravine. Overhead, a cluster of vultures let the riders know the mounds were anything but sand.

The nearest proved to be the broken, twisted carcass of a horse. The one on which the whimpering, imploring figure bounced proved as well to be a horse, but an old, froth-dappled plow horse that had dropped dead from sheer exhaustion while running in circles.

The figure in green, glancing fearfully back at the four riders, began pounding on his horse, kicking its rawboned flanks, tearing at its mane, and begging it to move. To fly.

Moments later a bronze-shod staff tapped Vasu on the shoulder, and he reacted as if the staff had sucked all the energy from him. His head hung, hair dripping, chin against chest. Without a word, he got down off the plow horse. He stared reproachfully at it, betrayed.

Two fair-wards led him back to their horses, left him standing while they mounted up. The remaining two members of the group, Vasu saw, were dressed in the hooded robes of priests. One of them was just returning from the broken body of the stallion. The priest paused in passing to look at him; Vasu found himself staring into the face of the one who had called himself Sardofa.

Vasu gaped in incomprehension. The priest started away.

Vasu grabbed his shoulder and one of the fair-wards raised his staff dissuasively. "But how?" Vasu implored. "How did you know to be there before me, how?" The priest turned around. "And why the cruel deception when you knew from the first?" The one who had played Sardofa made to answer but was stopped by a voice that answered for him, coming from the other hooded figure.

"We had no choice." The voice was female, familiar to him. Though he could not see her face beneath the hood, he imagined her short hair and the charm worn in her earlobe; his first question had been answered. She went on, "Most of the priests have taken to deriding the tales of the Sky Lords. They have traded their belief for the proceeds of their usury. Only a small core of true believers still exists, still converses with them. And it was they who told us you were here. But we had to satisfy the fair-wards of your intent—you committed no discernable crime until you invaded the temple. Now they satisfy our justice by bringing you back to the shrine. The Three Lordly Ones await your disposition there."

Vasu went cold. He watched the priest who had been Sardofa walk away, and his eye was caught by the priest's hands: the man carried an oversized pliers in one hand; in the other he clutched a bundle of iridescent black nails.

Vasu whirled around and stared across at his horses— the stallion unshod and the other still wearing the badly applied gold shoes and leather boots.

"The nails," he said as if in apology to the plow horse. "The nails!" he screamed at the priests.

A quarterstaff rapped against his skull, directed him to turn around and take his place between the two fair-wards. They started off toward the temple.

On the outskirts of the fair, an early morning crowd

watched the party and their prisoner, and everyone speculated as to who he was and what it all meant. Among them stood a wall-eyed blacksmith. He did not watch the four riders but stared out across the plain toward the ghostly mountains, where three swirling dust devils spun away, as if in pursuit of the dark storm cloud that even now was withdrawing over the horizon.

THE RUBY WAND OF ASRAZEL

Joseph Green

The shallow chimney in the adjacent rockface grew too narrow even for his lean frame when Arun Elem reached the base of the huge nest. He had to cling precariously to the outer edge of the cleft for the last few feet, breathing heavily in the thin, cold air, until he could finally throw a leg over the intertwined branches and seek frantically for solid footing on the rock point beneath.

As Arun stood erect, gulping huge mouthfuls of air and waiting for his fatigued legs to stop trembling, the two Alt-eagle fledglings in the nest increased their already loud squawking. Scrawny and ugly in their immature feathers, they vigorously waved their newly thatched wings and hopped into the air, displaying their short but growing spurs to the enemy. The commotion was so loud Arun turned to scan the sky; but neither of their giant parents was in sight.

Working quickly and watching his footing, Arun sifted through the debris at the bottom of the nest, tossing old bones, animal heads, dried baby feces, and assorted vegetable trash over the side. The young Alts huddled together opposite him, as far away as the five-foot-wide enclosure permitted, still squawking and making their threat displays.

A deep violet glitter attracted Arun's eye. His hand starting to shake, he dug carefully through the dung-and-leaf mixture to extract it without letting the stone fall through the latticework of now dry supporting branches.

Arun lifted the glittering object into the bright sunlight and wiped it clean on his sleeve—only to see it was a common amethyst. For a moment he had thought he held a magic stone of real value, a Seeress's Eye.

Still, it was a good find. Arun tucked it into his belt-pouch and continued searching, working as quickly as he dared. Every minute spent in or near this great nest was dangerous in the extreme. If one of the fierce parents made an early kill and returned . . .

Arun moved toward the angry and frightened young birds, forcing them away from the last untested area. Their outraged cries rose to new heights of noisy indignation as they separated. One fledgling edged past Arun safely, but the other did not recognize harmless intentions, and Arun was too close. It hopped into the air, skinny wings flapping desperately for support, and tried to bring the short spurs on its shanks together inside Arun's reaching hand.

"No you don't, little fighter." Arun chuckled as he yanked his hand back, caught the bird in an immobilizing grip as it was forced to land again, and gently deposited it by its sibling. Then he turned his back to the pair and hastily went through the final area of nest bottom. He found nothing else of value.

These great Alt-eagles hunted far and wide over the Rusty Mountains and their forested foothills, their twelve-foot wingspans carrying the forty-pound bodies vast distances as they rode the turbulent thermals and updrafts. When they swooped down on the large tree-climbing packrat in its high hidden nest, a favorite prey, they swallowed his possessions as well as the rodent. The inedible glittering objects were regurgitated in the nest along with the meat, falling to the bottom when ignored by the hungry fledglings. And sometimes the avaricious packrats had stolen jewels from the merchants in the many caravans following the main trade road through the mountains and nearby Galzar Pass. . . .

Arun had never found a truly valuable stone, nor one with powers for which a magician would pay heavily. Often, after a long and grueling climb to these high nests, he found nothing at all.

It was a precarious living at best, but since his father had died from a fall in these mountains six years ago when he was fourteen, Arun had helped support his arthritis-crippled mother with occasional finds such as the amethyst. Those; and the vegetables the two of them forced from the thin red soil of their foothill home, sustained life in their bodies—but little more.

It was time to go. Arun climbed carefully over the edge, trying not to depend on the nest itself for support. He was a tall young man, lean with privation but muscular from frequent mountain climbing and hard work at home. He had learned to climb with his father, who robbed nests for the smaller types of falcons and swifthawks who could be taught to hunt. Arun would have become a falconer also, but the business had grown so crowded it was now hard for a new birdseller to succeed.

Instead, Arun had entered the dangerous business of robbing the nests of the untamable Alts, the largest of all the raptors. He climbed to every nest he could find during the season of nesting fledglings, or searched the ground below, if he could reach it, after the great birds demolished their high homes before departing in the fall. This second and safer method was only rarely fruitful.

But there was always hope, the sustaining strength of the real possibility of finding a diamond, a glittering green emerald large as a pigeon's egg, a wizard's coal-dark nightsight—others had, and had lived well for years from a single sale. Arun and Anyanna, his mother, deserved no less. They had worked hard and been poor all of their lives, while warriors, priests, and nobles lived fat and happy throughout this land of Ithkar. Their turn must come.

Arun squeezed one arm and leg into the narrow chimney and started downward, remembering his father's words: "Cling tighter going down than going up! You weigh more!" He went carefully, and was fully in the shallow chimney and setting a faster pace, some twenty feet below the nest, when there was a great *swoosh*! of wings and a huge shadow swept across his face.

Arun twisted his neck, to see that both parents had returned; the female had an animal in her claws. The male was stooping at him as his mate landed above him in the nest.

The cleft was shallow, and he could not wedge his body in deeper. Arun ducked his head to shield his eyes, just in time. Spurs as long as his middle finger stabbed at his head, one drawing blood as it sank through flesh to hard bone. With miraculous skill the giant raptor whirled away without hitting the rock, falling momentarily but rising again with powerful beats of the great wings, to where he could dive at Arun once more.

Arun ignored the puncture between eye and ear at the hairline, letting it bleed as he scrambled rapidly downward, trying to move fast enough to throw the bird off course as it returned. If one of those spurs entered his neck, he was as good as dead. But missing a single grip could start him on a downward slide from which there would be no recovering. . . .

Arun was not going fast enough. The fierce eyes of the giant Alt were fixed on his face as the hunter dropped toward him, able to counter any slow move. Looking downward, Arun saw a narrow ledge he remembered from the climb up, the length of his body below his feet. As the searching talons came toward his face he released the pressure of back to rock and let himself drop. A protruding ridge scraped his back and right shoulder, bringing a gasp of pain, and then his feet hit hard on the narrow, flat outcropping of gray stone, a shelf of granite protruding from the rusting taconite of these iron hills. Desperately he struggled for balance, hurting one hand as he thrust at the opposite wall. This was where he had entered the chimney for the final part of his climb; the ledge was open to the sky.

The Alt had whirled away as Arun dropped, and was again beating for altitude. Arun was now more exposed than before. Desperately he looked to either side for shelter, and spotted the dark shadow of a deeper recess to his right, where the granite led.

Arun waited, and this time when the attack came—with a piercing screech intended to paralyze, and a beak reaching to maim and tear—he slipped sideways at the last instant, able to move very quickly on the narrow but flat ledge. The Alt missed again, and before he could seek altitude once more Arun had sidled along the narrow shelf and entered the sheltering darkness of the cleft.

To Arun's surprise, he found no inner wall as he hurried into the shadow. The rock beneath his feet was flat as that of a floor. He walked carefully between the rising walls, around several S-turns, and into an open chamber, where little light penetrated.

The cave was tiny, little larger than the Elem shack. It had an ancient musty smell, as though no breeze had stirred here for millennia. And it was lighted, though dimly, by an object glowing in the darkness by the inner wall, a slim rod of some silvery metal that stood alone on a rock pedestal, its jeweled top on a level with Arun's eyes.

The rod was no longer than Arun's forearm, and the width of a finger. The jewel at its top was a strangely formed ruby the color of old blood, in the shape of a long teardrop. It glowed with a baleful red gleam, a shadow of hidden flame, like light escaping from the athanor of some powerful old necromancer, working directly with fire borrowed from hell. . . .

Arun felt the breath catch in his throat. Suddenly he seemed cold, despite the heavy jacket and leather pants he wore against the chill at these heights. He had never seen this magician's wand, but there was no mistaking it. The old tales said that a hundred generations before Arun's birth it had vanished from human ken, secreted away by the three white magicians who had finally overcome its ambitious master, the great and learned wizard Asrazel. This was the Ruby Wand, the most powerful magician's tool known in all Ithkar, and the one with the most evil reputation. In the hands of an experienced wizard it could bring riches, power, and the rule of the kingdom.

As he stood there, frozen, his gaze fixed almost hypnotically on the deep redness of the single jeweled eye, Arun remembered more. Asrazel had been a *white* magician before acquiring the wand, a benevolent and kindly man who ruled his small duchy well. But with power came overweening ambition, followed by war and conquest, death and destruction, until finally all Ithkar combined against him. Asrazel was defeated only after being tricked into a separation from the all-powerful Ruby Wand. A shaky peace was restored at his death, a balance between competing warlords and wizards that seldom threatened the whole kingdom. It endured today.

To the man who wielded the Ruby Wand . . . Arun pulled himself away from that thought. He was no magician; he might well do himself more harm than good if he attempted to master its powers. But then he remembered that the yearly Fair at Ithkar was only a few weeks away. He had planned to take his poor hoard of gems there, in hopes of getting a better price from the competing merchants. All the great wizards would be there as well, and any one of them would offer him a king's ransom for this wand.

Arun hesitated, and then the thought of riches for himself and the crippled woman who had raised him was more than he could bear. He grasped the wand at its haft. At his touch the glow faded, leaving the cave in near darkness.

He turned and found his way back through the twisting entryway into the light. A look around indicated both adult birds were in the nest, out of sight and no longer seeking him. Arun tucked the wand carefully into the waistband of his leather trousers, tieing it firmly in place with a string. Being careful to make no sound, he started the onerous climb down. Four hours later, well after dark, he staggered through his own doorway and sat down, weary in muscle and bone, before a tepidly warm bowl of vegetable soup.

Arun showed Anyanna the violet amethyst, and they worried and chattered over the number of silver pieces it would bring, and what they could buy in Ithkar for their tiny farm. He did not tell her of the wand, now hidden against his body.

"You have a magical device with you," said the gate fair-ward gruffly, watching the little talisman he held on a chain before Arun swinging vigorously back and forth. No wizard was on duty, oddly enough—the use of such a device was new to Arun. "Hand it over or you may not enter." He was a rotund, gray-haired, and red-faced man with beady little black eyes and an officious, self-important manner.

"Of course I do! I have my healing staff," said Arun, feigning high indignation. He pulled the large caduceus from his belt and thrust it at the fair-ward. "Protective and healing magical devices are perfectly legal, according to fair-law. *Now* check me."

The talisman indicated Arun was clean. When it approached the caduceus it swung so violently the fair-ward pulled it away and rehung it about his neck. "Very well," he said, and there was something sly and knowing in his look. "You may pass, young sir. And let us hope you will not need healing. Our patrolling fair-wards are very efficient. Thieves and mendicants, drunkards and troublemakers of all sorts are severely dealt with. Behave yourself and you will have no problems."

Arun nodded and picked up the caduceus. He tucked it

back into his sash and walked through the gate onto the fairgrounds.

The instant Arun was out of sight the stout fair-ward rose and handed the talisman to one of his colleagues. "Take over for me. And watch out for the highland warriors, they'll slip a knife through in places you don't want to examine too closely."

Arun was walking slowly through the bustling crowd just inside, on the main thoroughfare leading to the temple. The fair-ward stepped in the other direction, to where two loafers sat on a bench against the back of an adjacent booth, idling their time away with a small cask of ale. Quickly the fair-ward pointed out Arun. "The caduceus in his sash. Get it!" he hissed, bending low between their dirty heads. "And slice his liver when you take it. I want no complaint filed."

The negligent air of mild drunkenness fell from the two men like discarded masks. Abandoning the keg and cheap mugs, they took off in pursuit, weaving like hunting dogs through the crowd. Each checked the thin knife strapped to the inside of his thigh, reached through what seemed only a tear in ragged clothing. The fair-ward had passed them through himself, two days before. This was their third assignment.

Arun was both excited and somewhat distressed by the boisterous, noisy, and often rowdy crowd. He was accustomed to the peace and quiet of his isolated home or the lonely high places of the mountains. It was both interesting and nerve-racking to be among so many people, particularly those who shoved or jerked at you without notice or apology. He hardly knew what to think when the men appeared at each side, firmly grasping both arms and propelling him forward.

"A word with you, pilgrim," the older man said as they hustled Arun across the walkway toward an alley leading to the permanent building at the river wharves.

"What do you want?" demanded Arun, suddenly certain that he knew. The two men ignored him. He hung back, resisting but being dragged along regardless. There were no fair-wards in sight at the moment, and the crowd would not interfere in a private quarrel.

As they approached the corner Arun pulled back more strongly, but they easily overcame his resistance. He had a growing conviction that once they had him out of sight, a hand would go over his mouth and life escape out of a new hole in his throat. But they were too strong for him to hold back. He looked about desperately for help, realized none would be coming, and saw the corner of the wall a few feet ahead.

A desperate plan suddenly appeared in Arun's agile mind. Four feet from the alley corner he suddenly stopped resisting and surged ahead instead. The two thieves stumbled forward but were held up by their grip on his arms. Arun raised his right foot waist high to kick off the wall, hurling himself backward while at the same time exerting all his considerable strength to pull the two men together over his extended leg. Already off-balance, they slammed into each other hard, the forehead of the shorter one making a solid contact with the jaw of the taller. Momentarily stunned, both lost their grip on Arun and fell to the dirt.

And he was away and gone, weaving so swiftly through the crowd that he was out of sight by the time the would-be assassins recovered and got back to their feet.

When the two crestfallen thieves reported to the fair-ward in private, he cursed them so roundly both men placed their hands in the tears in their pants and on the thin knives. He ignored the threat; without his protection they could not function here.

"There's nothing for it now but to tell the Wizard of Iron. Maybe Ferrugo Rebar's soldiers can do what you two babies can't," the indignant fair-ward finally finished. "You, Jonash, get up to his river keep immediately and take a message. And give it to no one but Rebar himself. Understand me?"

"Wasn't that what you were supposed to do in the first place?" asked the other thief unpleasantly.

"I'll handle the thinking here. You two worthless lumps of dogmeat just do as you're told."

But when the message was delivered the Iron Wizard detained Jonash, and questioned him at length, and then had the fair-ward brought to him surreptitiously after he finished work for the day. In fear and trembling the stout official babbled all that he knew, admitting that never in his experience had anything approaching the power of that caduceus passed by his talisman. It had to be far more than it seemed, magic hidden by lesser magic. He lied valiantly, claiming he had only sought to steal it for his lord, but as he babbled the Iron Wizard glanced casually at the detector jewel on his left little finger. When he had separated truth from protective lies he had the fair-ward taken to an inner room of the warehouse keep and strangled. Rebar then ordered his inner guard to quietly spread word of the treachery, and his response. Finally, he sent his many metalsmith apprentices throughout the fairgrounds, armed with a good description of Arun.

And eventually, by slipping silver pieces to every tavern and hostel owner inside the fairgrounds, they found him.

Arun had intended to sleep under the stars, along with

thousands of others among the very poor, but the attack by the thieves had changed his mind. Watching birds and climbing mountains had developed in him a fine sense of observation. He had noticed the wide swings of the talisman and the change in the gate fair-ward. Arun was certain the two thieves had been sent by him. Which meant someone now knew he had a very powerful instrument of magic, and they would cut his throat quicker than that of a chicken to get it. He had decided to spend one of his two precious silver coins to sleep with four walls around him, and asked an innkeeper to allow him to stay inside the stable. Since the inn was long full, the innkeeper had agreed, for what should have been the price of a room with meals. He betrayed Arun to the Iron Wizard's young men with equal cupidity.

Arun lay in the darkness of the hay pit, wrapped in a blanket grudgingly furnished by the innkeeper, wishing he were safely home. He had sold two of his less valuable stones, but such items were in plentiful supply this year, and they had brought only a little money. The violet amethyst was his best, but even it would not bring more than ten silvers, enough perhaps to replace the cow that had died on them two months back. His whole supply of gems was not going to produce enough money to keep them from starving next winter.

But he had the Ruby Wand.

Arun reached beside him to the large caduceus, which he had taken off to sleep. The wand was small enough to fit inside its handle. He had hoped that the acceptable healing magic would mask that of the Ruby Wand, but his ploy had failed. Tomorrow he must think of some subterfuge to gain audience with one or more of the powerful wizards. Perhaps the wizard Ferrugo Rebar should be his first try. He had the largest private army in Ithkar, but everyone knew it was to compensate himself for being only a poor wizard. Although ambitious in the extreme, he had never dared attack one of the truly great wizards or the scholarly white magicians. Instead he operated Ithkar's largest foundry, not far from Arun's home. His slaves mined the Rusty Mountains and produced most of the steel shaped by others throughout Ithkar. Here he lived half the year, supervising his trade with river merchants. He had great wealth, but not the prestige of real power.

Arun, troubled in mind, was still awake when the six soldiers dressed in red uniform shirts approached the stable, making no effort to be quiet. He heard the quick, low orders of the squad officer as he stationed two men at each of the two exits. They could only be seeking Arun. He had been betrayed by the greedy innkeeper.

It was very dark inside the stable, but Arun had had a good look around when he'd settled in for the night. He tried to remember some way to slip past the soldiers, and there was none. Then a desperate plan occurred to him, and he had just a few seconds to make some preparations before the final pair of soldiers boldly entered the swinging front door, torches raised high and thick wooden clubs in hand.

There was a sudden loud neigh of anger from a startled horse, a scream of stallion rage, and a great black charger came hurtling out of the darkness toward the two soldiers. They sprang to the side, but one was caught by a massive shoulder and knocked off his feet. The second whirled back to face the interior, just in time to see a gray mare bolting for the open door, the running figure of a man on the other side. He sprang forward and tried to swing his club, but the lithe figure ducked so low he could not reach him over the horse's back. In seconds both figures were out the door, the human falling behind as the mare raced after the black stallion, but both now well down the narrow alley and past the two men waiting outside.

Arun looked back only long enough to see the six soldiers organizing into a squad for the pursuit, then set his eyes ahead and ran. It was only a short distance down the alley to the main street. He emerged and turned right, thinking to mingle into the crowd. But it had grown thin this late at night, and offered little concealment. Looking ahead, he saw another squad of red-clad soldiers, and now he recognized them as the Iron Wizard's. They spotted him at the same time.

Desperate, Arun turned back as the men spread across the street to block his escape. But the squad following him emerged from the alley only a hundred feet back, saw the situation, and spread out as well. He was trapped.

Arun looked quickly for an alley, an open door . . . There was none. He took a dozen quick strides toward the approaching soldiers in front, until he reached a large merchant's tent fronting the street. He bent and yanked a tent anchor out of the ground by main strength, then hastily wriggled under the strong cloth.

The interior was lighted by a flickering oil lamp. Strange sounds were coming from behind a separate partition at the rear, but Arun ignored them. The lusts of merchants away from their wives were not his concern. A sweeping glance indicated this was a jeweler's shop, of the cheaper sort, selling everything from children's decorated toys to poor stones such as his own, mounted in inexpensive silver or low-quality gold settings.

Arun's eye was struck immediately by a section for

children's toys that held several small wands. Two of these had pieces of colored glass mounted at their tops.

Quickly, while his willpower held, Arun removed the cap across the hollow bottom of the caduceus and extracted the Ruby Wand. He laid the wand in the case with the others and tossed the cap away, hoping it would appear the large staff had always been open and empty if he was captured. Then he fled toward the rear of the tent, searching for the exit flap. He found it in seconds and let himself through, just as a startled bellow sounded from behind the partition and a nearly naked man, stout, elderly, and more than half-drunk, came staggering out, waving a heavy club.

The soldiers slit the canvas door and burst inside at the same minute, their clubs ready but keeping deadly silent. Arun stepped into the alley in back to find himself almost within reach of four of the first squad he had met, coming toward him from his right. He turned left and fled, getting past the end of the large tent just as the two who had come around that way grabbed for him. Then he was free and running for his life, with the still silent servants of the Iron Wizard in hot pursuit.

In less than a hundred feet the narrow, twisting alley ended against the rear of one of the permanent warehouses. There were two more on either side, hemming Arun into a cul-de-sac. He looked around frantically for a way out, saw none, and began trying to scramble up the corner to his left, where the roughness of the bricks gave him a vestige of handholds. Only an experienced mountain climber could have gotten off the ground. He was over eight feet up and reaching for the edge of the roof when someone leaped from below, and powerful hands fastened onto his ankles, dragging him down. . . .

*   *   *

"Now, my young friend, you still have a chance for a nice profit out of this experience." Ferrugo Rebar smiled with his lips, but his muddy-brown eyes remained cold and calculating. He was a tall, muscular former warrior now going to fat at waistline and jowls, his black hair sprinkled liberally with gray. He looked more like a merchant than a wizard, and in fact his monopoly of steel throughout Ithkar made him one of its richest citizens. His paid magician, a minor wizard named Reynal, had just confirmed that each component part of the caduceus was indeed what it seemed, and not some disguised source of power.

"Describe the part that contained the power, and where you hid it, and you shall have ten standard gold coins," Rebar went on smoothly. "That will buy you a nice new home, and food for your crippled mother for years." He saw Arun's startled look, and nodded. "Oh, yes, we know who you are, young Arun Elem. You were offered service once as a guard at my mine, and declined. Insulted my officer, in fact. Your father was known to me also, as a fine trainer of hawks. A little too independent in his manner, however."

It was morning, and Arun had spent the remainder of the night in a dungeon cell below the Iron Wizard's great keep. He had dozed a little just before dawn, lying there in the darkness, filth, and damp. In the long slow hours before that, Arun had had little to do but think.

He had made a serious mistake in removing that ancient power of evil from its hidden temple. With it, Rebar would easily conquer all Ithkar, instituting a reign of terror and oppression such as the land had not known since Asrazel himself. Something had tempted Arun, some subtle influence he had not detected . . . and the Ruby Wand would find a ready vessel of corruption in Ferrugo Rebar, leading him up higher and still higher paths of glory and power till he overreached himself and tumbled down. . . . But before Rebar fell, thousands would suffer and die, the land lie ravaged under warring armies as the other wizards and lords fought back, death and destruction everywhere, the crops ruining in the fields and starvation falling like a great plague over the land . . . all because Arun had been tempted, and lacked the strength to resist the lure of gold and luxury.

But Rebar did not even know what he sought, only that it was powerful beyond any magic he now possessed. Arun cleared his throat, and determinedly told the Iron Wizard the real power had been in two small diamonds clasped in the snake's mouths, and he had pulled them off and tossed them away just before being captured.

Arun's trained gaze saw the several glances Rebar darted at the ringed hand turned casually up in his lap, where he sat in his seat at the head of his audience hall. Arun felt a surge of despair. Truth rings were very expensive, but routine for a man like the Iron Wizard.

"Enough!" A look of venomous anger replaced Rebar's attempt to look pleasant and reasonable. "You lie poorly, young man, and with little imagination. There are no such diamonds, and you did not throw anything away. Now identify the artifact immediately, and tell me where you hid it, or my torturers will drag it out of you."

Inside Arun quailed, but he lowered his gaze from the avaricious eyes of the Iron Wizard and stared at the floor.

"Send four squads of soldiers back along his track," Rebar ordered, turning to his captain of guards. "Search his sleeping quarters and the route he took when he ran, most particularly the alley you described where he was caught. Likely he hid it somewhere there. I have only two spare detecting talismans. Assign them to your most intelligent squad leaders. Reynal will instruct them in their use.'' He scowled angrily at Arun. ''And take this stubborn whelp to the cell in the interrogation room. Tell the jailer I'll be down this afternoon to help him work on young Mr. Elem.''

The Iron Wizard smiled, licking his lips, and Arun had a sudden understanding of how a warrior's love of combat, and the blood of enemies slain in battle, could easily, as he aged, become the bloodlust of the torturer . . . and he shuddered with fear and horror deep in his soul.

Two guards conducted Arun to a different part of the basement of this great house, a smaller room with a holding cell in one corner and dozens of devices spread around the floor. A misshapen, hairy, former giant of a man, now crippled and obese, was the jailer here. He smiled when he saw Arun passing into his care. There was something unclean and malevolent, beyond normal human feelings, in his bloodshot eyes.

The torturer promptly built fires in two different places, putting various tools on to heat as if preparing to roast a chicken. He hummed as he worked, occasionally glancing at Arun with that same hideous smile, yellow teeth gleaming. . . .

Arun resolved never to reveal the location of the wand— and knew that he only lied to himself. No one could resist what was coming to him. Sooner or later he would tell, to find the quicker death that would by then be so desperately wanted.

But instead of Rebar descending to the cellar, two soldiers came for Arun after three hours had passed. He was again taken to the audience chamber, where Rebar still sat on his near throne. The ugly scowl he turned on Arun would have made a nomad warrior quail.

"My men have not found the object, whatever it is. And it occurs to me you might just possibly take longer to reveal it than the time I can spare. Therefore I want its location, and I want it now."

Numbly, Arun shook his head.

"I thought so. Very well, you have my promise on this. You will tell me what and where it is, or I'll dispatch riders immediately to Galzar Pass, and sometime tomorrow they'll be back with your bent old mother. I will put *her* in the hands of my delicate cook in the cellar, and you can watch through the bars as he grills the meat. Speak immediately and she shall remain untouched. Make me wait one minute and her left hand will be fried off to the wrist. After two . . ." But there was no need to go on.

Feeling sick to his stomach, Arun tried to recover his composure. He finally said, "My lord, may I approach you? What I will tell you is best not said aloud."

"Certainly," said the wizard, waving a negligent hand at the two guards by Arun. "Stay where you are."

Rebar was certain Arun was unarmed, and he did not fear that the smaller man had any ability to harm him with bare hands. Arun climbed the steps and bent down by the waiting ear, noticing the bulge of fat in the heavy neck. The temptation to strike was strong, but he resisted it. That would gain him nothing. Instead he whispered, "Lord, I found the lost Ruby Wand of Asrazel. I brought it to the fair hidden inside the hollow shaft of the caduceus."

The wizard caught his breath. This far exceeded his highest expectations. Arun could see dreams of wealth and the true aphrodisiac, power, pouring through his greedy mind.

"And where is it?" demanded the wizard, low-voiced.

Arun told him but added, "It is best no common soldier should handle the Ruby Wand, lord. Think of the temptation, if one is truly ignorant enough to believe he can master it."

Rebar nodded. Now that he understood the true importance of what he sought, he wanted it in no hands but his own.

"I will go myself, this time," he decided abruptly. "Bind his hands behind him and slip a jacket over his shoulders to hide the ropes. You two come with us."

A few minutes later Rebar led the way toward the fairgrounds, Arun being hustled along between two burly guards behind him. They walked through the gate, brushing past the new fair-ward and his minions without ceremony, and out into the bustle and noisy activity of the teeming streets and alleyways. Arun guided them to the tent of trinkets and cheap jewelry, and inside. This was a popular shop, with a constantly milling throng of customers around its tables. Sharp-eyed servitors watched for nimble-fingered thieves, and the stout proprietor stood guard over his money chest, beaming and smiling.

Arun led the way to the children's toys, and smiled wryly when he arrived at the correct table. Only two wands were left, but one of those was the Ruby Wand. The astute owner had marked it up to a price almost twice that of its less flashy company.

Rebar spotted it immediately. He reached for the wand with a trembling hand, lifting it closer to his eyes to inspect the glistening ruby—and Arun struck.

Arun had expanded his muscles to their maximum size when they tied his arms, and the ropes were cutting across flesh made slippery by sweat accumulated in the heat of the torture chamber. While his hands were covered on the long walk here he had been pulling and tugging desperately at the ropes, until finally he had slipped one strand over his right thumb. With a little freedom of movement he had managed to reach a knot, and then another, and finally he was carrying the rope behind him to keep it from falling.

Arun put all his weight into one single, mighty blow, straight into the swelling belly of the Iron Wizard. The breath left the older man's lungs in a convulsive *whoosh!* The wand dropped as his hands involuntarily opened and Arun caught it in midstride.

Arun was halfway to the rear tent-flap before the startled guards could move. When they belatedly started after him one decided to pause and help their master, who was sinking to the floor, lost in pain and trying raggedly to breathe. "*Stop him! Stop the thief!*" the other guard shouted, but he was too late. Arun had reached the exit and was out it and gone, this time turning to his right.

Arun ran down the alley as fast as he could without tripping, turned to reach the main street, then moved out into its center and hurried toward the entrance. There was a commotion behind him as the guard reached the thoroughfare and paused, wondering which way he had gone. He began shouting and trying to get the crowd to help him spot Arun, but they paid little attention.

Ahead Arun saw two fair-wards hurrying toward him, staves lifted to the ready. He stood to one side to give them room and they dashed on past toward the noise, ready to do their duty.

Near the edge of the fairgrounds Arun used his last silver piece to rent a horse from a man he knew, an old friend of his father's. He rode hard for home, and had his mother out of the house and hidden in a cave up in the lower foothills when the soldiers came. The horse he had already turned loose, to find its own way back.

They had food, poor though it was, and were kept warm by blankets as they slept on the hard rock. Next morning Arun left Anyanna there while he set off into the mountains, promising to return before dark.

The red-breasted Alts were long gone, their nest demolished and lying crumpled deep in some unreachable gorge. Arun climbed the difficult path he had followed before until he could step out onto the ledge, and along that to the hidden temple. This time he felt a sense of evil presence as he entered, an ancient residue of overweening lust for power. He was growing more sensitive to the awful powers that sometimes lay buried in innocent-seeming objects.

Arun pulled the wand from inside his jacket and grasped its handle, to set it upright again on its rock pedestal. *And it throbbed within his hand, a presence as palpable as smoke rising from that ancient reservoir of strength and evil, enveloping him completely.*

Use me! the wand cried in a voice without words. *I am the power and the glory! Hold me in partnership and I will teach you all you must know! Worlds without end lie before us! Riches undreamed of and power unimaginable! You have only to ask. . . .*

And his old mother waited, poor and lonely, her aching bones beyond healing except by this magic. A long life stretched before him, one rich and full of joy instead of short and brutishly poor. The good works he could do with this power, the people he could help, the— And suddenly Arun knew this, too, was an intrusion into his mind, another effort by the malignant force of the wand, which

was gaining an understanding of how to tempt him. Had
Asrazel, too, been a good man, before temptation and fall?

Arun straightened his shoulders, took a deep breath, and
walked to the pedestal without hesitation. Moving quickly,
he felt in the darkness until he could place the end of the
shaft in its anchoring hole . . . and stepped back as the
tamed power of the Ruby Wand set its jewel softly glowing, an angry rose light by which he turned and left the
chamber.

The house had been thoroughly wrecked when they
reached it, but the soldiers had disdained to take any of
their poor possessions. Arun helped Anyanna gather up
what was left unbroken of their household goods and food,
making a travois of two long poles and their blankets.
Anything heavy was left behind.

They would go cross-country to Bear River, build a raft,
and float downriver to where the Bear joined the great
river Ith, below Ithkar. There he would work for their
passage on some ship heading back to the coast, where
they would make a new life for themselves, far from the
grasp of the evil Iron Wizard or his competitors.

We had little, and I have lost it all, Arun thought as they
set out before dark that same day, Arun dragging the
heavy poles as Anyanna hobbled along beside him. But I
have saved this land and its people from a generation of
terror and death. Should that not be enough?

To that he could find no answer. But suddenly he saw a
picture in his mind of Ferrugo Rebar, continuously searching the hills and valleys around the Elem homestead for
the Ruby Wand, not knowing how far away and high it
was, endlessly seeking, always frustrated, never knowing
peace or rest or the good feeling of accomplishment. He
thought of the Iron Wizard growing old and feeble, vulner-

able to his many enemies, with his most vaunting ambitions unfulfilled—and Arun knew he would eventually have faced a similar fate, had he yielded to the evil lure of the wand.

In the long run, Arun would lead by far the happier life—and in that thought he found a degree of contentment.

BIRD OF PARADISE

Linda Haldeman

Set upon a green mound just outside the fairgrounds but within sight of the Temple of the Three Lordly Ones stands, incongruous but beautiful, Papageno's Palace, an elaborate domed and turreted edifice constructed entirely from thick braided gold wire. The great Fair at Ithkar had more or less grown near it, for it was older than the fair; some said it was older than the temple itself, that it had been there when the Three Lordly Ones had honored the Ith Valley with their presence. Rumor persisted among the superstitious and a few conservative scholars that the structure had been built as a temple to the Earth Mother, long deposed primitive deity of the valley, and that the cagelike turrets had been used for unspeakable sacrifices of blood and flame. There was certainly no hint of this previous use of the palace as it now appeared, swept clean and polished to glisten in the bright sunlight, a gigantic bird cage, the roost and display case for some hundred or so exotic and rare birds. It consisted of one large cylindrical central cage, its roof forming the high central dome of the palace. Around this structure marched the turrets, composed of small cages set one on top of the other, each cage looking out on the fair and opening into the central chamber. Papageno, who apparently owned the palace or managed it for some ever-absent lord or entrepreneur, worked constantly keeping the place clean and polished; feeding, grooming, and nursing the birds; selling them to wealthy collectors at a grand price; and also apparently breeding them. For no cage remainded empty for more than a day. Within twenty-four hours after a tenant had died or been sold, a new bird of the same species or one of equal value had taken its place. It was something of a mystery where the birds came from, but since neither fraud nor impropriety could be proved and the palace and its inhabitants attracted visitors to the fair, no one investigated too closely.

Papageno himself was a rare bird. Corpulent and swarthy, he lived among his charges like an apprentice in his atelier, sleeping in a gigantic nest of straw and clay lined with the finest down avian nature could supply. There were those who contended that Papageno was a secret devotee of the Earth Mother and continued to perform forbidden rites.

It was an unusually chilly dawn on the third day of the great fair. Papageno rose groaning from his nest and waddled out onto the straw-littered clay floor, wrapping a tentlike mantle of multicolored striped wool around him, and blew into life the smoldering hearth in the center of the great cage. He poured milk from a jug onto a highly polished gold saucer and placed it with great care and

ceremony on the floor a respectful distance from the fire.
On his knees before the dish he raised his hands and
uttered a most remarkable chant, an elaborate and complex
birdcall replete with coloratura trills and decorations. The
birds asleep in their gilded apartments drew their heads out
from under their wings and joined in the chorus, each
contributing his own very personal and specific variation.
It was quite a din, but somehow it harmonized. The Earth
Mother in the form of a cat manifested herself in front of
Papageno, stepping, it appeared, from the fire itself, and
expressed her pleasure at and acceptance of his offering by
drinking every drop of the milk. She then climbed into his
ample lap, dug her claws into his flesh, pumping up and
down like a baker kneading bread dough, and finally
curled up, licking her paws clean.

"I'd be most obliged to you, my lady, for a bird of
paradise, a female to mate with my solitary male. His
display is most spectacular and would attract much attention from buyers, but it is a mating display, and he will
perform it only in the presence of a female."

The cat twitched her tail, then stretched herself out
comfortably. Papageno diffidently stroked her head, confident that his petition would be approved, for she found
mating and reproduction more to her liking than buying
and selling. After a bit, she stretched off his lap, sauntered
over to the golden staircase that spiraled around the wall of
the inner cage up, up to the domed roof, briefly examining
the respectfully quiescent inmates as she passed. When she
reached the apex, she looked down on Papageno with
fierce, narrowed slits of eyes, twitched her tail once, an
expression, it was hoped, of approval, and with cool fi-
nesse transformed herself into a pigeon and flew off over
the awakening fairgrounds.

Papageno slowly released a long held breath, and the hundred or so birds did likewise, each after his own manner, chirping, crowing, whistling, cawing all at once in a great deafening but somehow not dissonant cacophony. Papageno threw up his arms in a gesture of joyous welcome.

"Waken, O great Fair of Ithkar," he cried in a voice like a trumpeting swan. "The day awaits you. Arise and be about your business. Thanks be to the Earth Mother for locking the darkness away in her airing closet; let us honor her with cleanliness and industry. Praised be the stars in her crown and the soil between her toes!"

Having performed his morning devotions, Papageno bounced, rolled, and hobbled off to his morning chores. One pull on a silken rope that hung from the very top cage triggered an elaborate mechanism that opened the inner door of every cage, and a hundred or so birds, all sizes, shapes, colors, and configurations, flew out at once into the center dome for morning exercise. As they chattered and swooped about him, perching mischievously on his head, shoulders, and arms, Papageno, laughing in delight and affection like a nanny in a mad nursery, walked carefully to avoid treading on the highly bred chickens with high white plumes and wings like finely worked lace, moving from cage to cage, cleaning each tray and filling each dish with the prescribed and preferred seed. It was a prodigious chore for one man, one waddling wine tun of a man, to perform in the space of three hours, but perform it he did, pecked and fluttered at constantly by his affectionate and ebullient charges, up and around on the winding stairs, from the commodious communal chicken coops on the ground level to the very top of the dome where the larks and the nightingales held tandem vocal competitions like a troupe of Meistersingers in perpetual motion. By the third hour of the forenoon Papageno, his woollen robe filthy and soaked with sweat, stood once more at the foot of the golden staircase and gave one shrill whistle. A hundred or so birds spun and scattered, homing to their proper cells. Seeing all to be in order, Papageno gave the silken rope another pull, and the elaborate mechanism closed every door. Well satisfied with himself and his life, Papageno waddled down to the Ith for a well-deserved and much needed bath.

The Earth Mother retained the pigeon form for a while, though she found any material configuration frustrating and inhibiting. The form of a bird, she reasoned, could be useful under some circumstances, and just before departing, she soared easily over the wide fairgrounds, grown larger and more elaborate every year. She flew high for fear of the sporting instinct of some of the stone-throwing men and boys of Ithkar and took even greater care in approaching the courtyard of the Temple of the Three Lordly Ones, the cursed usurpers of her land and persecutors of her votaries. Upstart newcomers with their sky fire, they had overwhelmed her comfortable earth fire and established themselves as masters of her valley, driving her into exile. Then they had left to dethrone some other natural deity in some other valley. Now only a few scattered faithful remembered her enough to leave a saucer of milk for the cat in her. The bird in her cruised once around the inner court of the temple and then, seeing that no one was observing or threatening her, swooped in and dropped an avian offering onto the center of the sacred altar. Relieved in one way and satisfied in another, the Earth Mother relaxed into her customary formlessness and radi-

ated her presence over the sun-warmed valley, which could
never wholly reject her because she was in it and it was in
her.

Mormidor of Frigoland came down the East River in a
narrow, low-riding boat, propelling it through the rapids
and down the channel by means of a long pole. Carma
came down the road on hard bare feet, with a half loaf of
black bread and a hunk of aging goat cheese in a home-
spun sack slung over her shoulders. They met quite by
accident a mile or so north of the muddy, noisome encampment of gypsies, cutpurses, mountebanks, prostitutes,
and other undesirables that gather on the periphery of any
great event, like dust on a fine lady's petticoat. It was
midmorning, and Carma, seeing the cool ribbon of water
across a meadow, left the road, carefully scaled a fence,
adding another rent to her already tattered dress, and trotted
through the cooling grass to the river bank.

Mormidor of Frigoland, punting easily down the river,
glad to be in reasonably calm water at last, glanced shore-
ward and saw a woman sitting on the bank bathing her feet
in the water—a woman-child, so perfect a blend of light
and shadow that she seemed a child of the river bank
itself. Fascinated, he turned the prow of his little boat and
pulled into shore beside her. She showed no fear but
watched him disembark with her wide, curious gray eyes.
Her straw-pale hair, falling down her back in thick waves,
shone in the sun. Mormidor smiled, for the girl's rough
peasant beauty delighted him.

"Good morrow, mistress." He stepped from his boat
with a courtly bow.

"Good morrow yourself, master," Carma replied, studying him from boots to feathered cap with open curiosity. "Be ye hungered? I have but black bread and old cheese, but you be welcome to share."

"For such bounty I thank you, mistress. I ran out of provision last night and thought not to break my fast until I reached the fair."

He took from the belt of his tunic a short bone-handled knife and neatly sliced the bread and cheese into equal, easy-to-handle portions.

"The cheese is quite good," Mormidor commented, discreetly cutting away spots of greenish mold. "Did it come from your goats?"

"Aye." She looked with full eyes toward the meadows to the east. "We had a lovely herd of goats, but they are gone now, as is the gentle milch cow. We had a fine farm—wheat and oats, and a garden laden with every manner of greens and roots most pleasing in the pot. Now all is gone save the stone-and-sod house my father built, and now with no one to care for it that will in time be devoured as well by the earth and the sun and the rain. All abandoned things return to the Earth Mother, it is said."

Mormidor shook his head but said nothing. Ancient superstitions hang on amongst the ignorant, even in enlightened Ithkar.

"What happened?" he asked.

"Everything went badly all at once. My mother said it was the Earth Mother angered because we have forgotten her since the Three Lordly Ones came to Ithkar; my father insisted that it was the Sky Lords who were wroth because my mother sacrificed to the Earth Mother. I do not know, but some great force must have been very wroth indeed. Fire destroyed what crops the blight spared. The milch

cow went down with distemper. My father said that that
proved it was the Sky Lords, for the Earth Mother would
have taken the goats first and spared the cow, for milk is
the Earth Mother's incense. My mother must have thought
so, too, for she sacrificed herself to the Earth Mother by
eating red mushrooms. She told me, 'You bear my seed;
do not let it die,' and prayed to the Earth Mother to keep
me safe. She died in great pain, calling with joy the
forbidden names of the Earth Mother.'' Carma's gray
child's eyes glistened with excitement. ''She was magnificent! And as she fell a great storm came with a whirlwind
that carried away our barn. My brothers, such fine, valiant
fellows, fled with the clothes upon their backs and were
not seen again, I know not where they be. After that day
no person came near to us, nor friend nor foe nor kin nor
stranger. Naught grows on our land save thorns and thistles. Only the goats thrived. Goats, said my father, were
beloved of the Earth Mother. He grew old, my poor father,
before his time, and but sat before the meager fire and
dreamed of my dead mother. She was the Earth Mother,
he told me, and he told me not to fear, that she would
provide for her seed. I do not understand such things, but I
smiled and said yes, for that made him glad. I was not sad
myself; I am never sad. Every day the sun is golden, and
every night the crickets sing. So long as that be so, I am
golden and I sing. 'You be the Earth Mother's child,' said
my father. And so I think I must be.''

She stretched out on her back in the grass like a basking
cat, spreading her hair about her head in an aureole.
Mormidor smiled on her, suddenly finding himself filled
with a happiness he had not known for many years.

''We lived on goat cheese,'' the girl went on, ''and the

old bread the village baker cast out. I came in dark of night to raid the bin behind his oven. If he knew I came, he said naught, but the bread was not always stale.

"One night in early spring when the small pale blossoms were just opening along the road, my father called me over to the fire where he sat and spoke to me thus: 'At summer's end, when the thistles begin to bloom and the nuts drop from ripeness, at the time of the great golden moon, take with you what provisions ye have and your finest dress and follow the road south to the Fair at Ithkar. Go not to the temple—the temple is the Sky Lords', but the valley yet belongs to her. She will provide for you a fitting mate and a new life. I go to join her now.' He kissed me and sent me away. When I returned he was dead, smiling, in his corner by the fire. That night the goats died, I know not why. I think they must have been his.

"That is my story. Now tell me yours."

Mormidor sighed, returning to the reality of a fly humming in his ear and damp grass under his legs. "My story is not very interesting."

The girl gave him a wise grin. "I be not so sure of that. You be not what you seem. You come down the river like a stranger from the mountains, but your speech is of Ithkar."

"You are an observant one. My speech is of Ithkar, for of Ithkar was I born. My mother was a weaver, my father a tailor, both descendants of a long line of masters in their craft. Their marriage was, I suspect, an arranged matter, an affair of convenience rather than of love. I am the culmination of that union, conceived on the loom and born on the cutting table. All the gifts of both houses showered in full abundance on my cradle. All save love, which I knew not from birth. At first I was trained in my craft, but the gift was strong in me, and soon I found I need not follow my mother's tedious puzzle of warp and woof or my father's painstaking fit, measure, cut, sew. I could weave anything, straw, flowers, the thread of spiderwebs, the summer-shed hair of dogs. With the proper movement, the right words, I could shape these cloths into the garments of my choice. I know not how I learned the words; no one taught me. They came to me when I had need of them, the gift of some unknown power. I was young and did not question. All the same, having been brought up in a house of ambition and unscrupulous avarice, a hearth where there dwelt neither love nor joy, I was secretive and told no one, especially my family, of my gifts.

"We have booths at the fair, of course, lavish tents dominating both the cloth and garment trades, my parents' families controlling both crafts. As a child I was brought to the fair appareled like a young lord in the best of the families' wares and sent to wander about the grounds, especially those parts nearest the temple precincts, where the wealthy congregate to speculate on money or buy jewels and other luxuries. I was stopped frequently by fine ladies and gentlemen admiring my garb. I dutifully sent them to my parents' shops as I had been commanded, but secretly I smiled, for already I could make superior garments with my own hands."

Carma, who had been listening to all this with increasing agitation, could keep silence no longer and burst out.

"You be a wizard man. I knew it. When I marked ye floating down the river like a young prince of old, I did think ye more than common man. When ye came to shore I saw that ye were in no wise special and just a trifle old.

But now I perceive that though there be little to commend your face and form, there be wondrous magic in your hands.'' She caught his hands in her small ones and examined them carefully. They were long and thin and very white. The palms were soft, but the balls of the fingers rough and callused. ''Show me, wizard man of the North. Make me a fine gown for the fair, as I have ruined my best dress in my wanderings.''

Mormidor smiled, enchanted more than offended by the girl's blunt appraisal and, flattered to have his services requested, accepted the challenge.

''You wish to be properly garbed for the fair, do you?''

''Oh, indeed. The Earth Mother is to provide a mate for me, and I must look my best for him.''

''Perhaps she already has provided,'' Mormidor said.

Carma looked at him and giggled, just slightly, and shook her head. ''I think not.''

It was impossible even looking closely into her gray eyes to interpret her response, for she showed no concern or embarrassment. Perhaps in her innocence she had not properly understood his statement. Then again, perhaps she had.

''Come,'' he said. ''Let us gather branches from the willow yonder that droops so gracefully over the water, and I shall weave for you a skirt of willow and a bodice of soft river-bank moss trimmed with white asters. And as I work, I shall tell you of my youth in Ithkar.''

They gathered the willow branches, cutting them off at the right length with the bone-handled knife, taking care not to spoil the beauty of the tree by taking too many limbs from one place. The Earth Mother hovered unseen over them, blessing their converse with morning sunshine and soft breezes but keeping guard over the welfare of her willow tree.

"I had to be careful," Mormidor continued as his fingers moved rapidly, binding the willow branches together, "for I could feel my uncles watching me even when they were not watching me. I have many uncles, both weavers and tailors. They have always been suspicious of me, all of them, though I had told no one of my secret gifts. They objected always to sending me out to roam the fair at freedom while they sat all day at their labors, but they were overruled by the patriarchs of the families, because I brought in money. They were right, though, to so object, for I brought back with me much more than orders for tunics and gowns. I looked as I wandered among the booths and shops of the great fair. I looked at everything, finely wrought chairs and bracelets, gems cut to reflect the power of light, carpets and tapestries of intricate design and luminous texture—made things and natural things, colorful, vividly shaped plants brought in from the swamp and from islands beyond the western sea, marvelous animals with striped and spotted and many-colored coats, and exotic birds. Do you like birds, Carma?"

"So I do," she said. "Especially the brightly colored ones, red and blue and yellow they be sometimes."

"Ah, but you cannot imagine the birds at the fair, orange and purple and green and silver. Birds with serpents' necks and regal trains spreading out behind them and crowns of golden plumes. Just outside the fair, yet older than the fair, there is a house, a great golden palace filled with birds of all manner, hundreds of them. Quite a sight. I never fail to visit it."

"Oh! Oh!" Carma clapped her small, perfectly formed but work-callused hands. "I want to see that, so I do."

"And so you shall." Mormidor smiled upon her, his eyes stroking her unkempt tangle of hair and lightly touching her cheek. With effort he forced his gaze back to his still rapidly working hands, which seemed to move under their own command, and continued his story.

"The fair was my school and my entertainment. I learned shrewdness from the merchants, dishonesty from the money-changers, hypocrisy from the priests, the power of illusion from the strolling players and puppeteers, an insatiable appetite for what is truly beautiful from the artists and artisans, who came bearing what they had made with their dreams and their hands and set them on display to the world, saying, 'Look what I have done that is beautiful and of my own making. Look and marvel, even as I do.' I looked upon those things and wept at their beauty, then watched, choked with misery, as their creators laid a price upon them and sold them to strangers. That is the part I could not bear. Had I wanted to join in this terrible sacrilege I could have sold the lovely things I made in secret for great profit, or I could have bartered for them fine gems and soft leather boots and delicate sweetmeats and even the lovely sunrise-colored birds that sang and trilled in the turrets of the great gold palace. But this I could not and cannot do. As I grew older I realized that I lacked the tradesman's heart. I cannot bear to part with anything I have made, and consequently I have not the courage to take possession of that which another has made. In despair I abandoned my own works and in self-defense took on the character of a simpleton to avoid the anguish of being set to work in the family shop. Seeing no profit to be made from me, my enterprising family sent me out to beg, for I had learned from observing the player show to be an attractive and appealing simpleton. It was a most gratifying way of life for a youth of my temperament, for I had the freedom of the fairgrounds and leisure to look my fill at all the beautiful and fascinating artifacts on display. When the fair closed I did not have to return to the town, but lived on the deserted grounds by the indulgence of the temple priests, who for some reason regard simpletons as holy and privileged creatures. I loved the fairgrounds, for they are the only home I have ever known. I kept them and the buildings clean and in repair. The priests kept me warm and fed. Naturally I clothed myself, for my gift had not abandoned me. I dared not indulge my love of beauty in the making of my clothes, but I did indulge at times my love of whimsy, attiring myself in all sorts of strange motley as befits a simpleton.''

"I should like that," said Carma, "living at the fair. But does it not get lonely there when all have left?"

"It's never really deserted," Mormidor explained. "There are always a few derelicts around, old beggars with no proper home seeking shelter, outlaws, and occasional genuine simpletons. They always welcomed me to their company, though they knew full well that I was an imposter. And there was old Papageno and his birds."

"The birds?"

"Yes, the bird cage is a permanent building just outside the grounds, and Papageno keeps his feathered menagerie there all the year 'round. I used to help him clean and care for the birds. Now there is a wizard man of the first rank. He is a secret devotee of the Earth Mother, very likely a priest, and I've always suspected that he gets his birds from her, unless he creates them himself. No one knows where they come from. Most people assume they are imported, but I have never seen any cages come up from the docks. A very interesting fellow. Here, try this.''

He held up a long flounced skirt of pale green cloth that was like a very fine velvet lightly embroidered in an oval leaf pattern. Flushing with delight, Carma pulled it over her head and fastened it at her waist.

"Oh, you be sufficient wizard man for me," she cried. "Now am I beautiful enough to win my promised mate. What be you doing now?"

"Making a bodice of river-bank moss trimmed in white asters."

She sat on the green bank beside him, carefully spreading out her skirt. "You have not yet told me how ye came to leave Ithkar."

"I left Ithkar because I finally found what I had been deprived of all my life—love—and made my first sale. It was at fair time in my twenty-first year by my calculations. She was the daughter of a chief of one of the nomadic tribes of the northern mountains. And she was beautiful, tall and dark with bright, tormenting black eyes. Her father and brothers had come to the fair with a great store of pelts and tanned hides and had bargained well. Now they swaggered through the grounds spending gold recklessly, childishly. I stood to the side watching them, reminding myself that if I did not profit from their innocence, someone else would, to be sure. But she was there, her eyes searching me out, challenging me. I could not beg in her presence, nor could I rob or cheat. As I watched they entered the shop of my Uncle Marlo, the tailor, a miserable miser of a fellow, famous for shoddy goods and thin seams. She meant to buy a robe of him? No, I could not tolerate that. I presented myself to the leader of this horde, a leather-clad giant with a black mustache as proud and shiny as a cockscomb, and offered to sell the lady a robe of the finest silk available in Ithkar, embroidered with threads of gold and silver, and for a better price than Marlo, no matter how low that would be. He was dubious at first; after all, I did look like a beggar. But I was young and filled with passion, and what chance has any ordinary barbarian chieftain against a determined enthusiast?

"But she would have none of it, for she had found what she thought she wanted, a tacky satin gown of ugly purplish mauve, very unbecoming. Impulsively I seized the garment, spun it around several times to confuse the color, and ran, holding it before me, through the booths and shops, calling upon all the beauty I had honored and worshiped all these years to bless the gown. It came through the bakery bleached white as fine flour; the jeweler's ran it through and through with silver threads; and the confectionery sparkled it with a fine spray of spun sugar. And as I dashed out to the great bird cage, fine down floated onto the borders to form a soft, delicate trim. Running back to the cloth sections, I paused to pluck a single red rose from a tree and made of it a broach for her to clasp at her neck. Then I stood gasping before her, seeing no one else, caring for no one else. She smiled at me. She took the gown and put it on. I was dazzled by the sight of her and forgot where I was and what I was doing. Her father pressed something into my hand. A purse filled with gold coins. I had sold the work of my hand."

"But you won the heart of your dark princess," said Carma.

"Aye, even as I am to win yours."

Mormidor turned away from her and chanted incoherently to the pile of moss and tiny wild asters he had been shaping between his hands. She watched, somewhat in awe but in no fear, until he had finished and rose ceremoniously to face her, holding up a dark green bodice trimmed with the finest white lace. Eagerly she squirmed out of her rough peasant blouse and fitted the new one on, paying not the least attention to her admirer's excitement.

"There, see how lovely I am?" she cried, kissing him lightly on the cheek. "Lovelier than all the dark beauties of the northern mountains, for I am the Earth Mother's child, as are you, else you could not use her gifts so well." She turned on him suddenly. "How is it that you took to wife a barbarian princess and left the sacred valley of the Ith?"

"Not by my own design, little one. I was offered on the spot the dark hand and a princedom in the North, but I would not have accepted it had not my dear old Uncle Marlo come upon the scene and threatened to haul me before the fair-court for theft and fraud. It was then that I realized what I had done in the name of love. The chieftain, no stranger to corruption, bought off Marlo and bought me in the bargain. I could not face public opprobrium, so I fled with my new patron and my love to the pale, sunless tundras of the North, where everything is black and white and occasionally gray. I am a full-fledged prince there now, with a steppe I can call my own and three tall, dark sons who hunt great furry beasts and care nothing for beauty. I make weavings of dried bark now and then to keep in practice."

"And your princess?"

"Northern people do not age well. Perhaps it is the climate. I find it hard to remember how she was in those days when I loved her. My heart, I fear, never left Ithkar, and if I do not undertake my annual journey down the rushing mountain streams, through the gaps, into the rapids— disdaining the tame canal—down, down, down to the great river Ith to the fair, I should, I fear, go quite mad. My royal father-in-law, my consort, my three enormous mustached sons, none knows where I go or why, for they would insist I bring pelts for barter, and that I will not do. I keep my distance from the cloth section and dear old Uncle Marlo, who threatens to live forever and never forgets a grudge, and I drink my fill of beauty and warmth and color to last me through the dark, hard winter.''

''Then come,'' Carma cried, pulling him to his feet and leading him across the meadow, over the fence, and onto the road, now crowded with pilgrims and pleasure seekers. ''The sun is high, and the fair awaits us. You must be my escort that none dare insult or molest me. You will show me all the things of beauty and help me find my proper mate, for the Earth Mother has sent you for that purpose.''

Panting a little in his effort to keep up, Mormidor objected somewhat shrilly.

''Could it be that I am the mate the Earth Mother sent you?''

She stopped abruptly, ignoring an oxcart that nearly ran her down, and studied him hard for a half minute, then shook her head.

''No.''

That was all. The matter settled, she continued on her southern way, melding into the general parade. Mormidor trotted behind, miserable yet absurdly content. She was so lovely. He did not know whether to curse the Earth Mother or bless her.

*   *   *

The afternoon sun shone down on the Fair at Ithkar, drying the ubiquitous mud into hard cracked plaster, lulling the wild creatures in the menagerie into soporific siestas, accenting the reds and violets of the cut roses and poppies, and raising the color in the faces of the girls who sold them along the crowded midway. Papageno climbed laboriously up the wide spiral stairs to the domed roof of his palace, daughter of the golden sun. He raised a narrow square gate at the top of the stairs, eased himself out until head and chest rose above the golden dome, and he stood resting his folded arms on the roof, looking over the merry pandemonium of the fair, so close he was to the grounds, and so high above. Anything worth hunting? Not really; not today, not this season, just magpies and the usual contingent of common sparrows and blackbirds. His small, bright black eyes skimmed over the finely dressed patrons of the skilled artisans, magpies all, loud in self-praise, with little justification for their vanity, on beyond to the scrappy, dandified jays strutting about the horse stalls, and the starlings and sparrows, wily, opportunistic survivors who flourished amidst the sequins and squalor of the players' stalls, stealing food from occupied vendors and pilfering free pinches of passing whores. Then he saw her and gave a gasp of wonder and delight. His bird of paradise: a glowing green bird of paradise, standing in a crowd gathered around a haywagon, where players performed the *Play of the Three Lordly Ones and the Lecherous Priest*, hanging on the arms of a stalwart green heron. Too bad; he didn't need another green heron. But the bird of paradise, that he must have. He squirmed back through the door, locked it, and eased himself with all cautious haste down to the ground. They were coming this way. He must act quickly, but not before prostrating himself on the clay floor of the cage and offering his thanks to the great Mother who always provides.

Carma was delighted with the bawdy, scurrilous, libelous, blasphemous comedy, as she was with everything at the fair: the cloying sweetness of the honey-dripping confections, the tuneless twanging of strolling musicians, the gaudy opulence of boldly soliciting whores, the flashy patter song of barkers seducing marks to the gaming booths. Mormidor walked proudly at her side, aware of the admiring and covetous looks that followed them. He breathed deeply the marvelous bouquet garni of odors, all familiar, yet in combination all delightfully strange, and he felt at home again, a boy free to wander incognito, unencumbered with responsibility. It was for this, this time of freedom in the company of outlaws and urchins, observing, experiencing, absorbing life as a camel takes in water at an oasis before heading back into the desert, that he braved the rapids and dodged the shallows.

"See, over there, my dear, is the great castle of birds."

Carma looked where he pointed, and for the first time since beholding the banners and pennants of the fair from afar, she was awed into silence. Just beyond the bounds of the fair, the enormous golden cage glittered like a great jewel in the sun. Every outer chamber was tenanted by one of the more showy specimens; the upper cages, being far above the sight lines of the populace, housed the more showy singers. Just as there was at the amusement within the fair, there was always a crowd gathered around Papageno's Palace, for the show was ever-changing—and free. Carma pushed through with all the charming rudeness of the young and planted herself firmly in front of a small apartment above her eye level that housed a solitary brilliantly colored bird of paradise, fantastically decorated with swirling white plumes on his head and back and strutting in full appreciation of his own beauty. The bird saw her and stopped in midstrut, giving a weird, high-pitched cry. Then he backed off a few paces and broke into an elaborate minuet, bowing, scraping, ruffling his magnificent feathers while accompanying himself with a melancholy warble punctuated by high-pitched piercing yelps, in an effort to get her attention. He had it. She laughed, blushed, clapped her hands, and jumped up and down in a human version of the mating dance.

"Oh, Mormidor, dear Mormidor, buy him for me. He is so beautiful, and he is the delight of my life."

Mormidor turned away, feeling distinctly uneasy. He had taken great pleasure up until now in indulging the child's every desire, buying her anything she showed the least interest in. But her fascination with this bird and the bird's fascination with her alarmed him. In spite of all his generosity, she did not look so on him.

Papageno himself materialized beside them, resplendent in a varicolored silk robe, bobbing like an overfed pigeon, rubbing his greasy hands together.

"A bird of paradise, a living precious jewel for your lady? A handsome, stylish pet, sure to steal any girl's fancy and cause her heart to fly to you."

"I hardly think so." Mormidor flinched away from the birdseller, repelled by something in the man that he could not identify, something that the primitive child-man hiding in his soul recognized as inimical.

Carma sensed no danger. She clapped her hands together and hopped up and down on her bare brown feet.

"Oh, do, do, dear northerner. Buy for me this lovely dancing bird, for I do so love him."

Mormidor took the girl by the shoulders and turned her to face him. "I would have you love me, Carma."

"Oh, that I do, you know I do."

"Then leave off this foolishness and come with me now. In me you will find the mate you have been promised."

She frowned and shook off his hands.

"Here now. Ye know better than to fall in love. It was your undoing before and will be your undoing again. 'Tis not you who will be my promised one; 'tis yonder bird. If ye will not buy him for me, I shall find one who will or else perish here of love-longing."

She ran to the great cage, her filigreed green skirt billowing out like a showy tail behind her, and laid her cheek against the bars. The bird bowed and strutted and spread his colorful tail feathers in the manner of his species, while she whispered indecipherable sounds to him.

Papageno stood in Mormidor's path, his hulk blocking the view.

"Only five coins of gold, sirrah, and the magnificent creature is yours."

"You have bewitched her, you old devil," Mormidor growled. "You have ensnared her in your gaudy trap."

Papageno chuckled, making his belly jump ludicrously.

"I do not deal in flesh, my dear sir. That sort of trade is relegated to the fields beyond. I am a respectable merchant plying a respectable trade. You, on the contrary, are a renegade, are you not? There are hounds sniffing about this fair who would be overjoyed to flush you out."

Mormidor shrugged. "At this point I don't care. I must see the woman of my heart enamored of a plaything or return from whence I came to the cold, hard kingdom of cold, hard people, where I will be always an outsider, more than I am here an exile. So betray me, if that please you. It makes little difference to me where I am imprisoned.''

Papageno clucked his tongue. It really was too bad he didn't need a heron.

''It matters to her,'' he said, for he did need a bird of paradise. ''See how she smiles and dotes on the creature? In her heart she has almost joined her feathered lover in my golden palace. Only the grille and the bonds of flesh separate them now. It is in your power and mine to grant her happiness. What a waste of our poor old lonely lives if we do not.''

''Warlock,'' said Mormidor. ''I see your game now. I did not observe you in the years of my growing up without marking how it is that you keep your palace supplied. You want her, don't you, in the cage with that miserable dandy? But you will not have her. Come, Carma.''

He pulled the girl by the arm, but she resisted, clinging to the golden bars of the cage. Papageno made a motion, barely perceptible, with his plump hand, and the cage shattered with a golden shudder, releasing the bird. Faced with sudden freedom, he bent his wings upward, soared once, a trifle awkwardly, around the cage, landed on the ground in front of Carma, and bowed his head to the ground, raising his magnificent green-and-gold-and-orange tail and spreading it out like a fan before her. Then he fluttered off toward the palace. With a cry the girl ran after him, following him without hesitation in through the suddenly open main gate of the palace into the great central hall where the hearth blazed up a welcome.

With a despairing cry Mormidor threw his body against

the closing gate and before he was thrown back by the force of a wild gust of wind saw within the flames the form of a woman, slender as a willow tree, golden as the autumn sun, reaching out from the fire to embrace Carma. Then the hot wind rushed upon him and knocked him senseless.

He was lying on a grassy bank of the Ith when he came to himself. He was facing west and the rose-and-gold setting sun. Old Papageno, bending over him solicitously, offered him a drink from a silver flask.

"Be at peace, tailor's son," he murmured. "I brought you here out of sight of the wards until things quiet down."

"Carma."

"She is content; be you as well."

"How can I when I have once more lost my heart? I knew not how great a boon my parents granted me when they denied me love. It is naught but a curse and a grievous burden."

The old birdtender laughed. "Without doubt it is. But if you should wish for it again, the Earth Mother will provide. She always does."

Mormidor sighed, still not sure whether to bless or curse her. "She is beautiful," he whispered. "I never considered the possibility that she might be beautiful."

"All mothers are beautiful," Papageno said, "at least to their sons."

He started to waddle off in the direction of his palace, but he turned back when he saw that Mormidor, rather than following him, had gone down to the river bank and was busily plucking reeds and cattails.

"What are you doing?" Papageno cried. "The priests will have your skin for defacing their land."

"Be not concerned," said Mormidor. "Go back to your birds. I have my own work to do, and I must work quickly while there is yet light."

"What are you doing?" Papageno persisted.

"Making a gown, of course. The most beautiful gown of all. For her, my true and only love."

Shaking his head, the old birdseller lurched up the bank and out of sight. Mormidor sat upon the river bank in the twilight weaving reeds and cattails into a long flowing robe. The Earth Mother rose like a mermaid from the waters and came to him.

The nightingale in the dome of Papageno's Palace trilled gloriously into the coming of night, and all the birds that sing by day tucked their heads under their wings and settled content on their golden perches.

FLAMING-ARROW

R. A. Lafferty

Peter Flaming-Arrow from Kara Cove was in trouble with the men and masters of half a dozen trade-guilds. His own trade was that of a fletcher, one who feathers arrows.

"But a fletcher may fletch anything," Peter argued. "Not only can he put feathers or wings on arrows, but he can also put them on wagons or boats or himself."

"No, he cannot put feathers or wings on wagons," said the wainwrights or wagon-carpenters. "If there is a reason to put feathers or wings on wagons, that would pertain to our trade and not to his."

"No, he cannot put feathers or wings on boats," said the boatbuilders. "If there were a reason to put wings or feathers on boats, that would pertain to our trade and not to his. Indeed, the sails that we *do* put on boats *are* wings, if you will forgive us our metaphors. Beyond that, the boats that this Flaming-Arrow man does build are illegal and defective, for they have no bottoms in them."

"It's true that the boats which I build have no bottoms," Peter admitted, "and it is for this reason that I claim that they are not boats and they are not illegal. They are arrows, though not in the regular arrow-form. And where I intend to sail them or shoot them they will not need any bottoms in them."

"No, Peter Flaming-Arrow may not put wings or feathers on himself," the magicians said. "If there were reason or possibility for putting feathers or wings on human persons, that would pertain to our magic trade."

"What I am working with is *not* magic and does not pertain to the magicians' trade," Peter Flaming-Arrow insisted. "What I am working with is the arithmetic of flame and air; rather simple arithmetic, rather simple flame, rather complex air." Well, Peter irritated people when he talked in that complex and airy way of his.

"This man Flaming-Arrow has no right to deal in flame at all," said the candlemakers, the lamplighters, the fire-swallowers, and the weapons-makers (Greek fire division). "He has failed in his apprenticeship in all of the flame trades and he has no business with fire at all."

"Oh, stuff it, the whole bunch of you!" Peter always cried out, but he laughed when he cried out such things. Peter was as pleasant a person as you would ever meet, and it was possibly for that reason that he remained unhanged. Indeed, it was pointed out that he'd been born with the red mark of the hanging noose around his neck and that he had it yet. And it was argued with passion that one who was born with such a red mark around his neck would unfailingly end up on the end of a rope. Peter Flaming-Arrow, however, was one great red mark all over.

His complexion was a ruddy-red flame color entirely, as was his hair, and even the pupils of his eyes. People could just barely see the redder mark around his neck even after it was pointed out to them. Well, it was there whether they could discern it from the rest of him or not. If he hadn't been such a laughing and friendly fellow, this would have been held against him even more than was the case. A barefaced young man himself, as well as a wrestler that none of them would tangle with, he mocked all the beard-wearing and mustache-wearing men as cowards who hid their true faces behind their whiskers. Since the great majority of the men did so hide their faces, and as Peter Flaming-Arrow said other abrasive things as well, there was sharp resentment against this arrow man. It was even said that he was not so barefaced as he seemed, that he wore a red mask at all times, and that his true face was otherwise.

Peter Flaming-Arrow also tangled with the scribes, the antiquarians, the astrologers (meteorological division), the fortune-tellers (bird-entrail division), the bards, the priests, the herbalists (psychedelic and hallucinatory herbs division); he tangled with them all on the question of conflict of occupations and trades.

"A man should be able to fletch feathers onto arrow shafts without meddling in a dozen other trades," some people argued with fair logic. (Other toes that Peter Flaming-Arrow stepped on were those of members of the logicians' guild.)

For a man who generated so much goodwill because of his laughing and pleasant personality, Peter Flaming-Arrow also generated a lot of ill will by overstepping the narrow bounds of his trade and tongue. The good and the ill tendencies slid past each other with much friction, and a resolution of forces began to develop.

"What Peter Flaming-Arrow is generating is a cyclone," several persons of the weather predicters' guild remarked ponderously. "That is what is generated when things of contrary tendencies come together and become entangled."

"No, I am no cyclone man," Peter always argued. "What I will really generate by these antipathies is up-drafts. Oh, how I love to ride on updrafts!"

In that particular year (the annalists refer to it as the "Year of the Black-Footed Flying Fox," but that name has not yet received popular acceptance), Peter Flaming-Arrow of Kara Cove came to the great fair at Ithkar as he usually did in odd-numbered years. He did not come by the main trade road, not by any of the minor trade roads; nor did he come by either the East River or the Bear River. He came up the Ith River from the sea or from somewhere very near the sea. (Nobody knew where Kara Cove, which Peter said that he came from, was to be found.)

Well, many persons came up the Ith River from the sea, and then used the canal to come into the Harbor of Ithkar itself. But Peter Flaming-Arrow (in his boat that had no bottom) came up the Ith River all the way. He did not use the canal bypass for the last part of his voyage. There is some dispute about how he did this, and in a boat without a bottom. His own explanation, that he did it by the "arithmetic of flame and air," did not seem a sufficient explanation to all the people.

At night, when rich people get together, they talk about their conspicuous acquisitions and their conspicuous consumptions. There is a lot of fun to be had in talking about these shining things.

(Various sorts of peoples do get together almost to excess at night at the great Fair at Ithkar.)

At night, when the ruling people get together, they talk about the machinations by which they rule. No, the rich people and the ruling people are not the same. A rich ruler would be like a fat athlete. Though both are common, both are bunglers. Rulers are no good when they carry the load of property. Ruling for the love of ruling is the thing.

When the people of the Floating Island are together at night, they talk about the arts and the magics, about the exciting angers and the blood-spillings, about the novelties and the ever-more novelties, and about the concupiscence of the flesh. The talk of the Floating Island is always quite fleshy. And people of this floating middle-world, more than others, need novelties and excitements.

When poor people gather together at night, they often talk about the ultimate things, about the philosophies and the strange things of the world, and also about the skies and the sky-dwellers. This is because the poor people (more than other people, and especially at the great Fair at Ithkar) sleep under the open sky and so are reminded of the ultimate things and the sky things. Other people sleep under various roofs and so are reminded of their own varieties of things.

Peter Flaming-Arrow was a poor person (in odd-numbered years at least), so he slept under the open sky and talked about sky matters with his poor peers. Also in the group were two poor magicians. This in itself was interesting, for most magicians are not poor.

The name of one of the poor magicians was Draoi (you may pronounce this name as "Dree," if you wish to be correct). And the name of the other poor magician was Asarlai. Draoi had one striking trick, striking to all except other magicians, at least. He would disappear of a sudden, and in his place there would be a talking crow. "Draoi is gone for a moment," the crow would croak. "Whatever you may wish to say, say it to me. I am his familiar." But some people thought that the crow was more than Draoi's familiar. They thought that the crow was Draoi himself.

"The reason that I am poor is that I once made an enviable deal," Draoi said now. "The deal was that I should be totally rich for one year and then poor for the rest of my life. It happened so, and it's been worth it. I was not merely totally rich: for that one year, I owned the world and everything and everybody in it. I was the all-powerful Midas of the universe. That was the 'Year of the Golden Plover.' It was only seven years ago, but now it has been dropped out of the total of the years. People even affect not to remember the year. Aye, but they *do* remember that wonderful year in their underminds!"

"I remember it, Draoi," said one muddle-faced poor man there. "Seven years ago, yes, that was the year when I was totally poor. Oh, how totally! I pawned everything I owned. And then I had to pawn my skin itself. I had to take it off, too, and leave it hanging on a peg in the pawnbroker's shop. It may have been a wonderful year for you, but it wasn't for me. It may have been worth it for you. It wasn't worth it for me."

"As I think about things and lie on my back and look up at the flinty stars, I'm convinced that there are two skies," Draoi said now. "One is the low sky, which is a fraud. The other is the high sky, which is genuine. There is a Little Bear in the low sky and a Big Bear in the high sky. There is a Little Draco (Dragon) in the low sky and a Great Dragon in the high sky. There is a false Cross in the low sky and a true Cross in the high sky. These two crosses are in the southern skies below the tropics. I sailed there in my youth.

"And there are, no more than a mile over our heads, the Three Lordly Ones. These, though they are in league with the secret rulers of Ithkar and the whole world as well, are grubby fakes and servants of Thotharn. They are (usually but not always) one man, one woman, and one skrat or hermaphrodite. They are the false Three on the Floating Island in the low sky.

"But high above them are the true Three, *they who made the worlds,* they who live in the true sky. Such are my night thoughts in these rocky hills above the great Fair at Ithkar, where even now the shills are playing that 'Come in. Come into the Tents' music on their flutes and penny-whistles, and will be playing it all night long."

"Be careful," a poor woman said. "The very stones here have ears."

"I'll *not* be careful." Draoi chuckled. "I have not a care in the world, nor ever shall have again. I know that the stones have ears. And yet, by their stony nature, they're hard of hearing, if you'll permit me a poor man's joke."

"Draoi, you speak like the Seven Seekers, who came here and talked like that," said a poor man who had a lively way about him. "They also spoke about the Three in the high sky. And now those Seven Seekers lie rotting in the swamp, each of them with a sharpened cross driven through his chest."

"Yes, that's always a hazard for those who indulge in speculations." Draoi smiled in the starlit dark.

A meadow mouse came to Peter Flaming-Arrow, climbed up on the stone that Peter was using for a pillow, and seemed to whisper something into Peter's ear. Then the

mouse ran into Peter's breast pocket and was seen no more
for a while.

"Simplicity is good," said the other poor magician who
was named Asarlai. "Complexity is often good. *But* between them is the doubleness that is sometimes called
duality and sometimes duplicity. It isn't good. The Floating Island in the low sky isn't good, nor are the Three
low-sky people who live upon it. Yes, you hard-of-hearing
stones, I said it. And I know that you have mouths as well
as ears. Inform on me, stones, if you will. And when you
have done so. I will still be a man, and you will still be
stones."

Asarlai was a poor magician who carried around with
him gold coins equal to his own body weight. Whenever
he attempted to spend one of the coins, the coin would
whistle and then shout: "Shopkeeper, know that I have
been stolen from Hudspeth the Horrible, the man who is
vengeance itself. Accept me in payment only if you wish
to die today."

So shop people would not accept the gold coins from
Asarlai, nor would anybody else, even though they had no
idea who the horrible Hudspeth the Horrible might be.
Magicians often play such irreversible tricks on each other.
Moreover, Asarlai was under a compulsion to carry the
heavy gold coins with him wherever he went. But this kept
him strong and healthy. He was a happy man. And many
of the other magicians were not.

"I also believe that there is a false lower sky and a true
higher sky," Asarlai continued. "The Floating Island in
the low sky is the key to the falseness. And I also believe
that the Three who live on the Floating Island, they who are
called 'the Three Lordly Ones' and other such praiseful
names, are servants of Thotharn and in league with our

own anonymous rulers. My own personal familiar creature is this high-flying kite-bird here. I send him up to spy on the Floating Island, and he goes. But when he comes back from up there he is always in a daze, and he mumbles, 'My lips are sealed, my lips are sealed.' Dammit, kites do not have lips as such.''

"My lips are sealed, my lips are sealed," the totemic kite-bird now spoke in imitation of Asarlai's imitation of him. And then the kite winked, as could easily be seen in the starlight. He was a good-natured bird, but perhaps not intelligent enough to be a good familiar to a magician.

"Oh, I'll go up there in the morning and find out just what the Floating Island is and who lives on it," Peter Flaming-Arrow said. "If the updrafts are right, I can fly higher than this kite-bird. And the false powers of the low sky will only be able to seal my lips with real fire, with hot fire to be remembered.''

"Peter Flaming-Arrow, before you go skylarking in the morning, know you that there are three of us magicians here present now," Draoi said. "Three of us can effect a covenant between you and the mouse in your breast pocket. And you *do* need a covenanted familiar.''

"I see only two magicians, you and Asarlai," Peter Flaming-Arrow said.

"There is a third one present who will not identify himself. But he will be the third one in our effecting, and we can effect the covenant.''

"Perhaps the mouse and I already have our private covenant.''

"Yes, you two do have a private covenant, Peter; but it has not been magicked. We can magic it for you. It will make a difference.''

"Magic it for us, then," Peter Flaming-Arrow cried.

Then the three magicians, Draoi and Asarlai and one other, confirmed by magic that the mouse (it stuck its head out of the breast pocket of Peter Flaming-Arrow and assented to the pact) was now a covenanted familiar of Peter Flaming-Arrow, who could ride on updrafts in the boat without a bottom.

At night, when the secret ruling people are together, they talk about the machinations by which they rule. They plot and conspire; without such interests, ruling would hardly be worth carrying on. This night, the first night of the great Fair at Ithkar for the Year of the Black-Footed Flying Fox, some of them, from Ithkar and also from the outlands, were together in a plush house on a hill above the fair.

"The main expense of our wireless system is the wires for it," one of the secret rulers was giving an account. "Copper hammerers do not hammer out fine wire for nothing. And we need the wire-wound kick-coils to talk by wireless with our eye and thunder-base in the low sky. We should invent a cheaper way to do it, but at the same time we must not let our inventiveness spread to the people. We saw an example of unauthorized inventiveness on the day just past."

"You mean the inventiveness of Peter Flaming-Arrow, I suppose," said another of the cryptic and anonymous rulers. "Well, his laughable boat-without-a-bottom *did* rise out of the water and waft itself in the air for some distance above the river Ith. And by that device, this Peter came into the Harbor of Ithkar from the Ith River without using the canal. It was a small thing, I suppose, and the onlookers were undecided as to whether they should be amazed at what they had seen or whether they should forget that they had seen it. About half of them did the one thing and half of them the other. Well, he is only a fletcher who puts feathers or wings on arrowshafts. And this time he fletched wings onto a light boat and flew it briefly. But we have to have an explanation, or at least a name for it."

"Skull, tell us the name for it," another of the covert rulers said to a futuristic skull on the table there.

"The name of it is 'glider,' " the skull said. "And the additional trade of Peter Flaming-Arrow is named 'glider pilot.' The light and broad fletches or wings on the light boat will let it raise itself on updrafts of air, and will let it slide along on level air, also."

"We understand how the bird-mockery of a boat works," said another of the rulers (if you didn't know them, you could hardly tell these purposely inconspicuous rulers apart), "but we are a little bit dubious as to how the mind of Peter Flaming-Arrow works. How is it fletched?"

The futuristic skull on the table had been dug out of a future stratum of earth that in clear truth had not been laid down yet. This suspect stratum was in the Improbability Hills not far from the Galzar Pass north of Ithkar. This skull that had been dug out of future time would answer simple questions out of its future-based knowledge. But the ruling persons had learned not to expect great things from this skull. The skull had not been (or rather, it should be said that the skull would not be) the skull of a genius.

"Suppose that the magnetic motor, that toy devised by the cooper (copper-cask division) John Slackwit, should be combined with the 'glider' of Peter Flaming-Arrow?" one of the rulers asked the skull. "What would the result be?"

"The result would be a flying boat capable of flying anywhere in the low sky at will," the skull said.

"We have too many fakeries stabled in that low sky to

have person's meddling around there. And yet we have the interceptors angle on Peter Flaming-Arrow and on anything he might try to do. If he thirsts, he will have to come down to our spring and drink. What we need now is some creative destruction. We will make Peter Flaming-Arrow fulfill his own name and legend. Indeed, it is time that we gave another legend to the people, and here is one almost ready-made. What do you call that new device of the armorer Jasper Shortlegs, skull?''

"Rifle is the name of it. It's a crude, handmade rifle, too heavy by ten times, and it fires the messiest incendiary shots that I've ever seen. It should be cleaned up or else done away with. It isn't made for stylish shooting.''

"We will use it one time, skull. And then we will do away with the messy flame-shot thing. And with Jasper Shortlegs, also, and with John Slackwit, and most of all we will do away with Peter Flaming-Arrow. Skull, we are not greatly impressed by you even though you were dug out of the future. In all honesty, are you greatly impressed with us?''

"I'm impressed by your irrationality. It's beyond anything I ever met with in my own time. I'm impressed by your illogic. And above all (or should I say 'below all'?), I'm impressed by your reeking magic, your cloying magic, your suffocating magic. I don't know where you got it, unless from Thotharn.''

"How odd that you believe in Thotharn in the future when we've left off believing in him in this present.'' .

"You don't believe in him? I thought you used him,'' the skull said.

"Certainly we use him. And now that we know him so well, now that we have him on our own payroll, we find him the least believable creature anywhere. What little bit we get from him is hardly worth getting. Not only that, but we find him the least impressive creature anywhere, except maybe yourself, manless skull.''

Then all the rulers who were present pronounced a ritual:

"Indeed, the people are becoming like us in their knowing. Lest perhaps then—" The ends of the sentences were never verbalized by the rulers; they were only thought. And after a short pause they pronounced the first part of another verse of the ritual:

"This is the beginning of what they would do. Hereafter they could not be restrained from anything which they determined to do. Let us go, then, and thereby confuse—"

So the secret rulers of Ithkar, and of other places, also, conspired how they would confuse their ruled ones with shot and fire and legend.

> "In the middle of life, every lightning man, every arrow man, must be wrapped in the dismal clouds of death, and he must die that death. But if he is a true lightning man, a true arrow man, then the limit of his death will be seven years. When the mouse shall trumpet with the voice of thunder on the mountain, then you will know that the lightning man has wakened from his death."
>
> —*The Book of Jasher*

"The mouse must not go with you, Peter Flaming-Arrow," said the poor magician Draoi the next morning. "The mouse must remain here. The mouse must *be* you here until you come back again. The mouse will be you, but to the eyes and ears of the people he will still be a mouse."

"Yes, all right," said Peter Flaming-Arrow.

"Yes, all right," said the totemic mouse familiar. And it came out of Peter's breast pocket and found itself a safe nook in the rocks.

Then Peter Flaming-Arrow was almost ready to begin his morning flight. He had tested the winds and currents and drafts, and they were right. He lacked only two new long feathers. In reality, the feathers played a very minor role in fletching his boat-without-a-bottom. But he was a trained fletcher and he retained his fletcher's superstitions on the necessity of two new feathers on any new enterprise, and about the luckiness of the feathers of the coppertone eagle.

Peter Flaming-Arrow whistled a coppertone eagle down from the low sky. All competent fletchers are able to whistle birds down to them. He killed the eagle. He took the longest feather from each of its wings and added them to the wings of his flying boat. Then he tore the bird apart with strong and canny hands and spread out its entrails for the fortuning of himself.

"The entrails indicate that I will die this morning unless I forego my flight," Peter Flaming-Arrow spoke with great shock. "This is intolerable to me, that I should die in my flaming youth. It is also intolerable that I should give up my sky flight. I was born in vain if I give up the flight now, just when I have brought it to possibility. I must think about this, and I ask that you magicians think about it, also."

"Maybe there are compensations for dying, Peter Flaming-Arrow," the poor magician Draoi said without a lot of hope.

"Oh, the dead clearly have knowledge of things that we are ignorant of," Peter agreed. "But when one encants up dead men and questions them, they answer with such great sorrow and agony as to make it seem that, for all the special knowledge that they have, they've got the worst of the bargain. What I want is the best of both worlds."

"The eagle entrails indicate that you'll die only in a special way," the poor magician Asarlai said with a little flicker of hope. "But they do not indicate wherein your death will be special."

"Do it, Peter Flaming-Arrow," the dead coppertone Eagle suddenly spoke in his harsh eagle voice. "You'll have my two greatest feathers with you. They know the way up the tall and tipsy air. Do it, Peter Flaming-Arrow."

"After all, I'll be you, and I'll still be here," the mouse said thoughtfully. "And the time for you to fly is right now. The warm fetid air from the swamp (I was a swamp mouse before I was a meadow mouse) is now blowing as strong as it ever blows in the mornings. But try to die some place where I can come to you easily."

"Thank you, my friend, my mouse, my covenanted familiar, my self," Peter Flaming-Arrow spoke. Then he gathered his light boat-without-a-bottom about him and ran down the slope toward the cliff edge. The warm swamp wind was at his back, and the cool wind from the ocean was almost in his face. He ran past the edge of the cliff, and then he went up instead of down. The warm swamp wind overrode the cool ocean wind, and Peter rode the bucking updraft as if it were a stallion.

Now he did the things that he had been born to do. He was cousin to the little heading winds and brother to the updrafts. The fabric-bark-feather lifting fletches of his light boat were like extensions of his own skin. And the rudder was his legs, which dangled and flailed and tipped and guided his boat. None except a bottomless boat could have been so guided by him.

The early sky was overflowing with sunshine that spilled down and drenched the air and the earth below with leaping light. There were only two or three skimpy clouds in the sky, and Peter Flaming-Arrow didn't know which one of them was the Floating Island.

"Speak to me with morning thunder so I'll know you," Peter called his cheerful greeting upward. And one of the clouds did speak with a curious bronze-throated thunder that was the special mark of the Floating Island. No other thunder had ever been like it. It wasn't overpowering, it wasn't great, it wasn't even extremely loud, though it tried to be. It was only unmistakable. Peter rose and wafted and steered to the cloud of the thunder signature, knowing that it was the Floating Island.

Oh, it wasn't large, half an acre in area maybe, and not more than ten cubits thick, a thin rough floating disc made out of air-filled and cloud-colored tufa-rock. But how did it float?

"The masters of the Floating Island are *my* masters at the arithmetic of flame and air," Peter Flaming-Arrow said happily. "Here we have real magic, and yet magic is only the advanced form of the arithmetic of flame and air."

He wafted and soared a bit above the Floating Island. Then he landed in the middle of it. He stepped out of his boat and was confronted by the Three Lordly Ones, and a talking post, and behind them a little gibbet or gallows for hanging people on. And behind the gibbet were three great sheets of green bronze hanging from stanchions, and three ponderous hammers with which to beat the characteristic thunder out of the bronze sheets. That is what a thunder machine consists of. It is almost the most simple machine anywhere.

"The goof has landed," one of the Sky Lords said to the talking post. The Sky Lord was a rough-looking sort of man.

"Hang him, then," said the talking post. "You can be sure that he has the prophetic red mark of the noose around his neck, for you can plainly see that his whole body is one ruddy red mark. Hang him, and be sure that you break his neck."

"Aye, we'll hang him, and then we'll cruise with him through the buzzard sky until his bones are stripped. And then we'll put his bones with the others."

Peter Flaming-Arrow noticed that there were six skeletons on the tufa-rocks behind the gallows. "Six of them," Peter said in wonder. "Six persons have been here before me and have died here. Did they all use the same device I use, or did they use six different devices?"

"Yes, six of them," one of the other Sky Lords said to Peter, "and you'll be the seventh. It's always good luck to be the seventh of anything."

"Somehow you three don't seem like the Three Lordly Ones," Peter said uneasily.

"Oh, we're the alternate team," one of them told him. "We're up here only one week in the month when we let the first team take a rest from it all. They're more lordly and noble than we are, but we can do what needs to be done. The only thing that ever needs to be done is to hang persons who've become too inquisitive about the thunder and the bullhorn."

But the talking post was protesting something:

"No, no," the talking post said. "Hang him and break his neck. But what pieces the buzzards get of him they'll have to get on the fly. When he is properly hanged and broken, then put him back into his funny boat and push it off the island. His will be a flaming fall.''

''Yes, all right,'' the third of the false Sky Lords said to the post. He was the roughest-looking of the three. But Peter Flaming-Arrow was fascinated by the talking post.

''I can figure it out!'' he cried. ''I can discern how it's done. It has those copper coils in tune with copper coils on the earth below. And the voice of the post comes from down below. Give me an hour and I can figure it out in every detail.''

''Not an hour, not even a minute,'' one of the false noble and very earthly Sky Lords said. They put the noose around Peter's neck right where the red mark on his neck indicated it. They hanged him on the gallows, and they made sure that his neck was broken.

''Six sets of bones on the rocks behind me there,'' Peter Flaming-Arrow said. ''Six persons have been here before me on this Floating Island in the low sky and all have failed, even as I am failing, to balk the mystery and rectify the deception. Six sets of bones I see behind me there, but if they are behind me, then I am not seeing them with my proper eyes. I am dead and I'm seeing them with my death eyes.''

Then the three false Sky Lords put Peter Flaming-Arrow back into his funny fletched boat and pushed it off the sky island. It started down toward earth at an easy glide.

''Seven long years,'' said the covenanted mouse familiar as he again studied the entrails of the dead coppertone eagle. ''Well, I can't let myself get mouse-hearted over this,'' he said. ''I'll shorten the time if I can, and I'll spend every free moment in careful planning. I'll not fail us! Most of all I must practice my thunder voice. That will be the hardest of all. But will I ever *have* a voice again? When they hanged the other me, they hanged myself, also. When they broke his neck, they sympathetically broke my neck, too. Oh, woe. Oh, rue!''

The crowds below the Floating Island, on the sunshiny second morning of the great fair, had already been alerted by the bronze-throated thunder from above. Now as they looked up they saw that funny, floppy boat leave the sky island at an easy glide. This was between the stormy petrel sky and the firebird sky.

Then the crowds gasped as they saw the little gliding boat burst into flame to the accompaniment of a series of barking roars from a plush house on the hill.

The handmade rifle of the armorer Jasper Shortlegs was a powerful one, for it took three men to hold it. And it had a device more futuristic than the futuristic skull in that plush house on the hill. By this device, the rifle would hit anything espied through its sights. The shots had no trajectory. They were as straight as light itself. And the incendiary shots that the rifle fired were the hottest things this side of the east meadows of hell. They hit the funny boat in the low sky and they hit the funny arrow man in it. And the flaming arrow man hit another coppertone eagle as it flew by. And then there was a conflagration overhead as bright as ten suns. And bullhorn voices amplified from the Floating Island belabored the point for persons who might not understand.

''I saw a demon fall like lightning!'' came the amplified bullhorn voice from the low sky in what was supposed to be an imitation of the voice of the Lord of the universe Himself. The people shuddered to hear this, and they said to each other:

''That pleasant and gifted funny man Peter Flaming-Arrow was a demon, and now he is falling to the doom that was prepared for him. So it is seen that all who question the Three Lordly Ones are evil and will come to an equally fiery end.''

Again the amplified bullhorn voice spoke in bronze thunder from the low sky, prophetically in futuristic verse:

> From morn to noon he fell,
> From noon to dewy eve,
> A summer's day, and with the setting sun,
> Dropt from the zenith like a falling star.

And all the people at the fair groaned at this, partly in compassion for the man burning in the low sky, and partly from the great heat that blistered them all.

Oh, the strong odor of heroic flesh roasting in the middle of the low sky!

Oh, the inexorable logic of the arithmetic of flame and air!

Oh, the strange earth-and-sky road from Kara Cove to Bleak Mountain!

Actually the wobbling, flaming fall of Peter Flaming-Arrow lasted no more than eleven minutes and covered no more than twenty miles. Then he crashed in the swamp east of Ithkar. Quick rumor said that the final ashes of him and his boat came to rest on a low mountain named Bleak Mountain in the middle of the swamp. And so Peter Flaming-Arrow was dead—

—except for a flickering ember of him in the brain and body of the covenanted mouse familiar, for the mouse and the man were one. A thing is not dead when any last ember of it is still alive. The mouse had suffered the pains of the damned while the man burned, but its resolve was strengthened in that fire.

It was six weeks before the mouse recovered its reason. And then it set itself to do what had to be done.

"I know from studying the entrails of the second coppertone eagle (the one that was split apart by the lightning man) that it will be seven years before there is a summer dry enough to allow me to come to Bleak Mountain in the middle of the swamp," the mouse recited to itself. "But in seven years I will be there. And I will wake up the other half of me, the man half of me, if I am able to do it. I will prepare myself for it. The world has not seen the end of this arrow man, nor of this arrow mouse."

The mouse pored over dusty tomes in obscure bookrooms when there were no persons there, to acquire the necessary knowledge. The mouse exercised his voice morning and evening in the open places, the meadows, the rocky wastes, the swamps. He has caught the tone of the thunder already. He does it well. All that is needed now is that he strengthen his voice a hundredfold or a thousandfold. He is working on it, he is working on it.

"When the mouse shall trumpet with the voice of thunder on the mountain, then you will know that the lightning man has wakened from his death"—so it is written in *The Book of Jasher*.

The mouse is working on it, he is working on it.

THE SHAMAN FLUTE

Shariann Lewitt

Khadil was whistling when he reached the fair gate, and he tried to stop. Unfortunately, he broke out into a grin and had the most difficult time suppressing it. Steppe riders didn't show feelings in front of southerners, especially not if they belonged to the Iduai clan. Still, it was a glorious late-summer day, and there were sights and smells that he had never encountered before. In front of him was a rich cloth caravan, the wagons painted bright blue. He could see the plum and turquoise silks, the yellow-orange cottons, and the fine white linen in the minds of the horses who carried them. Negat would love the stuffs, and thinking about her made him really smile. He would have to buy many good sheep so they could marry at the spring lambing.

He didn't notice the guard of the cloth caravan who regarded him with disdain. The man had the features of the steppe, the flat nose, the upturned eyes, and the long black braids. The guard recognized the Iduai markings tattooed across Khadil's nose and cheeks, and pulled his helmet closer down on his head. It would not do for his clan tattoo to be seen. Iduai! Why weren't they all dead? That had been the promise of the Thotharn priest. It had been their pay. There should be no Iduai at all, and above all not one so close to smiling.

The horse beneath Khadil shied from the crowd, and he touched its mind gently, reassuring it. It was not his horse, nor were the two he led. They wore the tree brand of a friendly clan over ten days north of here. He had traded down the clans but had not dared once he'd entered the war zone. Now, though, he was at the fair, over the Galzar Pass and into the rich lands of the South. The pastures he had seen made his mouth water for the sheep, and that made him sad.

The sheep. The flocks were all dead on the early spring pasture. The Iduai would starve if he didn't accomplish his mission. That was the hope of the Hoyda.

The Hoyda clan were the traditional enemies of the Iduai. There had been blood feud between them for seven generations. There were different stories of how it began, but the beginning did not matter. It was only a feud at first, a way for young warriors to prove their valor and to raid for sheep and servants. It was nothing different from what any steppe clan did all the time. But that had changed.

When the war began in the South, several Hoyda had gone. They had wanted the money, pretty coins for wives and sweethearts to sew on their dresses and kerchieves, cloth, iron tools, and horses. The Hoyda had been like any steppe clan then. Of course they had gone to those who had offered the most. And they had come back different.

Khadil could not say how they were different. They seemed more cruel. Before, when they raided the flocks, they would do no more than steal, which was expected. Then they began to kill, but only a few at a time.

What had happened this past spring, though, had been beyond the imagination of the Iduai. A man had come, a southerner with a beard the color of rain, who wore a second face below his own. He spoke the language of the steppe reasonably well, which had surprised them, Khadil most of all. Khadil had been studying the southern language because a shaman must be at home everywhere, but he had never heard of a southerner who could speak their language.

This one did. He said that he had been wandering lost for days, and that he was cold and hungry.

They feasted him. They gave him the very best, the small store of fermented cow's milk and the meat of a sheep flavored with roots. There was cheese and bread, hard and soft of both, and the fresh white goat cheese that Khadil loved.

To this man, who was old and so must be wise and honored, they gave a place in the very best tent, right in the back where only the most honored visitor would be put.

He stayed for three days and no one asked him any questions or disturbed him in any way, as was proper. They noticed his accent and commented on it, but he had eaten with them and slept in the best tent. He might be from the South and wear a golden face on his chest, but he was old and must be wise. He said that he was a priest, the servant of the great god Thotharn. Khadil wondered about that. He had never heard of this god.

On the third day it was time for him to go. He was

asked politely if he needed assistance to reach his destination. He asked for a horse, which the clan gave to him. It was an old gelding, but they gave it without even a hint that it had been impolite for him to ask more than directions. The clan grandfather rode him off and wished him well. They had honored him as they would any who were wise and kindly.

That evening the sheep did not come home. The boys sent to guard them did not come home, either. A group of young warriors rode up to the spring pasture. Khadil was glad that he had not gone with them. He would never go near the place again. The clan would have to find a new pasture for the flock this spring, if he could sell enough rugs with the help of the Sky Lords to buy a new flock. That pasture was now haunted.

The warriors reported that all the sheep were dead. The pasture had been thick with garbage-birds with bloody claws. There was not a single lamb alive.

There were no marks of the killing, neither arrows nor a Hoyda honor-staff. The boys lay dead, too, all together with their bread untouched. It had happened early in the day. There was no mark on the boys other than the marks of the feeding garbage-birds.

The clan mourned. Women cut their hair short. The clan was dying. The great Iduai were condemned, for without their flocks, how could they survive? Where would they find food in the winter, with no sheep to milk and cheese to put away? Such a thing had never been done before among the clans of the steppes.

Mekhet, the ancient shaman of the Iduai, understood it all and told them. Their guest had helped the Hoyda, he explained. They knew from stories of other clans that the Hoyda had fought for strange priests who wore a false face under the true one and served a strange god called Thotharn, just as their visitor did. Some said the Hoyda had begun to worship this god, too. The other clans didn't know about that, but they did know that the Hoyda were well paid, and not just in coin.

So, Mekhet continued, this was part of their payment. This priest, who had the powers of a priest, had come to kill the Iduai sheep to pay the Hoyda for their fighting. The southernmost clans had said that these strange ones were not doing well in the war recently, and they wanted more fine steppe fighters.

It was no longer a proper steppe feud. To abolish an entire clan of the people, that was unthinkable. Yet the Hoyda had thought it. Now they wanted to destroy all the Iduai hopes of regaining their lives. They wanted the Iduai to die over the long winter, hungry in winter quarters without cheese or koumiss or lambs for the spring. They wanted the Iduai to die badly. The Hoyda had changed.

"Come on, you, wake up," a voice yelled in his ear.

Khadil started and broke from his recollections. He was being motioned into the giant gate, and assailed by the scents of spices and baking breads, he entered the fair.

"Your weapons," a bored fair-ward demanded.

"I don't have any," Khadil answered lightly.

The man scowled. There was a moment when he felt the light twinge of examination, as his master Mekhet had examined him, and then no more. Puzzlement crossed the fair-ward's face as he realized that Khadil was telling the truth.

Khadil shrugged. Steppe shamans neither killed nor ate flesh, and even though he wasn't a full shaman yet, he had to keep all the taboos. Besides, he was almost a full shaman or Mekhet wouldn't have proposed him for this journey. And the clan had accepted Mekhet's suggestion, too, which meant that he must be very close to full power.

Another fair-ward gave him directions to his place in the fair in exchange for a few coppers. The coppers had holes in them from where his mother and Negat and other women had sewn them onto their clothes. He felt bad about giving their baubles to this man, who hadn't seen them crying over their ruined best dresses.

He had to wait while the priest beside the wizard-of-the-gate checked his goods for magic, and the length of time it took surprised him. There was no magic here, unless one counted the magic of simple beauty, and it was that magic alone that had bewitched the priest. The rugs and saddle-bags had been woven for Iduai comfort and were only to be sold in this time of extremity.

Still, the man took his time, feeling the texture of the knotwork of each piece and running his fingers over the soft wool. At the bottom of the pack the priest stopped and made a soft sound deep in his throat.

The rug he was holding was small but wonderful. The knotwork was so small that it was barely visible, and the horse and omen-bird pattern was as clear on the back as the front. The brilliant blue background and medium purple had taken a long time and a lot of charms to prepare, but the colors were fast and true. Even the fringes at both ends had been patterned, although this was most unusual. No, this was a very special rug, the most beautiful the Iduai had ever produced.

Both Khadil and the priest were so involved in the glory of the rug that neither of them saw that one of the guards of the cloth caravan had lingered behind. It was normal for a caravan guard to spend a few moments inspecting his horse's hooves. It was not normal that, once inside the safe enclosure of the fair, he had retained his helmet. Sweat dripped down this man's face, but his back was carefully turned to the two inspecting the merchandise. He could hear them well enough.

"And how much do you wish to sell this for?" the priest asked.

Khadil smiled. "We need the aid of the Sky Lords. This is our offering."

"Their aid isn't going to help you any," the helmeted guard muttered to the ground.

Dismounted, Khadil led his three geldings on their woven leads into the crowds of the fair. It was a good way to the space he had been assigned, and there were more people here than he had ever seen in his life. This crush of humanity made the horses nervous, and he had to touch their minds quite often to quiet them. This place was too small and difficult to move in, and full of strange and fearsome smells. Man-scent was different here, and the air was redolent with it.

Khadil kept his touch careful and light, as Mekhet had taught. The small creatures, the little friends of the Sky Lords, were not slaves to command but gentle, simple friends. It was for the shaman to care for them and guide them, just as it was for him to bring them to the arrow when the clan needed their flesh, as it was for him to gentle the young horses and read the omen-bird's warnings in the sky.

In the strange animal's mind, a yelping bark distracted him. Without thought he melded with it, contacting the poor creature. He cringed. It was being beaten.

He pulled the horses aside and dropped the leads. They were well-enough trained that they would stay there; steppe riders were very careful with the training of their animals.

The Hoyda caravan guard, shielded by the crowd, permitted himself only the smallest movement. He came around the horses from the back, and they did not react. As a clansman of the steppes, the guard smelled comfortable and familiar to the beasts.

"Stop it," Khadil yelled as he ran to the yelping dog.

In front of him a fine gray hunting hound whimpered as a man wearing a fine leather tunic whipped it again.

"The beast was hungry," Khadil said, not bothering to explain how he knew.

The man brought up his arm again, and then lowered it slowly to his side, staring at Khadil intently. Khadil scowled at him, angry at the treatment of the dog, which was a good dog but without the reason of a man. The frown did him good.

"He's hungry all right," the man in the tunic said, "and he'd be more than happy to eat your hand off."

In response, Khadil went over to the great animal and began to pat him absently. A crowd had begun to gather, but at some distance. They had heard the rumors about steppe riders with their savage magic and warlike ways. They might be uncivilized, but they were to be feared.

Khadil had first laughed when Mekhet had told him about these stories, but now he needed to use that reputation. He tried to look as menacing as possible. From his wide red sash he drew a thin painted stick with two large black feathers, and shook it at the man in the tunic. The civilized southerner blanched.

"Feed the dog," Khadil said evenly, "and do not mistreat those who do not have the reason of men."

The other nodded mutely.

A fair-ward strode up and placed his heavy bronze-shod staff between them. "What's going on here?" he asked.

"Nothing," said the man with the dog. "This gentleman was telling me how to better care for this fine animal."

The fair-ward looked first at the man, then at Khadil, and back to the man again. There was no response. As the fair-ward shook his head and gestured for the crowd to leave, a helmeted Hoyda melted from the periphery of the gathering.

For Khadil's part, it took all of his discipline not to break into a run and laugh as he returned to the horses. Someone turning white at the sight of a fly-whisk was the funniest thing he could imagine. It would make Negat laugh all winter.

To make up for leaving them alone in the great fair crowd, Khadil fed the horses a few stringy carrots he had been saving. Their owners would probably say that he spoiled the beasts terribly. The pack animals were old and probably had only two or three good seasons left in them. Surely they deserved some recompense for their long service to man.

He picked up the lead again and headed into the second section of the fair. Somewhere in this overgrown cacophony of sellers there would be a space for him.

The people were packed together closely and he often felt a brush against his shoulder or leg, which made him flinch. He could smell them, too, full of sweat or damp wool or perfume or food. It was pleasant that the food sellers were here near the woven-goods merchants, of which he was now one. He had heard stories of the southern delicacies and had hoped to try some. Maybe he could even bring something pleasant back to Negat and his mother to make up for the coins they had donated to his enterprise.

He walked slowly, gazing at displays of wares set out to

entrance the eye, oblivious to the figure that still followed him. Staying far from the bright displays, the Hoyda managed to avoid detection like the veteran he was. He used the distractions of the fair.

Here were heavy silks embroidered all over with flowers and ribbons of white and red and yellow all fluttering in the soft breeze. Here were people tall as trees with hair the color of sunshine. In front of one small tent sat a group of men in white caftans moving colored stones and drinking a pungent liquid from thimble-size cups.

Why should Khadil turn and search faces in the crowd? Here there was law, with priests and priestesses and fairwards with their heavy staves.

The Hoyda sneered, observing how the Iduai gazed at the goods and people around him. Obviously the Iduai clan had never had the advantages of civilization, of the South with its richness and finery. The Hoyda had no need to look at the things around him. None of it was new. No, he had only to mark the Iduai gawking like an idiot through civilized society.

Khadil was entranced by the fair itself. That embroidered material, what a beautiful wedding skirt that would make for Negat. He wondered at the stones the men in white were moving so carefully. Perhaps it was some form of divination, or maybe just a game. But grown men didn't play games. He heard merchants yelling words he couldn't understand and thought that some of them must be the names of the exotic items displayed for sale.

Then he heard words that he understood very well. "Thief, thief!" they were screaming.

There were two fair-wards running toward the sound in front of him, and the crowd pressed around so thickly that he had no choice but to follow. There was shouting and argument in high-pitched voices, but there was so much noise at first that Khadil couldn't make out the words.

The fair-wards were pulling two figures apart. He rose on tiptoe to look over the shoulders of the tall southerners who were in front of him. In his mind he felt fear and confusion, the fear and confusion of an animal without reason.

"That, that ragpicker stole my hyn," a lady in an elegant gown said. "See, it's in her arms and she won't let it go. I'm from a noble family. I only came down here with my little darling to pick out some fabric, and that little pickpocket stole my hyn."

The girl was certainly poorly dressed. Her feet were bare and her dress a little too large for her figure. Over her arm she carried a large basket full of something Khadil didn't recognize. In the other arm was a small fluff of white fur. The girl didn't say anything.

Khadil had heard of hyns but had never seen one before. He knew that they were prized as very expensive pets and that they could travel through the spirit world at their own will. In this way they chose their owners, no matter who had paid for them—a very sensible animal indeed. Although it was a kind of beast mind he had never touched before, he reached out gently as Mekhet had taught him.

Nice, nice. Smell good. Cuddle, cuddle.

The animal was too young to be taken from its mother, Khadil thought. It was shivering with fear, afraid to move at all. And it seemed to feel more secure with the girl.

The fair-wards were pulling the hyn from the girl's unprotesting arms, but the hyn just nestled closer to her. Tears were slipping down her face. Still, she said nothing. Then the hyn found its courage and disappeared.

Khadil pushed his way through the crowd, slipping

under shoulders and using his elbows against massed ribs. He had to get out and get a priest. One of the Sky Lords' servants would understand the problem.

"Help, help, we need a priest. Priest!" he yelled at the top of his voice, which had been trained to yell across wide pastures.

A priestess materialized at his side. She was not particularly old, but she had a mature and dignified air that made Khadil confident.

"They're saying the girl stole the hyn," Khadil explained breathlessly, "but really it's only very young and likes her. They do that, you know. And she won't speak up for herself. But you can't force a hyn to do anything, not even a baby one."

The priestess blanched. "Hyns," she said, her face a study in controlled anger.

Seeing Khadil completely involved in the situation, the Hoyda crept up behind the gray geldings with the tree brand. He was slow and careful, as if he were on an ancient raid, creeping low and unnoticed in the confusion. Everyone's attention was on the priestess, who marched forward to brave the mob.

They parted before her, and Khadil trailed, mostly because it seemed to be the only thing he could do. The fair-wards had already tied the girl's hands and were leading her off, the noblewoman following, when Khadil and the priestess arrived.

"Stop," the priestess commanded. "What is going on here?"

One of the fair-wards explained, and the priestess nodded, attentive.

Then the noblewoman interrupted sharply, "She's a thief and that's all. My husband spent an entire ith on my little white hyn and she took it. And she won't give it back to me. You see, she doesn't have anything to say. She can't say anything. Lock her away. Hang her! That's what little thieves are good for, so they don't grow into big ones.''

''That will do,'' the priestess said coolly. ''Now, girl, what do you say?''

The girl just looked at her with the tears still falling.

''I don't think she can hear,'' Khadil said.

The priestess appraised him very carefully, as if considering for the first time what he had said when he had fetched her. He felt almost the beginning of a touch, and then nothing. The priestess was concentrating on the child with a look that reminded Khadil of Mekhet when he was looking into their thoughts. Then the priestess turned to him.

''You,'' she said. ''What did you say to me about the animal's opinion? How do you know?''

Khadil pulled himself up to his full height, which was still a good bit shorter than that of the southerners. He wished he had on his good caftan and not the old one he used for riding. ''Sister,'' he said, ''I am Khadil of the Iduai clan of the northern riders. I am the student of Mekhet, shaman of the Iduai. We are servants of the Sky Lords, who care for and command their smaller creatures, and speak to them. The hyn was very young. All I know from touching it is that it likes the girl. It said she smells good.''

The crowd began to laugh and the priestess looked distressed. She spoke quietly to the fair-wards, who took both the noblewoman and the girl under charge. They began to walk in the direction of the shrine.

Khadil sent a reassuring thought to the girl, although he

wasn't certain she would understand. He had never communicated with those with reason. Not even children.

The day had begun warm and was now really hot. It wasn't the hard dry heat of the brown pastures of high summer, but a damp and cloying blanket that clung to everything that moved. Khadil's caftan was soaked from sweat and his boots and leggings were red from dust. He only wanted to find his place, wash, and make himself presentable to make his offering in the temple. He had not even been at the fair for a whole day, and already he had enough stories to tell all winter.

He found the space assigned by the fair-ward at the gate. It was small, barely a gap between a large tent with cloths brightly displayed and another carpet merchant. At first this worried Khadil, but it needed only a second glance to tell that these carpets were of a very different kind, made with pale colors and cut in strange ways. People who would like one would not want the other. It was good enough.

He dropped the horses' leads and pulled off their packs. Then he produced large carrots for each of them, telling them how wonderful they were in the crowds of the fair.

He had a small felt from his mother that would make an adequate shelter. It would not be large enough to stand in, but it would provide privacy and warmth at night. Besides, the felt was made of the finest goat's hair, not common wool, and was brightly embroidered with Iduai designs. That should attract some attention.

It took no time at all to set the stakes and lash the felt. He hung the cheese, fermented milk, and hard bread in goat bags on the back stake, and the place began to appear quite homey. He brought in the large pack of rugs and a smaller pack of his personal items. There, wrapped carefully, was his best quilted caftan made of trade cloth. Black omen-birds were embroidered around the hem and shoulders. The omen-bird was his spirit-friend from his shaman vision, and his sister had made this caftan after he had returned to the clan and told them. He wore it always as a remembrance of his special duties to the clan, the small ones, and the Sky Lords.

From one of the heavily quilted sleeves of the caftan he pulled out his shaman flute. It was bone, narrow and simple and without design, the flute by which the shaman dreams were made, the animals commanded. It was the flute that was the essence of his magic, and yet the thing had no magic in itself. It was the playing that counted, and the desire in the music.

He lifted it reverently and placed it carefully in a small bag which he suspended from the center stake. That was where it belonged. It was not his flute, as he was not a full shaman, but Mekhet had loaned this one for the journey.

"If you have need of it, and use it well, then it shall be yours," Mekhet had said before he had left.

Turning aside from the flute, he washed his face and rebraided his hair. Donning the good caftan, he was almost ready for the temple.

He opened the large rug pack to search for his temple offering, the offering that must impress the Sky Lords to aid the Iduai now in their time of greatest need. One by one he flipped over the rugs he had brought for sale, the large red one with the diamond pattern and the dark blue one with the flowers all over. He found the smaller red ones with the black omen-bird pattern and the gold ones with the trees and stars. The saddlebags were there, too, with their bright tassels and deep pockets, and the cheese bags and the lead reins. He was nervous. He was excited.

It was easy not to look carefully. He went through each piece again, pulling it from the bundle and placing it carefully aside.

He pulled out one of the saddlebags and turned it. Out of it rolled a stick painted white at both ends and red in the middle. The ends were wrapped with human hair and there was a deer tail attached on one side. It was a Hoyda honor-staff, Khadil knew, and he resumed his search with an air of desperation.

The Hoyda honor-staff could mean only one thing. Still, he searched the pack for a third time to no avail. The offering rug was missing, the most valuable rug he had to purchase the aid of the Sky Lords. The Iduai would die. Negat would die. The Sky Lords would be angry.

He sank on the ground and pulled the felt flap shut and began to moan softly. He knew. He understood only too well what had happened. He had never seen the Hoyda, but that made no difference. There was one of that accursed clan at this fair, one who meant him and his people ill, as all the Hoyda did. They were responsible for the death of the flocks, and now they would not let the Iduai try to recover, even if they had to sell their own bedding and saddlebags to do it.

Khadil hung his head in the darkness of the small tent. The felt was snug and secure around him, blotting out the light and the activities of the fair. Only the hurting was real. He had failed. They had believed in him, believed in his powers and gifts from the Sky Lords. Mekhet would be disappointed. Negat's parents might even decide that they couldn't let their daughter marry a no-good wastrel. Khadil didn't know what to do.

"When the sun does not rise and the pastures are full of

sadness, that is the time to play the flute,'' he remembered Mekhet saying.

With a minimum of movement, Khadil took the flute from the central stake. In his fingers, the bone seemed slightly warm and still living, vibrating with his own need. He began to play very tentatively. His fingers barely touched the holes, his breath was a butterfly's wing. There was only the rasping, faint echo of what could have been music. There was a deadness in it.

''When you play, you must play with your whole heart and your whole soul. That is where the magic is,'' he heard Mekhet's voice in his mind.

His heart was unhappy and his soul was as dry as the pastures in midsummer. The pure high notes carried the time of the winter wind, the killing time, in them. All of the pain and fear in him, the hopes of his people and their loss, wrapped around Khadil, and every feeling became part of the music.

He played. He played the death of the flocks on the high-summer pasture. He played the work of the summer, the knotting and setting of the carpets. He played the tents of the Iduai, denuded and joyless and silent. Need gripped him intently and he wanted to cry, but his only tears were the long notes. The music itself vibrated and glittered, almost visible in the dark tent.

''Capture it in a picture, and let the music carry the picture,'' Mekhet had said.

Khadil imagined the rug as he had last seen it, glowing under the wizard's fingers. He could see the pattern in his mind, and the colors in the glory of the sunlight. He needed it. It was more than need, more than desire. Without this he would die.

It all became the music, drifting from the felt into the

fair itself, so the entire fair would know had they the ears to listen. But this music, though woven by a man, was not made for men. It was the ancient right of the shamans, who were given leave to ask a favor of the Sky Lords. Khadil asked. His whole spirit begged. It was the will of the Sky Lords and the small spirits, and the spirits of the Iduai who had died. It would have to be the will of the whole world, of the earth itself, and then, maybe, there would be the magic that would save him. He did not hope because he knew that he didn't deserve that miracle, but he hoped because he needed it so badly.

No one would have cared or noticed the great black omen-bird that flew in lazy circles over the fairground. There were always birds. This one, though, came lower. It inspected and watched, changing patterns as a searcher might. There was a thing it must find more than food, a thing of bright colors and a special pattern. In the whole world there was only one, and the bird sought it.

Below, the fair spread out to all sides, great and sprawling. In three large circles, the omen-bird was drawn closer to the ground. Several tents stood close together in this area, poor ungainly things that smelled from too many seasons of weather. Men sat on the ground playing with dice and knucklebones and colored pebbles.

One of these men had the Hoyda horse tracks tattooed across his forehead, and he watched the omen-bird carefully. These others would not understand what that bird could mean. The bird stayed above, and then dove suddenly, straight at the Hoyda. The man ran into his tent, followed by the bird.

There, in that tent, omen-bird saw what he had sought.

He rose back into the sky and marked the location of the thing he would lead the others to.

The great hunting hound lay watchful at the feet of a man in a leather tunic. Suddenly the dog jumped up and began to bark at a black fleck in the sky. The man reached for his quirt and stopped in midmotion as he remembered the curse laid on him by the steppe magician. The bird came closer and the dog watched quietly for a moment, and then ran off. The man almost began to chase it, and froze. Very faintly he heard the strains of a simple bone flute.

The dog ran quickly through the fair, following a scent it barely knew. It ignored food, men, and animals until it came to three gray geldings standing nervously still, their leads dropped in the red dust. The dog approached the greatest one and ran back and forth, urging the gray to follow. The large horse let out a whinny of relief and broke the stern steppe discipline to follow.

Guiding the horse, the dog kept looking at the great black bird above them. The bird circled, dove, and swooped, keeping the company together.

The three animals moved slowly through the crowd, through the places of the woven-goods merchants out to the part of the fairgrounds where the brigands and caravan guards had their tents. For the first time the dog and the horse saw the unsavory men sitting, throwing their dice and smelling of rancid meat and corruption. The sounds and smells were frightening to the horse, but the dog nipped at his hocks. The dog would not let the horse shirk the task.

The omen-bird came to perch on the high pole of one of the old, greasy tents in this company. Only one man, the Hoyda, stared at the bird and began to curse. He knew that the omen-bird was friend to the Iduai. He tapped one of his companions on the shoulder to point to the bird, but just then a white ball of fluff appeared just beyond the perimeter of the caravan tents.

"Hey, look at that. A hyn!" one of the men exclaimed.

"Sit down, you're seeing things."

"No, really, look."

"It probably belongs to someone."

"They're worth a lot of money. And if it belongs to someone, there must be a reward."

The white hyn seemed to shake. It blinked out and appeared again on the other side of the group.

"Is it worth the trouble?" one of the men asked no one in particular.

"Probably more than you'll ever see in a year," came the reply.

All of them, even the Hoyda, lumbered up and began to chase the quivering fluff. It ran. It disappeared and reappeared. The men were all very large and they ran heavily, first this way and then the next.

The dog watched carefully. The hyn was very young but very intelligent, and it was led by the same strange music. The men were being led farther and farther from the tent. With a speed that would have won many races, the dog darted into the dark tent.

There should be a special smell, yes, the smell of a friend on it. There. The man had hidden the thing, but he could not hide the smell. The large dog ripped open the hide pack with his teeth and pulled out a small mat.

After the dog dragged it into the open, the omen-bird crowed quite loudly. It was the right one. The friend smell was there. The colors were there.

The bird's call attracted the attention of one man, smaller

than the rest. He turned and saw the dog carrying the Iduai offering rug, and the man bolted straight at the hound. Yelling a steppe war cry, the Hoyda lunged at the dog.

The dog ran and dodged through the openings between the tents, but the man was fast. The Hoyda was almost within reach of the brilliantly colored rug when his legs were kicked powerfully from behind.

A gray horse with the tree brand of a more southern steppe clan reared over him. The man rolled, but the horse continued. It had been trained for war on the steppes. It reared and snorted, bringing its hooves down close to the Hoyda's face.

Terrified, the Hoyda lay perfectly still. The horse stood over him for long moments, guarding. In that stillness, the Hoyda heard a faint sound, and knew that he was beaten. It had been a very long time since he had heard a simple shaman's flute.

The horse caught up with the dog and flanked him through the crowd. He would not let any of the humankind come near his companion, none except the shaman friend. Man friends were rare indeed.

The music in the black felt tent was soft and restful now. The dog scratched carefully at the felt flap and entered without invitation. It was good to enter here. This was the place of a friend.

The music died slowly. Khadil looked down and his eyes misted. Even in the lightless tent he could discern the patterns of the offering rug and the dog beside it. Even in his best caftan he embraced the animal and let his feelings of gratitude wash over it.

Outside, the horse and omen-bird waited. Khadil stepped out and greeted them, giving them the full satisfaction of his emotions. These were to be thanked greatly, but there was nothing he could give them. A fourth creature appeared from nowhere into his arms, and he began to weep openly.

Khadil put down the hyn, which disappeared. The dog ran off and melted into the crowd. With the omen-bird on his wrist and the offering rug over one arm, Khadil began to walk to the Shrine of the Three Lordly Ones with his head high. He was one of their priests, too, their shaman who guarded the small ones. And the small ones guarded him in return.

All fear and doubt had drained from him, and a smile crossed his face. There were bright ribbons in the stall next to his, and he would buy one for Negat, for their wedding at the great spring lambing.

SHADOW QUEST

Brad Linaweaver

One moment there was the sound of celebration—bells and horns and the beating of drums, with some hearty cheers adding merriment to the whole. Then this was brought to an end . . . at least in one part of the fairgrounds. The Fair at Ithkar was famous for strange occurrences, but nothing in its four-hundred-year history had prepared any participant for what caused that bone-chilling silence.

A crowd had gathered on the outer fringes of the fair before one booth. The young man who seemed responsible for the present distraction was as wide-eyed as any passerby at the thing struggling on the floor. The creature started to crawl in his direction, a snake's head wriggling forth from a hump covered by feathers. As it moved across the floor, the young man involuntarily jumped back.

"So!" rasped a voice like a dungeon door slamming shut. "You conjure monsters *here*! Curse my folly for ever making you my apprentice, Jad." The crowd turned as one at the approach of an old man. His reputation preceded him: Kesnir the Brooding. Few would claim him as a friend; none wanted to have him as an enemy.

Kesnir stalked past Jad to appraise the creature. Above was the full moon, menaced by a great cloud suggesting the shape of a crow's head. The moon seemed to pause when it was in position as the night bird's white eye, while an orange radiance played under the cloud—the light from the fairgrounds' many fires. Jad wished that a cloak of darkness would fall to hide from view the proof of his bungling. For, attempting a simple spell to amuse his bored customers—a low-order illusion that was within the rules of Ithkar—this monster had unexpectedly appeared.

"Jad," said Master Kesnir, and the young man could feel the weight of his name so uttered, "do exactly as I tell you. We will send this creature back to whatever black gulfs spawned it."

As the old man raised his hands and began to chant, it dawned on Jad that, at rare moments of crisis, an experienced magician does not waste time on threats. He saves them for later.

The apprentice watched his master pull his old body taut as a bowstring under the fine, silken robes he always wore. As Kesnir raised his arms, the jewels on his belt glowed with green fire.

Noticing that a fair-ward had joined the company of interested onlookers, standing quietly with a quarterstaff at his side, Jad swallowed a lump in his throat and waited for his master's instructions, which came as: "Take up the vial of ghoul's powder and throw it when I give the command."

The thing on the floor had managed to move only a few inches, leaving something wet behind. Keeping his eyes on the creature, Kesnir moved his hands over his head as if he were playing invisible harp strings. "Now!" he cried out.

Jad tossed the powder, which was evenly distributed over the aggravated monstrosity. There was a flash of light, a terrible smell . . . and it was still there.

"How?" asked Kesnir of the universe at large as the monster unfolded surprisingly large wings, rose for an astounding moment, and exited the booth. In so doing, one of its claws brushed Jad on the arm as the bulk of its body knocked him to the ground.

It flew over the gasping crowd into the night. Regaining his feet, Jad saw that once the oddity was in the sky, it moved with an obscene kind of grace. Outlined against the moon, it seemed as if an ungainly, crippled bird had devoured a large snake that was coiling itself free through a place where a beaked head should be. Yet it could fly without twisting.

"The snake-bird," whispered Jad. "How did I ever bring you into the world?" Examining his arm, Jad saw that he had a slight scratch. He could barely feel it. He felt strangely peaceful.

His mood was broken by the voice of the fair-ward addressing Master Kesnir: "A word with you, magician." Jad knew that he was in for it.

The animals kept in the largest precinct of the fair had panicked when the snake-bird had sailed over them. The authorities were immediately beseiged with complaints by owners of the various beasts. In some cases, animals had hurt themselves; in others, dealers were hurt by the thought that they might not realize any money after all their trouble. At any rate, they received satisfaction, the deserving and dishonest alike. Fair-law had emergency provisions for making a careless participant wish he had never saved his money, just so that it could be paid out in such a fashion. Kesnir learned how swiftly he had to part with a pouch of gold.

The old magician was at least grateful that the Fair at Ithkar did not hold him responsible for the sudden darkness that had enveloped the grounds for a few minutes after the departure of the snake-bird. "Well, Jad, they couldn't prove that your monster is the cause of every ill."

Shortly after they had satisfied the last claim, the magician and his apprentice were standing in the ruins of an abandoned tower near the fairgrounds overlooking the river Ith. Kesnir had told Jad that this place had been used as a place of worship for the Three Lordly Ones long before the temple shrine was even constructed. It was a well-kept secret, Kesnir confided to his apprentice, that such had ever been the use of this tower—and most people had no idea that power from the Three still remained here.

"But I wished for darkness," Jad said, half in awe, half in worry.

Kesnir allowed himself to chuckle before answering: "I doubt that you have that kind of power!"

Jad took the moment's humor as an opportunity to apologize: "Master, I had no idea—"

"You never have!" Kesnir was never happier and Jad more intimidated than when the old man was insulting him. The apprentice had given up trying to understand so long ago that he couldn't remember if it had ever been different. He braced himself for abusing words . . . those that didn't come this time.

"Jad, as this tower stands guard over the river below, so must I stand guard over the mistakes of an eager apprentice who believes himself competent to practice the art unassisted."

"I swear that I don't know what could have gone wrong. My spell was meant to show a silver fountain in the moonlight."

The conversation continued with a melancholy sameness, the younger repeating the theme of inexperience, the older insisting on the necessity of blame. At length Kesnir's purpose became clear: "I do not say that what you have done through carelessness cannot be corrected. I do insist that you set it right. For I believe that the monster you have called forth comes from the sinister Thotharn."

There was a shocked moment of silence. Jad dreaded the dark god, in whom belief was generally stronger than it was in the reputedly benign Three Lordly Ones. Kesnir drew back a dusty curtain that revealed a purple window taking up the space of a wall.

As if guilt were a hand pressing down on him, Jad sat on the floor, his head slumping forward on his chest. "I didn't mean to do it. I want to change everything back."

Master Kesnir smiled, which, if Jad had noticed, would surely have struck him as odd under the circumstances. "You can help me, Jad, and do our world a service in the bargain. I have a scroll that I wish you to deliver to the Three Lordly Ones."

The casual manner in which Kesnir suggested a meeting with personages for whom Jad, at the very least, held some doubts concerning their reality, was not so surprising as the other implication: namely, that there was a *place* where he would find them. "A quest?" Jad asked.

Pointing with his bony forefinger, Master Kesnir drew his apprentice's attention to the purple window. "There lies a portal to another world," he said. "It is the home of the Three. I have a spell to send you through."

In the shadows of the altar was a leathern bag. Jad noticed that his master appeared just as well prepared here as in his own tower. The old man's hands played across its surface, like pale, white spiders, then held two items before Jad: a flask in one hand, a tightly rolled-up scroll in the other. "You must not open the scroll, Jad, for it will turn your mind to ashes if you read it. Once you arrive, trust your instincts to help you find the palace of the Three. It is a barren land you will find, and the palace is its only structure."

Already Kesnir was giving Jad the flask and scroll, all in one smooth motion that seemed to push him toward the window, as well. The degree of Kesnir's preparation bothered Jad. The sudden change in his demeanor—from sullen to cheerful—seemed an exercise in unwelcome haste.

"Wait a minute!" insisted the apprentice. "I have no provisions: food, weaponry, sacks, torches . . ."

"They would merely slow you down," came the brisk reply. "Water's enough to keep you going. Now listen: Once you present the scroll to the Three, they will send you home again. You must make haste. Every second lost is a second the snake-bird—I rather like your name for it—remains where it doesn't belong. The Three will know what to do."

Standing directly in front of the window, Jad seriously questioned whether he wanted the life of a magician. He still had enough wits about him to ask: "What of dangers?"

"Minor obstacles, no more," Kesnir said, but there was little conviction in his voice, now beginning to hold a note of irritation as Jad hesitated. "If you get into trouble, throw the scroll away from you, and all will be well."

"Hey, hold on a—" Jad never finished. Master Kesnir had given him a helpful shove. Then he was surrounded by a veil of purple so pervasive that it was as if the drape had been pulled *through* Jad's body. A stubborn part of his mind was astonished to have met no resistance from a pane of stained glass that, apparently, was never there.

The transition was virtually instantaneous. It took several seconds before he noticed the marked decrease in temperature. He stood on a flat, featureless landscape of dry clay, hard as stone—stretching away in all directions. The sky was as dark purple as the vanished window.

A cold breeze touched his face. Jad was slightly astonished that such a barren place would be visited by even the wind. Shivering, he pulled his cloak more tightly around him. There was no sign of a palace anywhere in sight.

"Which way?" he asked aloud, searching for the barest sign of habitation. A mound of bones attracted his attention instead—the skeleton of a human being. The skull had fallen so that its vacant eye sockets were turned toward the merciless sky. It was impossible to tell from the arrangement of the bones the direction in which the dead had been traveling when death came.

The unpleasant sight made Jad think through the events of the last few hours. So much had happened that it felt as if a lifetime lay behind him. But the most peculiar aspect of the affair was not the advent of the snake-bird, whatever it was, wherever it came from. The really strange thing was what had gone on between Master Kesnir and him; the speed with which his usually cautious instructor had sent him on his bizarre errand, with essentially no preparation, and hardly any explanation.

Was this the man who doubted that Jad could handle the simplest spells on his own? Who had rules that he kept secret until Jad unknowingly broke one and chaos was loosed? Who set traps for his apprentice throughout the tower in which they both lived—practical jokes that never caused permanent damage but worked effectively to undermine the victim's pride? Why entrust something of this importance to—what had he called it?—Jad's instincts? It made no sense.

The skull grinned. There was something about its absence of life that suggested great wisdom. Jad had to find out what was going on, and obviously there was only one way. Find the Three Lordly Ones.

He started walking. One direction seemed as good as another. His eyes strained at the vast expanse of purple sky and brown earth, hunting anything that might be a stronghold in this wasteland.

He walked for hours. Every thirty minutes or so, he would stop, slowly turning in a full circle, hoping to sight even the slightest difference in his surroundings. An occasional bone was the only change. Any guess as to how these bones had come to be scattered was, in itself, disturbing. The clay underfoot was so hard that no prints remained behind to show his own passing.

When the wind resumed, its icy needles forced him to huddle in the folds of his cloak. It never lasted long. The bones that appeared after a while were clearly not human any longer. Although most appeared to be those of animals, some suggested things he did not care to imagine clothed in flesh. He guessed that all had died from exposure or simple loneliness. He wondered how it was that any of them had arrived in this place.

The sporadic wind came to scour the bones. Jad had no intention of the same fate befalling him, although he was becoming tired, very tired.

His legs and chest felt thick and heavy. At last he was too worn out to continue without a rest. Even the hard ground felt good to sit upon.

He swallowed dryness. Pulling the flask from inside his cloak, he resolved to take only one sip. The thought of the full bottle gave him a sense of security.

Suddenly the scratch on his arm began to itch wildly, a touch of fire, like a line of red army ants lancing pain into his skin. It was such a surprise that he shook his arm and cursed. Abruptly as it had come, the pain vanished. He had to remind himself that he was still thirsty.

Uncorking the flask, he tilted it to his lips . . . and retched as a vile, green liquid began erupting from the spout. He threw it from him and watched the ichor ooze into the hard ground, steam rising from the spot where the liquid had splashed. He was about to turn away in disgust when he received another flash of irritation from the little red line on his arm.

"Damn that scratch!" he cried. "I'm lost, I lose my water, and now this!" The pain vanished the moment he mentioned the word "water." He noticed.

Looking at the ground where his discarded flask lay, he saw something else. Picking it up, Jad upended the flask and sadly watched a few clear drops fall. Instead of a smoking piece of ground, he saw a simple darkening where the water had spread.

The time he had spent working on illusion spells had seemed wasted when it appeared that he had no talent for it. Now he thanked his stars for the real gift work provides: memory of how things are done.

He knew all at once the curse of this place. He was wandering in a land of illusion. His only hope was to take care and look for the signs of deception.

Sitting once again upon the hard surface, Jad stared ahead to where the straight line of the horizon promised nothing but more unbroken terrain. This succeeded in giving him a headache. Closing his eyes, he listened to the resonances of the silence. Eventually he heard the distant sigh of the wind, passing, but this time not touching.

He considered the horizon again, but without strain. He had relaxed, letting his eyes drift and his mind wander. The truth nudged him. The line of separation between ground and sky was somehow wrong. Then he did not so much see as realize that the plain was not flat after all, but curved like the bottom of a bowl. He had been walking around the perimeter.

Now he saw even more. Jad stood up and turned around oh, so very slowly. There was something in the distance. Upon closer scrutiny, he could make out two objects, still too far away for details. He started walking in their direction, feeling that he was approaching the center of this land.

He walked for a long time before the objects seemed to grow in size. They hadn't seemed *that* far away. Finally he was near enough to hear a sound of breathing like a thousand bellows full of ragged stones, rasping and wheezing in the thin air. The sound emanated from the first object. A few steps closer. He stopped dead in his tracks, dropped to the ground, his face grinding against the clay. The thing couldn't make that much noise if it wasn't alive, and he recognized it well enough.

For, however many shapes they may assume, and no matter the size, there is something distinctive about dragons. They can be taken for nothing else.

This one had wings and a long neck supporting a massive, horned head sprouting like an evil stalk out of a lumpy, scaled body. And just as there is no mistaking a dragon for any other form of life, so there is no mistaking a dragon with a purpose! This dragon was a guardian. Beyond it was the second object—a small, ugly castle. Fortunately, the monster appeared asleep.

The color of the scales was an incongruous bright green, the hue captured on leaves in early morning sunlight. The beautiful color on the hideous form made a strange contrast in the bleak tableau, and it was as if a light pulsed somewhere deep inside to give the dragon an ethereal quality, which was all the more disturbing because of its unbelievably colossal size. A mountain of quiescent reptilian flesh, it dwarfed the fortress beyond.

Jad asked himself the obvious question: Was it real? Did he really want to go over and touch it to make sure? As if his right hand had a mind of its own, it was rubbing the scratch on his left arm. The scratch. The mark remained unchanged from the time he had received it. Yet it seemed inappropriate to call it a scar. Just what the snake-bird had set upon him was a mystery.

He had felt pain when he was about to throw away his water. Was it a warning? Too many questions crowded his mind, foremost among them why the snake-bird would help Jad. He wanted to dismiss such a line of reasoning, but he also had learned long ago that in magic, there are no coincidences.

Another question that nagged at him was that if he had a warning device on his person, why was it not tingling now? Did that mean that the dragon wasn't real, or that it posed no danger? He had to find out.

He had some pebbles with him that he used for a game of chance. There was one for each color of the rainbow. Now he selected the yellow one, said a prayer to every deity he could think of, and tossed it in a wide arc toward that green flank.

The pebble bounced off the dragon. Although the creature didn't move a muscle, every organ in Jad's body responded to his reckless gesture. After his heart had stopped beating at the speed of a hummingbird's wings, Jad muttered to himself: "That's real enough for me."

Concluding that the Three must be within the castle, Jad crawled on his belly, as might a desert reptile foraging through the perpetual twilight. It was his most devout wish that the dragon would not awaken.

He hugged the ground until he found himself on a gentle ridge (a surprising break in the landscape's monotony) overlooking the castle. Searching for the best manner of entry was fruitless. Even at close range, the structure was oddly nondescript. Aside from the main gate, there did not appear to be any other breaks in the blank, gray surface. There were no turrets, and not even lines were visible between the stones. Yet even taking into account its diminutive size, it could be nothing other than a castle, however inappropriately humble a home for the Three Lordly Ones.

As Jad drew nearer the building, the hairs on the scratched

arm twitched. He halted a few yards from the right corner of the outer wall. Something was wrong.

As if on cue, the scratch began to burn. If it had hurt before, that was nothing compared to the agony he felt now. He had to bite his tongue to keep from screaming.

Could it be that the dragon had been roused from that heavy slumber? Turning his head, and lifting his body a fraction, he gained a clear view of the ridged back of the reptilian leviathan. It hadn't moved. Now that he was facing away from the castle, fear engulfed him. The mark on his arm had apparently reached its maximum discomfort. What was to happen would happen soon.

Later he was not sure if it had been a natural instinct for survival—a quality he wasn't sure that Master Kesnir had ever recognized in him—or a result of training in the art that had saved him. But he had rolled over, jumped to his feet, and run directly at the dragon. His sudden, wild hunch came not a second too soon. The castle began to move.

Odd how he hadn't noticed *its* breathing. Or was it by some acoustical trick he had mistaken the sound as coming from the dragon, whose sides—Jad now reflected—had not been moving? Hearing a wet, slushing noise behind him, he had the good sense to throw himself to the ground.

A long black tentacle snaked past his head, slapping the hard clay two inches from his body. Flipping over on his back, Jad viewed a sky full of more waving tentacles, all extending from the "castle." What he had taken to be the gate of the structure opened to reveal a red maw.

Possessing no eyes, it had to be relying on scent, sound, and the driving force of ravening hunger. Tentacles snapped back and forth, entangling themselves in a frenzy to feed.

Jad had no way of estimating the reach of those tentacles, but he imagined that he was quite some distance from what might be safety. The closest point of refuge was the dragon! Perhaps if he could provoke the castle creature into attacking that behemoth, the ensuing battle would distract them both sufficiently for him to escape unnoticed.

The exhaustion that had plagued him earlier vanished. Jad leapt up as another tentacle grazed him. Even the touch of the thing through thick clothing caused his skin to crawl. This was a terrible form of alien life, loathing all natural flesh. It might feed reluctantly on anything clean but would feed just the same.

As a choice of deaths, the dragon was preferable. Whatever risk lay in waking up the reptile, Jad knew, had to be taken immediately. He raced straight for the massive hulk. Just before one flailing tentacle touched his ankle, the apprentice succeeded in ducking down beside the nearest haunch. The questing tentacle struck against scales instead of yielding tissue.

There sounded a dull thud, as one would hear from the striking of stone.

Then he noticed a door's outline where the ribs of the dragon should be. There was no time to worry over whether or not the portal was locked. Jad put his full strength against it . . . and was through. Several tentacles converged on the spot too late. Jad wondered if the black monster was hesitant about assailing the edifice of the Three.

The dragon shape had not, after all, been entirely an illusion. Indeed, the structure had been purposely fashioned so. Given this outer design, it was relatively simple for powerful magic to cast a strong suggestion. The greater magic had been in the making of that eater which had worn the appearance of stone.

Torches burned on the walls of a corridor within. Traps might wait between those shadows. Echoes turned the softest footfall into an ominous pounding. Too many doors to choose from. Too many ways to be lost.

Jad started down a side hallway, only to halt as the scratch gave warning. He made two more attempts before he discovered a route taking him along just inside the outer wall. Naturally one would expect to find the Three at the center of their fortress, like spiders waiting in a web. Perhaps they were off to the side instead.

Jad's scratch suddenly itched, the same second his foot touched the metal plate hidden in the floor. He strove to retreat . . . too late. And he fell forward into darkness, but not the darkness of unconsciousness.

His tumble was brief, ending surprisingly on cushions thick enough to protect him from any impact. Feeling very foolish, he sat up with a deep drawn breath. Determinedly, he removed the scroll from inside his cloak. By touch he thought it had been crumpled but was not torn. Holding it tightly, Jad waited.

Voices sounded as if speaking from the end of a tunnel, then light flared. He saw three smiling faces, hovering at the end of a strange room. Everything was yellow—blending as one, floor, wall, and ceiling. The faces were palid globes, expressionless and alike. That in the center spoke: "You have proven yourself a worthy courier. Place the scroll before us and your task is done." However, to Jad that calm, reasonable voice carried a vaguely disturbing note.

"I have questions," the apprentice summoned the courage to say.

"Retain them, boy," came the prompt answer. "You'll find all such preferable to answers. Now give us the offering and you will be sent back."

Offering? Did not they mean *message*? This choice of term unsettled Jad, but he moved forward nonetheless. He would have dropped the parchment below the hovering heads, as bidden, if the scratch on his left arm had not suddenly deepened into a nasty cut, from which blood erupted with force.

Jad staggered but somehow managed to hold on to the scroll. Though his blood was flowing red, as the stream splashed to the floor it became light blue—the color of his own world's sky. And out of that growing pool formed a familiar shape.

Light vanished. He felt as if the room spun around. A whispery voice hissed through the thick dark: "I am what you call the snake-bird. We must help each other against these servants of evil."

Jad heard his voice rise in anger to reply? "No, the Three Lordly Ones can't be evil!"

"These are not the Three," hissed that dark, hidden other. "Look!"

Light again soaring from the flickering of large torches in sturdy iron holders showed that there was no blood on the floor. Jad's arm was bare of any wound. He hardly noticed this, for the scene before him held his full attention. Three grotesquely fat men squatted atop an emerald dais in a chamber now possessing recognizably gray walls of stone.

Jad, in turn, became aware of a set stare from three pairs of eyes. Three mouths wetly formed his name with a silent pursing of lips. Three sets of hands held up stubby fingers, like white slugs squirming up to the light from unknown subterranean depths, to gesture at the young magician before them.

"They are servants of Thotharn, and I am their enemy," said the snake-bird, whose reptilian head touched Jad briefly on the shoulder.

These three creatures—who had once been men—sat in monastic simplicity, wrapped in robes of coarse, dark fabric, even though they owned the riches of a dozen worlds. Their real wealth was displayed in folds of flesh bulging on bloated frames.

Theirs was a corpulent perfection, their obesity an art. Jad recognized them in all their perverted strength—did that knowledge flow from the snake-bird?

The first once had a name—Illmur—and he had clung to his goal in life with genuine dedication: a full knowledge of nature. The second's had been Enir, desiring the role of rulership: those Machiavellian satisfactions that went hand in hand with political intrigue successfully accomplished.

Though the first two had forgotten their names, the third remembered his—Aickly. His end was to have been a pious one. With the powers that would be his, he wished to invoke the wisdom of gods, to serve others. He longed for sainthood.

Each in turn had betrayed their dreams, settling instead for raw dominion, living increasingly hidden lives of quiet malice. Their satisfaction became to hate life for itself alone.

He who had been Aickly spoke now: "Kesnir never had a message for us. You were a gift, young Jad, a sacrifice. We could have taken you at any time, since you entered our domain, so long as you gave up the scroll that is your master's petition. We could have fooled you into doing that, but each obstacle you overcame made you . . . tastier.''

"You could have tried, you mean!" From within himself Jad found defiance.

"We were planning on giving power to Kesnir in return, a small matter for us, but much for him. We were going to provide him with this.'' The eyeballs of the wizardly triumvirate rotated to the left. Propped against the wall was revealed—as though it had just appeared—a scepter unlike any other. Golden, granted a pair of gossamer wings, it was crowned with a winking diamond, and it hummed as if a honey-mad bee. "With this, he can easily master his world.''

Jad held tightly to the scroll, as if to a lifeline. The exchange of it for this golden weapon must never be. He understood now that the art he himself sought was not a means to an end, as he had always thought; it *was* the end. For the true magician signs of worldly wealth were transitory, bait to catch the human fly. Kesnir wanted the same thing these three monsters sought: power over other people's lives.

The voice continued: "With this, he would begin by laying waste the Fair at Ithkar, and incidentally demolishing the temple shrine. All that would be left standing would be the remains of a tower dedicated to the worship of Thotharn.''

Jad had no doubts about the location of that structure. "I always half suspected I was a pawn," said Jad slowly, "but I told myself that was simply the lot of any apprentice. I wouldn't be one forever. I never guessed that death was to be my graduation.''

"But you are fortunate," said the one who had been Illmur. "Your new ally saved you from that.''

"Who *are* you?" Jad turned to demand of the snake-bird.

The answering whisper came promptly: "I am a wizard from a dimension bordering yours. Certain animals in your world are eyes for us. So we learned that Kesnir would have threatened us, after enslaving his own kind. I almost arrived too late, and the journey cost me dearly. I was so weak that I almost didn't survive. If I had not had the remaining strength to place my mark on you, I could not have shared this quest. Thanks be to the Three Lordly Ones that we prevailed!"

The one who had been Enir complained, "You, 'snake-bird,' have interfered with us too often in the past. We thought we had made it impossible for you ever to annoy us again. I now call you by your real name, which is—" There followed a series of syllables so alien to the human ear that Jad could not remember them a moment later. "And you were not allowed to enter this land directly. Thus you needed this inept boy to serve you!"

"Which he has done well," retorted the snake-bird.

The central figure spoke again: "We should have detected an enemy wizard when we cast the spell of darkness over the fair. Kesnir was our servant, but not a good one, for he detected no danger near this boy. We let Jad through the gate. Kesnir did not even tell us of any difficulty, no doubt fearful that any such disclosure would jeopardize our agreement. The fool! Well, we shall do nothing to save him from his current danger. As for you"—the unspeakable name was somehow spoken again—"you must have flown a good distance away after your arrival. If you had been anywhere near the fair when we looked, we would have sensed you."

"Oh, yesssssssss," the snake-bird hissed, "I traveled far. And now Jad and I will travel back to his world . . .

unless, of course, you three care to contest my will in this?''

Beady eyes regarded Jad from fleshy depths. The central one was spokesman for all: ''We only enjoy that which comes without effort. Begone!''

The hissing voice of the snake-bird reached Jad instantly: ''Hang on to the scroll.''

The return journey was quicker than the first. It *was* instantaneous.

They no longer were at the fair but rather inside Kesnir's own tower, that monument to his ambition standing alone among jagged rocks near the Galzar Pass. Jad had no idea how much time had elapsed in that other place. All he saw was that he and the snake-bird were now outside the door to Kesnir's library, a secluded room at the top of the tower.

''Now comes the time to use the scroll,'' hissed the snake-bird, jerking a claw toward the rim of light beneath the closed door. ''Read the words that burn,'' came the whispered order. Jad did not hesitate. Kesnir's warning did not deter him now. Opening the ancient roll of paper, Jad saw the letters clearly, even in the darkness, glowing in blood-red light.

Because at the fall of night Master Kesnir had redoubled the magical protection surrounding his tower, he now wrought his incantations in imagined safety. Uttering the final words of a spell, he started for the door. As his hand closed upon the latch, fire flickered from that along his arm. He leapt back, wildly rubbing his tormented flesh, crying out hoarsely.

The door burst open. Jad thrust his way in, accompanied

by the snake-bird. "Never thought you'd see me again, did you? After what I have been through, I'm happy to return a little taste of it to you."

Kesnir did an uncharacteristic thing. Instead of casting a spell—which Jad expected—he threw a knife. The blade was aimed at Jad's throat, but the snake-bird intercepted the steel with a whistled cry, and it clattered to the floor.

Jad pointed the scroll at the cowering Kesnir. "I called you master and served you as best I could. You know well my reward."

"Thotharn forced me," Kesnir protested weakly.

"Thotharn forces no one," retorted the snake-bird.

"*You* made the decision," growled Jad, advancing on the old man. "I was to die for your gain."

Kesnir's lips twitched; he plucked at the folds of his robe. "It was an experiment," he said lamely.

"You have told me so many lies that I have lost track of them. You lied when you didn't even have to! I don't see how you could call that horrible dungeon those three fiends live in a palace."

"*I* would have lived in a palace." The old man's voice betrayed his loss of hope.

"You've lived long enough," said Jad, hurling the scroll to the rough stone floor. The snake-bird laid its head on Jad's shoulder and wrapped its wings around the young man's body as the apprentice pronounced the words that were written on the parchment.

Gasping for air, Master Kesnir clutched his chest as if trying to make his heart continue beating. One word escaped his lips—"No!"—before a crackling flame licked out from his chest, bathing his shaking body with eerie phosphorescence. The skin on his already emaciated frame dried to the fine, tight leather of a mummy.

There was the odor of decay. The mummy became dust, which blew out of sight. All that was left was a robe, looking as clean and unwrinkled as it if had been washed and hung out to dry. The jewels on the loose circle of the belt continued to glow with the magical energy that had failed to save Kesnir's life.

"You're getting better at spells," remarked the snake-bird approvingly.

"Thanks to you. I don't suppose my magic had anything to do with your arrival in the booth?"

"Not really."

"I didn't think so," said Jad, picking up a nearby sack and beginning to fill it with implementia from Kesnir's collection, first among them the belt.

The snake-bird observed this procedure with its cold eyes and at length enquired, "Taking over your inheritance?" Jad nodded and started selecting volumes from the library shelves as his companion continued: "I've seen magicians in many life forms, and I think you have the makings of a good one. You'll have to study long and hard, especially now that your teacher is gone."

Jad paused long enough to say, "I've had enough. I'm giving up the art, aside from the few tricks I've already learned. Those are all I'll need for a good show in my booth. My own booth."

The snake-bird made a sound that Jad later realized was a laugh. "Maybe I'll visit you at Ithkar Fair again. It won't be any time soon. I need a good rest."

"If you do," said Jad, "how about another spectacular entrance? But don't bother scratching me. From now on I'll take my chances without that mark of yours. It's useful, but it also *hurts*!"

After a moment, Jad added: "I'm glad that we met. I was at last part of something important. You used me, of course, but what a difference from the way that Mas . . . that Kesnir used me."

"There is a goodness in you, Jad."

Jad reached over and touched the snake-bird's wing in a gesture of friendship. "Visit again," he said, "and you'll find that I have the most talked-about attraction at the fair." He rattled his bag of makeshift treasures. "These pieces of Kesnir's wizardry will lose their evil power if not kept together. I will sell each one to a different customer."

"Ah," said the snake-bird, fading from view, "you may not be a full colleague of mine, but you are no longer an apprentice."

KISSMEOWT AND THE HEALING FRIAR

A. R. Major

The bundle of rags and filth known as Brian the Cutpurse nearly made it. Earlier that evening he had left his comrades with the other camp followers on the outskirts of Ithkar Fair and picked his mark immediately. After lifting a fat noble's money pouch, he had slipped through the evening crowd. But an alarm had been raised and now he was trapped.

He could almost feel the breath of the fair-ward on his neck when he spotted torchlight gleaming on the brass helmet of another such coming toward him. In desperation, he dodged between two of the elaborate pavilions of the rich. An unseen tent-peg tripped him up, throwing him on, headfirst, against the wheel of a nearby cart. The resounding crack and the twisted angle of the crumpled neck told the fair-ward that Brian had filched his last purse. "Good riddance!" he mumbled.

235

"Canst thou restore life to that youth?" questioned a soft voice. "No? Then be not hasty to cast away what thou canst not create."

The soft-spoken speaker used the ancient tongue, one of the marks of a traveling mendicant permitted to beg at Ithkar Fair. But *this* man looked no ordinary beggar. His robes were clean, a mixture of forest green and light brown. His feet were encased in worn but sturdy travel boots. Blue twinkling eyes were set in an innocent-looking face between ears that stuck out like jug handles. The bald pate was ringed by a wreath of brown curls nearly forming a halo. A large leather wallet pouch was suspended by a strap from his left shoulder.

With experienced hands the little friar gently straightened out the crumpled neck. Suddenly the fair-ward found himself obeying orders: "Stand right there, hold the light exactly so, and *don't move!*" Reaching into his wallet, the friar removed a bright green stone and a small packet of herbs. From his lips issued a crooning sound, like wind singing through treetops. The torchlight focused through the stone in his right hand on the neck of the dead youth. With his other hand the friar dropped a pinch of herbs into the torch flame. There followed a flash of golden fire through the stone to center on the thief's neck, while the air roundabout carried the scent of the forest in springtime. Groaning, the boy squirmed and tried to sit up.

The little friar handed the purse that had been clutched in the boy's hand to the fair-ward. "Restore this to the owner, and forget what happened," he commanded.

In a daze the fair-ward moved away. Turning to the youth, the heal-all said, "I suggest, young man, that you change your occupation. Help may not be at hand in the future!"

Other eyes had observed the incident, paid eyes meant to report to the servants of the Three Lordly Ones. Within the hour, those of the temple would know of Askar the healing friar. Shortly therefore, Askar found himself being escorted by four fair-wards under the orders of a high-ranking priestess. These marched him into a small room walled with strange white stones that glowed. Before him the tall, pale woman stood behind a narrow table. She was flanked by six men, sitting three to a side. Each was robed as a servant of the Three Lordly Ones.

Askar, surprised at not being tried by the high priest, wondered why the lady stood in command. He decided it was safer to play the innocent rustic, smiling most disarmingly, as he asked, "How may I serve my lady and Your Worships?"

"You were observed performing a healing act, in fact, the act of restoring human life, on the fair premises. Did you not know that *all* of your sort must be examined by a lesser priest before being permitted any act, or even to beg?"

"My lady has been misinformed. My order never begs. We obey the forest goddess Nithra, who permits our services to our fellow man only if offered freely. Though we are permitted to accept small gifts from any who wish. I was on my way to report to the temple for permission to set up a healing booth when this fleeing youth stumbled and broke his neck. You see, lady, the healing art has *some* limitations. I can use the life-restoring charm but once a fortnight, and it must be used within minutes of the departure of the life into the shadow."

"Why is thissss?" hissed one priest, his voice unpleasantly toned.

"We know not why, but if the spirit is not recalled

within minutes, even though the body may revive, the mind is then dead. This is ever a mystery. Perhaps there is something in the air which unites mind and body, but cannot be withheld for long."

"The fool means oxygen," murmured one priest to another.

"He is not as big a fool as he who uses sacred words in the presence of the uninitiated," snapped the priestess. "Tell me," she went on, "does your order pay any allegiance to Thotharn, or know you of those dark mysteries?"

"Thotharn, to my limited knowledge, stands for all we healing friars are against. For us that one is the very essence of evil," replied Askar promptly and firmly.

After a brief consultation with the others, the priestess turned to him and said, "We will grant you the right to a small booth near the money-changers at the temple's main gate. You will be watched by the taxmen, and any 'gifts' you receive will be taxed accordingly. That is all."

"Not quite," replied Askar quietly. "Some of you carry burdens of sickness that I would remove. Do not forget: I am a heal-all, and when I heal, it is confidential if you request it so!"

At their nods of permission, he continued, "You sir," he said to the hissing priest, "are suffering from a bout of asthma." He reached into his wallet and produced a packet of herbs. "Before retiring, place a pinch of this in a candle and inhale the fumes."

"You, sir," Askar spoke with authority to that priest's neighbor, "have a wart on your index finger that has been growing. Now it interferes with your writing, within the year it can become cancerous, costing your hand, so let us remove it."

As the priest reluctantly unwound a bandage from the

offending member, Askar said, "A torch, please." Another priest went to the door and called for a torch. Again Askar focused the stone above the offending growth. The torchlight flared golden for an instant and the growth disappeared.

"You, sir," said Askar, turning brusquely to a priest with a very red nose, "are losing the battle to the wine bottle. Divide this packet of herbs into six parts, dissolve a portion in a cup of water each morning, and drink it for six days. Also, limit yourself to one cup of wine daily."

"Give it to *me*," said the burly priest on the right, "and I'll *see* that he takes it!"

"Spoken like a true friend," murmured the little friar.

One by one he prescribed medication, until only the priestess was left. "Perhaps the lady would prefer to discuss her problem alone," he said softly.

"No," she replied curtly, "you have already exposed disorders that would disqualify each of us from sitting on this court. I, too, need healing."

"It will not be necessary to remove the robe," he said hastily. "It is quite obvious to me that the carbuncle is on your left hip, that is why you did not sit down. Point to the exact spot and let the stone do the rest." Rapidly the miracle took place. "Now take one of these small potions each night for a week instead of your present sleeping drink. It will remove the desire you have developed for the mes-weed drink."

Thus Askar found himself in a small booth actually provided by those who were jealous of their own powers, near the temple main gate at Ithkar Fair—though it soon began to be obvious that healing was not the only reason for his being there. For each time he performed the healing art, he asked casually, "Have you ever seen such a healing

stone as mine, elsewhere?'' The last word was always
uttered with a hypnotic stress, leading his patient to a
search of memory; yet the answer was always negative.
When not involved in healing, Askar repeated the same
question fruitlessly at those booths where were sold various charms and amulets.

On the third morning an agitated man came to Askar
demanding bluntly, ''Would the good heal-all stoop to
heal a sick animal? I will pay you well.''

Askar replied readily, ''My pay will be to share your
noon meal—'' Then a soft, purring voice in his mind said,
*Please come quickly, holy man. It is I who know what you
seek.*

Askar strode hastily behind the tall man toward the
section of the fairgrounds devoted to the animals.

''I have many animals for sale,'' the other said as he
went, ''but not the hurt one. He is Barth, and Barth is
'family.' He was badly slashed while herding a boar-orsk.
Word around the fair is that you . . .'' Here his voice
trailed off as they entered a tent crowded with cages.

Barth lay on a pallet of straw, gasping for breath. A
crude bandage failed to close the gaping wound in his side.

*Well, Barth, old boy, I'll have to sew the edges together
before the stone can do its best work*, mind-spoke the friar.

My tribe's blessings be upon you, an agonized and weak
answer came to his mind.

Relax, have faith, go to sleep, and fear no hurt, replied
Askar.

He held the stone before the hound's pain-filled eyes,
moving it mechanically back and forth, crooning softly.
Soon Barth lay in a deep hypnotic sleep. Taking a needle
and thread from the pack, the heal-all sprinkled the wound

with healing powder before carefully sewing the torn flesh together.

The friar is seeking more than sick ones to heal. Can he mind-speak without hindering his task? Again that soft voice entered his mind.

Certainly, and to whom do I have the honor to speak? inquired Askar.

I am called the Lady Kissmeowt by those of the fair, replied the soft, almost purring voice.

Askar glanced sharply around. A small gray house cat fixed him with an intent stare from a perch on a bale of hay. He nodded respectfully and mind-spoke, *The Lady Kissmeowt?*

The house cat nodded gravely in return.

You are right, lady, Askar thought-spoke. *Two ten-days past one of my order was murdered and his healing stone taken. He managed to write in the dust with his finger "The evil ones at Ithkar Fair" before he entered the shadow.*

And, prompted the soft voice, *you are here to get it back?*

My lady, do you realize how much mischief that stone could cause in the wrong hands? For one thing, wealthy nobles might be forced to pay large sums of money to avoid a plague striking their dwelling!

You must also punish the criminal who sent your comrade into the shadow, and so restore the balance of justice, purred the house cat as she licked a paw, then scrubbed behind an ear. Secretly she thought the little man would be incapable of punishing anyone.

Yes—Askar sighed—*that, too. Can you indeed aid me in any way in my quest?*

I already have been mind-searching the camp. Last

night a war-horse reported that, while he was waiting for a blacksmith to repair a loose shoe, two men stood near him. One kept looking over his shoulder as if he feared he was being watched. He had a red beard and a long scar on his left cheek. War-horses are well trained to note such details, you know. The other man was dressed in a priestlike robe, but different from those of the temple. He was also wearing some sort of a mask-badge. There was a remark like "Fair trade, many stones for one stone." Then they exchanged packages and parted company.

So, said the friar, tying the last knot, *it just may be that an evil priest of the East has purchased the healing stone from my poor comrade's murderer.*

I took the precaution of having a night bird trail him to his resting place. The winged one can guide you there this evening. But beware! This strange priest is dangerous! I was able to shift some of his thoughts through the mind-link of the night bird. He has spent the entire income from his temple for three years to purchase the healing stone. Thus shall he face the most terrible punishment possible should he fail to deliver it.

Askar raised his own stone to the torch, completing Barth's healing. The hound's lick across his hand was a sufficient reward, but the stewpot in the corner gave forth delicious odors, and he remembered his request to eat that day with the dog's owner. While he was so feasting, he again mind-touched the cat.

So when does this masked priest propose to leave the fair?

Tomorrow morning; thus we must work fast, the house cat replied.

First. I must pass this information on to my superiors at the hermitage, thought Askar. *In case I, too, walk the way of the shadow, they will need to know what has happened. Unfortunately, my mind-touch is very short ranged.*

I have clear sending for over seventy-five leagues. Who is your contact at the hermitage?

We have a large tomcat named Manso; he looks like this. So saying, he projected an image of Manso to her. *How can I ever repay the lady for her aid?* added the friar.

The talent is not for hire, even as yours it must be used freely. So saying, she rose and stretched luxuriously. *However, a small present of fragrant herbs would be appreciated. . . .*

Of course, of course, replied Askar, helping himself to another bowl of savory stew. *One wonders just how much this evil priest knows about the healing stone's use. I have labored for years to learn what little I know.*

Then why not use that to trap the man? inquired the house cat softly. *You are the talk of the fair, offer to give a public display of ways to use a healing stone. He will come, he cannot afford not to. Then, just before your performance, there will be a diversion of sorts, and in the confusion your friend Brian just might use his talents to get the stone back.*

Well I might as well try that, since I have no better idea, Askar replied thoughtfully.

Make your announcement of a display of power to be presented between the watering trough and the red pavilion near the Weavers' section of the fair, sent the house cat. *Now I must busy myself concerning the diversion.*

As Askar left the tent, he stopped to pet many animals. No one noticed his leaving a small packet of catnip near a seemingly dozing gray house cat.

Kissmeowt was already in contact with friends. *Sir Ratton,* she mind-spoke a large white rodent hidden nearby, *I would make a truce with thee.*

So, the lady is in enough trouble to recognize that my ancestors, like hers, also descended from the ship of the Sky Lords? The answer was more mocking than angry, for he did enjoy teasing any house cat.

The lady held strict control over her feline temper. *For this favor, Sir Ratton, I would be willing to assure that my tribe grant a year's truce to your tribe.*

Such a boon was not to be taken lightly. The big rodent's little red eyes flashed. *Can the lady deliver this promise in truth, or is it only idle words?*

The lady can deliver, for the safety of the entire planet depends on this, and my tribe will readily respond to that appeal. Though I doubt if your tribe could understand.

He chose to ignore that last slur. *It must be a very dangerous act you desire, perhaps like stealing the ranking necklace from the throat of the high priestess while she sleeps?* This was as risky a thing as he was capable of imagining.

No, much easier than that. You are to start a riot. Here is how you will do it: Tonight in a weaver's booth an ozren must get loose to cause an outbreak of noise and confusion. This will draw all the fair-wards away from the area you are in, then you . . .

While the little house cat was doing her part preparing for the coming events, Askar, too, had been busy—doubly busy, for wherever he went people recognized him and he would have to pause and give freely of his art. Sometimes it was just a gentle word about a change in diet, other times it was a more lengthy healing. However, he no longer asked questions about anyone having seen a stone like his.

He finally found a lesser priest who would listen to his request for a platform to put on a demonstration of the many uses of the healing stone. Nothing like this had ever happened before in fair history, so the priest had to take the matter up with the high priestess.

In turn she was deeply puzzled. Such a request was unlike the image she had formed of the nature of the peaceful little man.

"Would such as he choose to exhibit his skill after the manner of a common juggler? Or did I misjudge him—has his success here gone to his head?"

At any rate, she *did* owe the little man a favor. What a boon to be able to walk and sit normally again! And her spies would bring information about anything needing her attention.

Digging into his small supply of coins, Askar then hired a crier to go about the fair. The crier's bell and cry of "Oyez, Oyez" soon had every ragamuffin around him, as well as the attention of every other fairgoer, as he boomed out the time and place to see "freely, one and all, a demonstration of the famous healing stone of Ithkar Fair." So important, this announcement! He gave the impression that he personally was responsible for making available this once-in-a-lifetime experience.

Then Askar must needs seek out young Brian. By a careful mind-sweep he located the youth pumping a forge for the very blacksmith who had shod the war-horse that had heard the thief and priest talking. Nearby another such beast was being prepared for new shoes. He resembled very much the fabled unicorn except that he had two horns growing out of the center of his forehead.

The smith greeted Askar warmly. "Sir heal-all, welcome to my shop! Thrice welcome are you! Since you removed that grievous birthmark from the face of my daughter Rosalind, she has had three young men ask for her hand in marriage! Even now she and her mother are in the weavers' section spending all I can make this week on her wedding gown. And they are welcome to it, sir! Our household has not had such happiness since her birthing day. Name your price, sir, name your price and you shall have it! How can *I* help *you*?''

Lapsing once again into the old speech, Askar replied, "Thy joy, O shaper of metals, bringeth payment enough to me.'' Then with a twinkle in his eye he added, "But I would like the loan of that youth at yon bellows.''

"Take him, take him, he is not much fit for forge work anyhow! I just 'prenticed him to keep him out of trouble. . . . Perhaps you could make a heal-all out of him, as his delicate hands are more fit for lighter labor than blacksmithing.'' With a roar of laughter the smith turned back to his forge.

"Surely, sir heal-all,'' complained Brian, "there must be *some* easier way to make a respectable living!''

"If you would be willing to train your mind as you have trained your fingers, you could make an honorable living with it,'' responded the little friar. "However, I must ask you once again to use your cutpurse talents. Relax your mind, have you ever seen a man such as this?'' Swiftly Askar projected a mental image of the priest of the East. "This man is pure evil, and has stolen a healing stone from one of my comrades, slaying him for it. He will use it for a stone of cursing, not healing. I must get it back, but such a deed will be very dangerous. . . . Do I even have the right to ask you to risk your life to help me?''

"Without you, I'd be already long into the shadow,'' replied the youth quietly. "I owe you a debt I can never repay. But why not take your case directly to those of the temple?''

''It would only be my word against his. One false faith against another in *their* eyes. With such a quarrel, they would not choose to become involved because of the truce of the fair, you know.''

They had reached the area where the priest of the East was reported to be staying in the pavilion of a rich merchant. There was a flash of sunlight off the mask-badge of a man fingering some weaver's cloth. The weaver, not wanting to do business with such an unpleasing stranger, had disappeared inside his booth.

''Notice how everyone avoids meeting him face to face,'' said Askar, ''so perhaps there is truth to the rumor that his mask-crest emits a perfume to upset the mind of anyone talking to him. We can't risk your being caught. . . . Can you work from *behind* him?''

''Hmm,'' mused Brian, squinting professionally at his proposed prey, ''he seems to be favoring his left arm. My guess is he has a sleeve purse weighting that forearm. I might get at it if something *exceptional* distracted his attention.''

''Like, maybe, a demonstration of healing, or a riot?'' asked Askar.

''You don't know the fair-wards, friar! They'd never let a riot get started. *They* know *how* to control a crowd!''

''*You* don't know Kissmeowt, either,'' the friar replied, for the brief meeting with the house cat had convinced him of her abilities.

''Kiss-me-who? What are you talking about, some healing secret?'' asked Brian.

''Forget it. You just be watching this evening when I begin my demonstration. Slip up close to the priest, and when the riot starts, take the stone, then get to safety. Also, make your mind as blank as you can. Such a one as he just might have mind-search talent.''

Evening came, and with it the illustrious Lord Roday, who was there to make a formal appearance, with his wife, at the trade pavilion of his county's merchants and traders. Planned to be an affair of much pomp and ceremony to draw full attention to his county's merchandise, it was hoped to increase sales for all concerned. Though it could be done better, Lord Roday commented to all within hearing. A pox on the regulations of the fair that all weapons be checked at the gate. How might any lord look impressive swordless, and his escort spearless? So Lord Roday had to ''make do'' with his eight men-at-arms brilliantly plumed, armored, and surcoated. The lord himself on a nervous white war-house and his men on contrasting black ones drew the full attention of the gathering crowd.

For the moment, the full troop was waiting impatiently before the red pavilion of his noble family. As usual, Lord Roday's lady was late, preening herself before her mirror. She was a vain lady, bringing a new and wondrous wardrobe to each year's fair.

''Drat that woman,'' Lord Roday fumed as his guards hid secret smiles. ''Why can't she ready herself before that charlatan healer starts his medicine show?''

For while many believed in the healing friar, Lord Roday was one of the new generation of cynics who did not accept anything except what he could see, feel, smell, touch, or thrust his sword into.

Now as a fair page advanced to the front of the small platform that had been erected across from Lord Roday's pavilion, a drumroll was sounded. The crowd pressed in closer for a better view. Roday's war-horse fidgeted and eased nearer to a watering trough.

Silence descended as Askar raised his hand. ''Dear friends,'' he said gently, ''some here have been skeptical of the power of healing. Others question the use of the healing stone. It is my desire tonight to set all such doubts at rest. First, I would like to show you how the stone may produce sleep. Will a volunteer please come forward?''

In his concern for his plan, Askar had forgotten to keep to the ancient form of speech, but no one seemed to notice. A young boy, urged by two companions, stepped uneasily up.

''What is your name, boy?''

''Cherbert, sir,'' the boy half whispered in awe.

''Very well, Cherbert. Sit you on this stool, relax, and watch well the stone.''

Once again Askar crooned in a monotone as he spun the stone before the youngster's eyes. Soon the lad was in a deep hypnotic trance. ''Now, Cherbert, you are no longer a boy, you are a house cat. How do you talk?''

To the amazement of the crowd the boy began to yowl like a singing house cat. However, as the crowd exploded in laughter, a voice mind-spoke the friar, *That is not funny, heal-all.*

Sorry, my lady, he thought back, *but it's all I could do on short notice. Where is my ''diversion''?*

It has already started. Listen!

Sounding at first faintly above the crowd's laughter came distant shouts. Then the cry that followed was desperate: ''Fair-wards to the weavers' tents, fair-wards to the weavers' tents!''

Almost as if the commotion had been a war-horn signal, strange action disrupted the gathered assembly—things happened that would be discussed with relish for years to come by those lucky enough to be present.

A large white rat appeared out of nowhere to dart under Lord Roday's war-horse, nipping at its heel. How would mere people know the war-horse and Sir Ratton were acting in concert? What master could rightfully blame a war-horse for rearing under *those* circumstances? The unprepared Lord Roday was tossed, like any ill-prepared novice rider, straight into the watering trough, where, in a very unknightly fashion, he cursed loudly and floundered for a footing. The laughing crowd now turned full attention on him—*this* was more of a show than they had been promised!

Two men-at-arms sprang to aid him, only to have their own mounts bolt in mock fear, adding to the confusion. In the meantime Sir Ratton slipped under the wall of the Lady Roday's pavilion, bringing high-pitched feminine screeches. Lady Roday, never one to be backward in her own defense, charged from the tent, a fire poker in her hand, screaming, "Get him away, get him away!" Her ribbons and headdress askew, she bore down upon her bedrenched husband just as a large hound—Barth by name—repaying his own debt to the friar, ran across Lady Roday's path to trip her. With one final shriek she stumbled against her husband, toppling them both back into the watering trough, where their combined curses and screams turned to sputtering under the water. As the two men-at-arms fished them out, Lady Roday turned upon those unfortunates with all the fury of a woman who has been made a public spectacle. Having somehow managed to hang on to the fire poker, she proceeded to flail out in all directions.

The hilarious crowd was now treated to a symphony of sound as the poker crashed against the armored men, Barth howled, war-horses snorted, women shrieked, and men doubled over, weak with laughter. Barth, thinking it better to be elsewhere, pivoted and tore through the crowd, running straight into a troop of caterers carrying wine and cakes to a nearby banquet. The charging dog both upset and unnerved the servitors: wine bottles and pastry trays flew into the air, much of the far-flung debris landing upon what was left of Lord Roday's guard of honor.

In a matter of seconds, what had been a well-organized procession of pomp and ceremony had turned into a complete disaster. Even the priest of the East, who had been watching the friar closely from the shadows, was diverted. So hard did he laugh that he never felt the craftily concealed razor-sharp knife slit his sleeve, nor fingers probing inward to detach the purse there. He missed nothing, until he sought his own lodging. Then he shivered at discovering his loss, and knew the full chill of one with no reason ever to laugh again.

While humans were laughing, there was a little gray house cat who was not amused—she was much too busy—as she spied through the eyes of a friendly night bird, and bespoke two fleeing black war-horses, directing them to the outskirts of the camp where thieves lurked. Afterward, the fair officials would congratulate themselves that, in all the confusion, no one was hurt save one unknown red-headed cutthroat with a large scar on his face. None of the other thieves knew, naturally, what had happened to the well-filled purse he had been seen with earlier, though a select few had more money to spend at the food and drink booths.

Men might wonder a little, but the wise merchant does not ask questions, nor do wise thieves volunteer answers, at Ithkar Fair. But the animals knew, especially a little gray house cat, who worked well to balance the scales of justice, neatly and precisely.

Ithkar Fair being over, among those traveling the road to the West was a small healing friar, followed by a youth wearing a novice's dull-colored cloak. The novice's education had already begun, even as they tramped sturdily ahead—his companion pointing out certain plants growing along the road, how they were to be used and which ones must be avoided.

And, since rumor spreads even the best-kept secret, at Ithkar Fair, the fairgoers of that season have an odd saying to explain the unexplainable: "It must be Kissmeowt!"

THE CARDS OF ELDRIANZA

Mary H. Schaub

"Your license?"

Kereth extended the folded parchment to the fair-ward, who passed it to his scribe. The scribe ran his quill down a list strip. "Eldrianza the fortune-teller," he confirmed. "License in order, space reserved."

Now would come the difficulties. Kereth took a fortifying breath. "Mistress Eldrianza is dead," he announced. "She freely gave me her possessions, her cards, and her license to work here at Ithkar Fair."

The fair-ward gazed skeptically at Kereth, his dusty horse and travel-worn wagon. "You have a witness to this legacy?"

"Other than the horse, no. My mistress died on the road three days past. She had been ill during the journey, and hoped to find relief at the fair. When a chill seized her, I could do nothing." Kereth remembered her fingers, dry and cold against his, when she had given him her card box. "Take the cards," she had whispered. "They are yours by right. Find your way with them." Not for the first time, he wished he *knew* his way. So much that had seemed dependably solid in his world had vanished like morning mist thinning above the river's dark surface. The fair-ward's voice jarred his attention back to the present.

"We must have proof of your claim. You could have stolen these things. What evidence can you show?"

Images crowded in Kereth's mind: a life's memories, their journeys together in this creaking wagon since he was a child. Kereth reached into the leather pouch he wore under his shirt. His sole item of evidence was a curious thing, but Eldrianza had been a most curious lady. "Besides my word," he said, "this is all I have."

The fair-ward shook out the square of embroidered silk, pale in the morning light. His scribe leaned forward to peer at the writing, hesitating over the faded words. " 'I, Eldrianza, Reader of the Cards, do take this male child Kereth of the Southern Glades to be in my care and to rear as my assistant.' " He paused to scratch calculations, then exclaimed, "This date is more than ten years past."

"And you say you are this Kereth," the fair-ward began, but was interrupted by a rumbling bass voice whose owner shouldered his way to the front of the crowd.

"Young Kereth! Is the word true? Mistress Eldrianza dead, and you to take up her cards?"

Kereth stared at the man, trying to recall if he had ever seen him before. He saw a stocky, middle-aged man with close-cropped gray hair dressed in serviceable clothes. Kereth knew instantly that the man was a complete stranger. His shrewd, good-humored face was unremarkable until one saw the eyes—one cool gray, the other warm amber.

The combination was startling. Kereth tried to collect his wits. This stranger was acting as if they knew one another. Kereth decided to test him as an ally. "Yes," Kereth said, "Eldrianza is dead."

The fair-ward swung up his quarterstaff to keep the newcomer back a pace. "Who are you? Do you speak in favor of this man?"

"I do speak for Kereth. Many here know me." The man flourished his left hand so that gold discs seemed to flare for an instant between the fingers. "I am Prann the conjurer, attached to Nasik's stall over there, near where Eldrianza's was to be. I expected to help Kereth set up her stall."

The fair-ward lowered his staff. "So you have witnessed them working together. Would she likely leave her goods and license to this lad?"

Prann nodded with conviction. "Most likely. Kereth was a son to Eldrianza, in all but blood."

The fair-ward considered both of them and the restive line jostling behind them, waiting to have their licenses approved. "I hold you responsible for him, Prann," he warned. "If he causes trouble, you are involved as well."

Prann smiled. "I take his part gladly. Let us move along, then? Be sure to pack away your license, Kereth, and the mistress's piece of silk."

Kereth felt as if he were being swept along by an unexpected current. He managed to retrieve his license and the silk, scramble back aboard the wagon, and follow Prann's directions to a narrow alley beside a ramshackle stall on the edge of the section dealing in animals—a not impressive section. Prann jumped down from the wagon and began unloading. The momentum of habit, plus Prann's help, carried Kereth through the familiar tasks.

By the time they paused to rest, the stall had been transformed into a reasonable place of shelter and, on the inside, a relatively quiet haven suited for Eldrianza's readings. Kereth couldn't stop expecting her to raise the inner hangings and take her place on the reader's cushion. She insisted on blue-and-green hangings; dark enough to conceal travel stains, but lending an open, outside feeling to the reading area. Eldrianza preferred that to the more popular black, red, or purple hangings favored, she sniffed, by scoundrels and tricksters trying to impress and awe the ignorant. While candles provided the necessary light, she invariably put out a few small lamps burning sweet oil. They were unobtrusive, but Kereth realized now as he placed them that he had always associated the faint scent with her readings. But she wasn't there, and she wouldn't be coming. His bleak mood spilled into words. "It should be raining," he muttered. "It ought to be darker, colder." Kereth flinched from Prann's reassuring hand. He had almost forgotten the conjurer.

Prann's tone was sympathetic, but brisk. "She's gone, lad. You have to make your own life now. Take things as they are, that's the best way."

Restless, Kereth paced the restricted area. "Why did you speak for me to the fair-ward? I've never seen you before."

Prann leaned back against the cushions arranged for the customers. "I must admit it was a whim," he said frankly. "Fair-wards and rules are all well enough—things would be in a grand tangle without them—but when I heard your license being challenged, I thought the least I could do was put in a word on your side." He twiddled his fingers and looked as surprised as Kereth when an egg appeared in his hand. "Fancy that. It is past time we had some food. You didn't stop to eat this morning, I suspect?"

Kereth shrugged. He didn't remember. Food hadn't mattered much these last few days.

Prann carefully set the egg aside and stood up. "I'll find something to sustain us while we get better acquainted. Wait here."

He was back shortly with a woven basket packed with warm bread, links of sausage, and a flask of ale. Kereth found he was hungrier than he had thought. While they ate, Prann related his own recent misfortunes. The minor wizard he had been assisting at another fair had proved to have talents more theatrical than professional. When he clashed with a better skilled competitor, the outcome was melancholy. "Transformed my poor master into a toad." Prann sighed. "I was vexed. What good is it to be assistant to a toad?"

Kereth eyed Prann narrowly, suspecting that he was being teased. "Good only if the toad retains his magical powers, I should think," he ventured.

"Ah, but my master's powers, such as they were, had been quite dispersed. I carried him to the nearest marsh and left him in the company of the local toads."

"Did you find another wizard to take his place?" Kereth asked.

"Not yet. I live by my fingers." Prann plucked a gold disc from the air. "Folk enjoy such display, and pay enough for me to live in a quiet fashion. But what of yourself? Do you read the cards like your late mistress?"

This was a question that had been weighing on him since Eldrianza died. Kereth hesitated. "I intend to try," he said.

Prann surveyed him critically. "You will have to dress more imposingly. What robes do you have?"

Kereth thought. "There's my travel cloak."

"No, no, you need something . . . noteworthy. I recall seeing Eldrianza once at the Pedregal Fair in a blue robe dark as midnight."

"Her special gown," Kereth agreed.

Again a tide of memories swelled, but Prann dispelled them by bouncing to his feet and exclaiming, "Where is her clothes chest, then? We should find something in it to suit you."

Prann delved industriously in the chest once they matched the key to the heavy lock. "Here you are," he boomed, extracting a soft robe of wildflower blue. "Brings out the color of your eyes. Now for a . . . ah, just the thing. I've seen caps like this far to the East." He pulled out a close-fitting cap so tightly worked with silver thread that it looked like fine chain mail. Prann adjusted it over Kereth's dark hair, draped the robe around him, and stood back a step. "Bright, but not too grand. Now I shall bring back a fortune seeker."

"But—" protested Kereth.

"Think on your cards," Prann interrupted. "Think on the mage of rings. Think on all the cards of rings, for that matter; you need to draw hither all the money you can." With a swirl of hangings, he was gone into the golden afternoon.

Kereth stared after him for a moment, then put the blue gown on properly. Sitting down, he ran his fingers over the intricate carvings that decorated Eldrianza's card box. Outside pressures—other people, even the friendly Prann—seemed to be shaping his life. He could still assert himself, break away from the imposed pattern and strike out on a new course. And yet, something had always drawn him to the cards. Many times, as a child, Kereth had watched Eldrianza lay out a reading for him. The sunken tower invariably showed among the great cards. Its watery greens and blues had appealed to him, brightened by flickering lines of silver fish. The chief meaning associated with the sunken tower was talents submerged, talents that might or might not be developed. Eldrianza had said that the link was through Kereth's mother, but she didn't know when or if Kereth's talents would surface. Intensely practical, she had insisted that Kereth should learn to read and write. Whenever he complained, she would say, "Be silent and learn. You can always earn your bread as a scribe if you can do nothing else."

He *could* be a scribe, he supposed. It was worth more thought, but he suddenly heard voices, including Prann's. Today—now—Kereth must be the reader. He settled himself on Eldrianza's blue cushion.

"Has studied the lore of the cards for many years," Prann was saying as he ushered in a short man wearing an verly ornate cloak. "Master Bost, I present you to Kereth of the Southern Glades, reader of the cards of Eldrianza. This is Master Bost, famed merchant of fine cloth."

The merchant strode importantly to the seeker's cushion and sat down, fussing with his cloak and the fat purse at his belt. Kereth decided he might as well have hired a lad to precede him, proclaiming, "Make way! My master Bost is a *busy* man!"

Kereth shuffled the cards carefully, striving to project a sense of calm. His years of watching Eldrianza helped to some extent, so that his voice was level when he asked, "What question do you wish to be read in the cards, Master Bost?"

Bost gestured impatiently, showing off to advantage

several fine rings. "My business is, of course, always foremost in my mind. Tell me how my trading will fare here at Ithkar."

Kereth selected the master of rings as the symbol card to represent Bost. "Place this card before you, to stand in your stead. Now, thinking of your question, hold the deck in both hands. Keep your question in mind while I mix the cards." As he dealt the cards in Eldrianza's favorite array, Kereth named them by position. "Below you, past, present, and future; and above you, the outside influence. To the side, in rank, threatening factors, favorable factors, and the outcome of your question."

A reluctant client, Bost fidgeted. Kereth tried to ignore all distractions as he turned the cards face up. He blinked at the display of swords and stars—action and conflict clamored from the swords, while chance, surprise, and the unexpected jangled from the stars. For outside influence, there was a great card, the broken cup, signifying even more confusion. Kereth touched it lightly, his finger tingling. The card showed a cracked goblet whose spilling contents obscured a page of writing. The card for the present was the ten of stars. When Kereth touched it, he had a fragmentary glimpse of a strange white creature, gone before he could properly identify it. He looked anxiously at the side cards—the threat was a reassuringly minor two of swords, the favorable factors card an encouraging eight of rings, and the outcome card an ambiguous five of stars. An impatient snort from Bost broke Kereth's concentration. He would have no time to make a reasoned narrative from the cards; it would have to be an instant summary of his impressions.

"Well? What do you see, reader?"

"I must be frank, Master Bost." Kereth decided his

best approach would be blatant honesty. "This array is itself confusing. The dominance of swords and stars indicates action and unexpected surprise. The broken cup here, representing outside influence, denotes confusion, obscuring factors at work that could be either planned or accidental."

Bost frowned doubtfully at the cards. "I deal in cloth, not confusion. What do you mean? Is something ill threatening my business?"

"The threatening factors card is quite minor," Kereth hastened to say. "The favorable factors card is most auspicious, boding well for your trade here at Ithkar."

Unconvinced, Bost demanded, "But?"

"The outcome card is not decisive," Kereth admitted. "It speaks again of chance, the unexpected."

"Bah! I did not come here to be told I am at the mercy of chance."

Kereth felt obliged to mention his one clear, if puzzling, insight. "I must tell you that I sensed in the card for present events the appearance of a creature, a rare, white—"

"Creature?" Bost surged to his feet. "An animal?"

Kereth also stood up. It was bad enough to try to talk to this self-important merchant when they were both at the same level; he refused to strain his neck looking up at Bost. "Sir, I regret that my mental glimpse was so brief I can say only that I sensed a white creature somehow associated with your present business here."

"Ridiculous. I despise animals, never let them near my goods. I am leaving." Bost fumbled in his purse and tossed a small silver coin on the cushions. "I will not recommend your 'visions' to my fellow merchants, young man. Perhaps," he snapped at Prann, "he could profit from more years of study."

The hangings were still swaying from Bost's exit when Prann calmly retrieved the coin. "Never mind, lad. For your first reading, this is no shameful fee. Come along outside and let me show you something of the fair. I know you have been here before but each year brings more changes—more dealers in all wares."

Kereth wearily pulled off the silver cap. "Thank you, no. I think I had better take Master Bost's advice and study my art more deeply."

"I fancy some sleep would do you more good," Prann said. "Lie down awhile. I'll close up the hangings so you won't be disturbed. When you waken later, we can go out for a meal."

Kereth started to object but yawned instead. Prann hustled him out of the reader's gown. A curtain of dreamless sleep fell over Kereth as soon as he stretched out.

The next thing Kereth knew, Prann was shaking his shoulder, urging him to wake up. Prann didn't pause for explanations but threw a cloak around Kereth and pushed him into the chill darkness. The conjurer was chuckling to himself, but when Kereth asked the reason, all Prann would say was, "You will see for yourself."

Kereth heard the uproar long before they entered a courtyard in the fair's middlemost section, near the area held by weavers, tailors, and cloth merchants. They had just passed through the animal dealers' section, where Kereth had heard various eerie cries of wild creatures roused by the humans' turmoil. As they rounded a corner, a crouching shape shambled in front of Kereth, who jerked back against Prann. An agitated group of torchbearers escorted by fair-wards hurried by in evident pursuit. In the wavering torchlight, Kereth verified his initial guess. "Prann, that was a stray ape!"

Prann's teeth flashed in a grin. "Apes are not the only beasts running free this night. Master Lukov, the animal dealer, has suffered a major loss of his stock. Here we are—Bost's stalls."

Kereth heard a musical squeak and saw a fast moving bundle about the size of a cat scamper past his foot. He had a brief glimpse of white, owlish eye rings and bright ruby eyes before their owner rushed nimbly up the side of a stall. An angry man erupted from Bost's doorway, exhorting his crew of retainers. "Lackwits! Clumsy dolts! I told you the ozren had to have special cages. They live to open closed latches. What apes can't open, ozren can."

Kereth peered up at the roofs with interest. He had heard of the lithe ozren with their gripping tails but had never before seen one. Now that he had, he decided they reminded him of animated ash heaps with red coals for eyes.

Bost appeared, presenting quite a different picture from the pompous master trader he had been earlier. His eyes were glazed, and his hands twitched as if he were tallying profits that were slipping through his fingers. "Surely, Master Lukov," he pleaded, "you can recapture your beasts. Those dreadful apes—my cloth—my stores . . ."

Bost's plaint was quite splendidly eclipsed by a series of eldritch shrieks from somewhere close by. Kereth felt his hair stir on the back of his neck. What living creature could possibly produce such a cry? Lukov alone seemed unimpressed; in fact, he appeared pleased. "Quick," he called to his men. "Follow me!"

Prann, Bost, and Kereth joined the chase after Lukov, who abruptly darted into one of the storage sheds lining the courtyard. When a torchboy arrived, Kereth could see that the small space was crowded with stacks of cloth in bales, rolls, and folded lengths. Bost groaned with intense feeling as he ran to catch up a length of spunfloss spread haphazardly over neighboring bundles. When he gave it a freeing tug, the weird shriek froze their blood. Bost joined in—at a far lower pitch—and dropped the cloth. There was a stirring from the upper reaches of the nearest pile, and Kereth caught his breath at the sight. Jeweled eyes glittered under an elegant ivory crest, gloriously backed by a spangled lace fan of tail feathers. Prann named the vision. "By the Lordly Ones, a white peacock!"

Lukov approached the bird cautiously, crooning soothing sounds to it. In a sudden rush and flurry of fabric, he and his helpers subdued the peacock, swathing it in folds of a most complimentary rose velvet. Bost wailed, "My best velvet!" but stood aside as Lukov bore his prize away.

Prann kindled a light before Lukov's torchboy left. He held the small lamp high so that Bost could see who they were. "And what do you say now, Master Bost? Was there or was there not a rare white creature suddenly concerned in your business, not to mention a certain amount of turmoil?"

Bost stared from Prann to Kereth. "You *did* say . . . it *was* here . . . and you did say my business would prosper." With that last thought, his voice strengthened. "It *has* attracted attention," Bost went on. "People will talk about Bost's cloth stall tomorrow. They will come to see, and many of them will surely buy." He seized Kereth's hand and pressed some coins in it. "You will ignore what I said earlier. I was mistaken. Say you bear me no ill will."

Kereth strove to keep his expression suitably severe. "I trust, in turn, Master Bost, that you will correct any wrongful impression you may have given to others concerning my skills in interpreting the cards of Eldrianza.''

"Oh, be assured I will," Bost promised.

Kereth nodded and stalked outside. On their way back, Prann was jubilant. "A fine stroke, lad. You have indeed made a notable start as a card reader."

The next morning, Bost's prediction proved to be correct. After a brief delay for the curious to survey the scene of the wild animals' depredations at Bost's stall, fairgoers strolled across to see the newly notorious card reader who had so brilliantly warned Master Bost. Some of the more curious asked Kereth for card readings, so he spent the morning busily engaged with a wide variety of questions.

It was nearing midday when a party of four merchants crowded into Kereth's stall. Three were talkative and demonstrative, but the fourth, a fair-haired man with a neat, short beard, seemed content to be a silent observer. While the talkative three argued over who should pose the first question, Kereth's glance kept returning to the quiet man. A subtle scent of spices clung to him, and he was wearing a simple silver pendant with the sign of the Three Lordly Ones.

"Come along, Emryk," one of the three called to this man. "Now that we've torn you away from the shrine, don't you want to ask some weighty questions about the spice trade?"

"You three have enough questions to occupy the reader," Emryk replied.

"Ha," scoffed another of the party. "Emryk doesn't believe in the powers of the cards. He gets all his answers from the venerable Sky Lords."

Emryk refused to be baited. "Each man chooses his

own beliefs, Delian. If you believe the cards can answer your questions, then for you, they are worth consulting.''

The third merchant demanded Kereth's attention for his question. During that reading and one for Delian, Kereth felt increasingly distracted. He sensed powerful forces swirling among them, centered somehow on Emryk. He hoped that Emryk would ask for a reading, but after Delian's question was answered, Emryk rose with the others and left the stall before Kereth could speak to him. Prann was away, so Kereth lowered the front hangings to assure himself a respite.

He felt troubled, pricked by a nagging worry he couldn't articulate. Quiet meditation should be calming, he thought, but Emryk's image intruded immediately in his mind's eye. Annoyed, but resigned, Kereth set out the master of rings as Emryk's symbol card. It was doubly appropriate, since the picture showed a fair-haired master merchant. Kereth noticed the tingling in his fingers that he associated with special insight. It was stronger than he had ever felt before. Stars, masks, and swords loomed in the array. The mage of masks and the master of masks denoted considerable influence from hidden lore, religion, possibly deceitful motives. Troubling as those regular suit cards were, the great cards were positively daunting. The cryptic rider in black could mean either good or ill fortune stemming from a meeting with a stranger, as well as outside forces bent upon the questioner; the aura clinging to it boded no good for Emryk. The card of the flaming tree showed a stately tree afire in all its branches, but not consumed. It indicated endurance, survival against odds, and knowledge to be applied to a serious problem. The last card almost scorched Kereth's fingers when he turned it over: the stone beast. No man knew what sort of creature was depicted on this card, but its meaning was fatally clear. It was always a warning of severe danger to the questioner.

The harder Kereth strove to make sense of the reading, the more urgently he felt compelled to find and warn Emryk. He was fastening his cloak when a new thought paralyzed him. Warn Emryk of what, exactly? The cards hadn't conveyed a specific message. Kereth couldn't say, "Beware of a tall assassin with a scarred right cheek," or, "Brigands await you on the third bridge over the Ith." He shook himself and hurried outside. It didn't matter that the warning wasn't precise. It was urgent and *real*, and however Emryk received it, Kereth was obliged to deliver it.

Fortunately, Prann had made him a rough sketch map of the fair area so that Kereth could find his way about. Since Emryk was a dealer in rare spices, he should be located somewhere between the midsection of weavers and cookshops and the temple outskirts. Kereth was squeezing through a throng of fairgoers in the animal dealers' area when a flash of silver beneath a fair beard caught his eye. It was Emryk, watching a performance by trained ozren. Kereth elbowed his way closer until he could call, "Master Emryk! A word concerning your business!"

Emryk turned at the sound of his name and waved to Kereth to retreat to a less crowded spot. The merchant looked wary, an understandable reaction to being hailed in a crowd by a near stranger. "What news of my business?" Emryk asked, then examined Kereth closer. "Aren't you the card reader?"

Kereth met the merchant's keen gaze. "Sir, I must warn you," he said earnestly. "While you were in my stall, I felt a strong sense of apprehension, so I consulted the cards after you left to see if I could name my fears."

He had Emryk's total attention. "Warn me? Of what?"

"The cards were not specific," Kereth admitted, "but you must believe me. There is a danger to your person, and within present time." By the cards, he thought, this is all too vague, but Emryk *must* listen.

Suspicion heightened the merchant's wariness. "You wish a fee for further illumination?" Emryk asked coldly.

Kereth was startled. "No! It's just that I had to find you—the sense of danger was so immediate."

Emryk's hand moved from his purse farther along his belt, where his dagger would normally be. Like all weapons, it had been confiscated by the fair-wards when the merchant had entered the fairgrounds. "I see," Emryk said in a puzzled tone. "You merely desire to warn me of some unspecified danger that looms over me and may strike soon."

At least he had grasped that much, Kereth thought, relieved. "Yes, sir."

"But you can't say more?"

"Only that a stranger may be involved, and . . ." Kereth hesitated, then recalled the potent cards of masks. "Religion may well be concerned."

Emryk touched his pendant. "As you see, I am a believer in the Three Lordly Ones. You may know," he added ruefully, "our belief is much scorned nowadays, even though this fair centers on our most sacred shrine. I have been away from Ithkar for several years, so my current opportunity for frequent pilgrimage to the shrine is all the more precious. Still, I can imagine no possible danger touching me from that quarter. My business would be a far likelier target. Some of my spices are valuable beyond price." He peered sharply at Kereth. "You called out to me concerning my business. What about it?"

"I was only trying to get your attention," Kereth confessed. "Every merchant thinks first of his goods."

Emryk smiled. "So we do, as I suppose you do regarding your cards, for they are your goods. Well, do not worry about me, master reader. I have stout lads to help me guard my stores, and I shall tell the fair-wards to keep special watch around my stall. Now I must return there myself, before my apprentice mixes the yellow peppercorns with the powdered tacq root." He clapped a friendly hand on Kereth's shoulder and turned to go.

Kereth longed to seize the merchant, but he knew he had too little substance to convince a nonreader. If only Emryk had *felt* the cards. Kereth sighed and started back toward the square, failing to notice a hooded figure that slipped from a shadowed doorway to follow Emryk.

The rain that Kereth had thought appropriate to mourn Eldrianza's death began to fall at twilight and showed no signs of stopping for the convenience of the evening trade. Prann arrived at Kereth's stall, bringing an odd but tasty collection of food for a late supper. His tent, he announced, leaked miserably, so if Kereth had no objection, he would spend the night. Still brooding over his failure to convince Emryk, Kereth absently said he didn't care where Prann slept. The conjurer waited for any further explanation, but Kereth wasn't in a communicative mood. Soon after eating, both men wrapped themselves in their cloaks and settled down to sleep, lulled by the drumming rain.

This time it was Kereth shaking Prann out of solid slumber. "Prann! Wake up—we've got to find Emryk!"

From long years of practice, Prann had trained himself to waken instantly, ready to fight or run. As he pulled on his boots, he asked, "Who is this Emryk, and why do we have to find him in the middle of a rainy night?"

Kereth fretted at the delay. "He was one of the merchants who came this afternoon while you were away. Oh, do hurry—it could be vital!"

"Your cards told you," Prann guessed. "Ah, the rain has stopped," he observed as they bolted outside. "That's one blessing to be thankful for. Where do we look for this Emryk?"

"Among the spice merchants' stalls." Kereth related his afternoon's unsuccessful efforts to warn Emryk of impending danger.

Prann listened carefully, grumbling only once when he stepped into a particularly deep puddle.

"I wasn't dreaming," Kereth insisted. "Just before I woke you, I had a sharp, certain feeling that Emryk was in danger *now,* and I had to help him."

"What kind of danger? Did you sense any details?"

"That's what he asked," said Kereth, exasperated. "My problem is that the cards weren't specific."

"The important question," Prann asserted firmly, "is do we know enough to call the fair-wards?"

Kereth shook his head. "I couldn't even get Emryk to believe me. What chance would I have with the fair-wards?"

"None," Prann agreed cheerfully. "We shall simply have to constitute a rescue party of two. An unarmed rescue party, I regret to say, but any adversaries should be at a similar disadvantage . . . I hope. You smell that scent? Spices." Prann took an appreciative sniff. "Shawl flower, lantern tree, tacq root. I'll ask about Emryk's stall." He poked his head inside a parked wagon and emerged with the needed directions.

Emryk's stall was tightly closed for the night and, they soon found, guarded by an alert retainer. At first the guard wasn't willing to say where Emryk was, but he finally disclosed that his master had gone to spend the night with Delian, a fellow spice merchant.

"I've seen him," Kereth exclaimed. "He was one of Emryk's companions this afternoon. I heard him say he had taken his regular space next to the outer temple wall, beside the money-changers."

"That area is no more than four alleys away," Prann confirmed. "Confound this wet! I knew I should have had these boots mended sooner."

Delian's stall was dark and unguarded. Prann rattled the door to no effect. He called Delian's name, then bellowed it. "Much of this," he muttered, "and we shall have the fair-wards down upon ourselves."

Kereth pressed his ear to the door. "Someone's snoring inside," he said.

A lounger who had been watching them with mounting interest crossed the alley. "If you're looking for the owner here, you've come a bit late. I saw him going off with friends a short while ago, probably for a drink, although I'd say he'd had too much to drink already from the way they had to carry him along." Their informant didn't smell or look all that sober himself.

"Where did they go?" asked Kereth, just as Prann chimed in, "How many were with him?"

The lounger pondered, counted several fingers, and announced, "Three, plus the fellow they were carrying—that makes four. They were going down that way, toward the shrine."

Prann slipped the man a coin and hurried to catch up with Kereth, who had immediately run in the direction pointed out. In this older quarter near the temple, the alleys were even narrower and more twisting. Kereth despaired of finding their quarry, but Prann snatched at his cloak and whispered, "Listen." The fairgrounds were seldom completely quiet, but Kereth heard the scrape of boots on wet cobblestones. He lunged ahead around a corner wall, then stopped short. By the flickering light of scattered cressets maintained by the fair-wards, Kereth could just distinguish a slow-moving clot of shadows half-way down an otherwise deserted alley.

"Quietly," warned Prann. "We may be able to surprise them."

The clot resolved into two dark-cloaked figures half-carrying a third, while a hooded fourth figure strode impatiently ahead. The hooded figure, turning back to exhort his fellows, caught sight of Kereth and Prann. They heard his voice, harshly accented.

"Put him *down*, dolts—gently, don't mark him! He must be presentable. Now rid us of those two spies."

"Two against two, is it?" said Prann, flexing his fingers. "Not such poor odds."

The two hirelings advanced warily toward them, drawing long daggers that had been concealed in their sleeves.

"Unarmed, I see," growled Prann. "Where are the wretched fair-wards when you need them? Guard yourself, lad."

Kereth was suddenly grateful for the season he'd taken wrestling lessons from a traveling acrobat. The assailant who rushed him met a firm grasp that converted alarmingly into a hard toss to the cobbles. He clambered to his feet and circled Kereth at a more respectful distance. Prann, too, seemed well schooled in rough-and-tumble tactics. After kicking his opponent smartly on the shin, Prann pounced on the man, and they lurched across the alley, grappling for best advantage.

Kereth risked a glance where the helpless victim had

been abandoned in the gutter. The hooded man was trying to balance Emryk—Kereth thought he could recognize the merchant's lolling head—on his back. "Prann," Kereth shouted. "They're trying to take Emryk away!"

His momentary distraction gave his own assailant an opening. Kereth felt a sharp pain along his ribs as the thrusting dagger tore through his cloak. In a desperate reflex swing, he smacked the flat of his hand across his assailant's ear. Yelping, the man fell back. Kereth raced down the alley after the retreating hooded man.

Although there were footsteps behind him, Kereth ignored them, concentrating on the burdened figure ahead. Why not try a bluff? he thought, and called, "We're coming, Emryk! The rest of your lads were close behind us, and should be here at any time."

The hooded man faltered, his victim slipping from his back. He whirled to face Kereth, flourishing a metal-tipped baton. "Meddler," he snarled. "You know not where you interfere. Begone!"

It was Kereth's turn to keep his distance. "The fair-wards will be coming, too," he asserted with more confidence than he truly felt. "You'll have to cut other purses than Master Emryk's—or were you seeking a ransom?"

"Purses? Ransom? Our stakes are far higher than such trifles, as you will learn to your cost." The hooded man darted forward a step and lashed out with his baton. Kereth threw up his left arm in time to protect his face, but the impact jarred him to his boots. Through tears of pain, he saw the hooded man gesture. A dull red glow radiated from the baton's tip, but no light penetrated the shadow beneath the man's hood.

Confused shouting broke out near the forward end of the alley. Fair-wards? Kereth's throbbing arm competed for his attention with the burning cut over his ribs. The hooded man emitted a night creature's keen cry. His hirelings staggered up, one supporting the other.

"Disperse," hissed the hooded man. "For now, we are betrayed." With a swirl of his cloak, he scurried toward a metal gate set in one alley wall. He touched his glowing baton tip to the lock, wrenched open the gate, and plunged through it into the building beyond.

Kereth tried to intercept the two hirelings, but the more agile one shoved his injured companion ahead and eluded Kereth's reach. The hubbub from the alley juncture clarified into distinct speech. Prann *had* roused out the fair-wards. Kereth abruptly sat on the dank cobblestones. Loss of blood, he thought, and wondered if he was fainting.

Prann was suddenly beside him, urging him to drink from a leather flask. "Restorative," Prann explained. Kereth dutifully swallowed the tangy liquid and felt much more alert. He caught Prann's sleeve.

"The hooded man went through that gate," Kereth reported. "The other two ran back the way we came. I tried to stop them, but . . ."

"No matter," Prann replied. "The fair-wards are searching this area. They'll find any folk out of place, hooded or no. Let us see to Master Emryk, if you have your breath back. Wait—your side—blood?"

"A dagger thrust," Kereth said, rising stiffly to his feet. "Mere scratch."

Prann looked dubious but followed Kereth across the alley.

"It is Emryk," Kereth confirmed, bending over the merchant's body. He recoiled, gasping. "Prann! What is that smell?"

"By the Lordly Ones," Prann swore, "he's been stupefied by zuthrumb. Quick, pull that cloth away from his mouth. Hold your breath until I can toss it away.''

The merchant groaned and plucked feebly at his face.

''You're safe now,'' Prann assured him. ''Friends! Take some deep breaths.''

Emryk complied, shuddered, and sat up, holding on to Prann's supporting arm. A pair of fair-wards arrived just in time for Prann to supervise their carrying Emryk back to his stall. Nearly recovered by then, Emryk promised to make a full statement to the fair-wards in the morning. The two who had assisted bustled back to rejoin their fellows in the search around Delian's stall area. In parting, they announced that Master Delian and his servant had also been subdued with zuthrumb, which explained why they'd been snoring.

Emryk invited Kereth and Prann into his living quarters and insisted on having Kereth's wound seen to before they discussed the night's events. Emryk then dismissed his servant and poured spiced wine for the three of them.

''I do not know why you came after me this night,'' Emryk began, ''but I thank the Lordly Ones that you did.''

''It was the cards, Master Emryk,'' Prann asserted before Kereth could speak. ''Kereth told me how he tried to warn you this afternoon, and tonight he had an even stronger premonition.''

Emryk nodded respectfully at Kereth. ''I approve of your persistence. Your cards must have given you a truthful glimpse of my near future, for I had no sooner settled down with Master Delian than a hooded man demanded entry on a matter of vital importance. He claimed to be distressed about a missing shipment of spices from the East. Only one of Delian's servants was with us, and when two more strange men rushed in and seized the servant and me, flinging those foul-smelling cloths over our faces, we had no chance to defend ourselves. The hooded man dealt likewise with Delian.''

"Could you see his face?" asked Kereth.

"No, he kept his hood low, saying he suffered from an affliction of the eyes and could not bear bright light.''

Prann's expression was unusually grave. "I do not like this business of hoods and the East. Did this man wear any jewelry?''

"It is odd you should mention that," said Emryk, frowning. "As you see, I always wear the sign of the Lordly Ones, and I note from habit whether others do the same. When the hooded man attacked Delian, an amulet swung out of his robe in view for an instant. Its metal was new to me—a sullen, reddish silver, but dull and heavy in appearance. There was a sign on it, so.'' He dipped a finger in his wine and drew a figure on the tabletop.

Kereth had just decided it was a stylized mask when, to his surprise, Prann gasped and gripped his own chest. Realizing he had drawn their attention, Prann drew from beneath his jerkin a silver medal that matched Emryk's. "Like you, sir," he said gruffly, "I respect the Lordly Ones. It is not always wise to display such an earnest of one's beliefs where I go, so I keep my devotions to myself.''

Emryk's hand sketched a salute. "The prudent man knows his surroundings. But why did you react so strongly to this drawing of mine? I have never seen its like before, although I travel widely.''

Prann's voice was grim. "Not much in the East, I'll wager. That cursed sign is one of those favored by the followers of Thotharn, the hooded one, who spawn in the eastern swamps. No good man knows much of them, but there is a taint of vileness about them, from what little I have heard.''

Emryk looked baffled. ''What possible interest could such people have in me?''

Kereth suddenly remembered the first orders he'd heard from the hooded man. ''Prann, didn't you hear the hooded man say of Emryk that he mustn't be marked, that he had to be . . . what was the word?''

'' 'Presentable,' '' said Prann. ''Yes, I recall it well.''

Emryk shivered, although the room was pleasantly warm. ''They must have wanted to present me somewhere, then,'' he concluded. ''Somewhere I would be known or recognized.''

''The shrine!'' Kereth grasped an idea. ''Do you have any special privileges, perhaps admittance to otherwise inaccessible areas?''

''It is true that I am honored to attend certain ceremonies not open to all pilgrims,'' Emryk conceded. ''But surely, if these people are as evil as you suggest, Prann, they would shun our sacred truths.''

Prann frowned. ''Consider, though, if they schemed to discredit our faith. It has been under attack for years, as you well know. They could not send an imposter, nor could they tamper with a priest. What cleverer way to gain entrance to the sacred core than by compelling a trusted layman to spy for them?''

''That is an ill thought, Master Prann.'' Emryk was deeply disturbed. ''We must warn the seniors of the temple at once.''

''These Thotharn folk seem both determined and devious,'' said Kereth. ''Will they not try again to capture you or some other unwary pilgrim before your priests can react?''

Emryk shook his head. ''The foolish may scorn the

Lordly Ones, but they have power to protect their sacred places and their believers. A timely warning such as ours will armor our cause against any future assaults. But we cannot wait until morning. Master Prann, will you come with me?''

"I will." Prann stood up. "What of our young friend?''

"Kereth," Emryk said, "I now see that your intervention has been vital from the first. The Lordly Ones move mysteriously, but always for the good. Will you testify how your cards led you to warn me?''

Kereth felt like a very small fish caught up in a current beyond his strength to master. And yet, he realized, no matter what the currents of life, choice remained: to fight or be swept along. He *could* choose. Eldrianza had been right. The cards—his cards, now—would help him find his way. At the thought of the cards, the image of a great card glowed in his mind's eye: the twin suns. It was another of the curious cards that seemed related to other places, for it showed two blue-tinged suns casting their strange light on a maze of paths. It signified opportunity, but also a difficult choice. The vision blurred, and he saw his friends were waiting for his answer. These *were* friends, who truly cared what became of him. He wasn't to be alone anymore.

"I shall gladly go with you," Kereth said, extending a hand to each. "My late mistress left me her cards and said I must find my talent. I begin to think perhaps I have.''

Prann grasped Kereth's hand warmly and managed to look uncharacteristically shy. "If you have room in your stall for a helper of various practical skills—" he began in a tentative voice.

"I do," Kereth interrupted, "provided that you bring me no toads.''

Emryk was looking baffled again, but Prann laughed

aloud and said, "My old master is content to be in his swamp; not *all* swamps are wicked places. Come along, both of you, before the fair-wards arrive to pester Master Emryk for his statement. We had best get the senior priests' advice on how much to tell of our joint encounter. There, look at that sky. It will be a clear day, I'll wager."

Kereth followed them into the predawn quiet. It was good to belong again, to care for others and in turn be cared for. As for himself, he thought, the sunken tower had begun to rise.

THE MARBLED HORN

Lynn Ward

It's not that I don't like Ithkar, or its people. The town has its pleasures, and the great fair is a pure delight. But gods, these townfolk do things in the most complicated manner! Let me tell you. . . .

I came to Ithkar on a late summer morning, sitting wide-eyed and gawking next to Master Hesketh on the seat of his wagon. We'd followed the trade route from just below the Galzar Pass and the wild lands I called home to the softer climate of the South.

Now Hesketh urged his ancient mare to pull the wagon through narrow, cobbled streets, coaxing and cursing the beast by turns. And no matter most doors and windows were shuttered still, or that those folk we passed were sleepy and surly. It all glowed in naive eyes.

"The fairgrounds, girl," Hasketh said, nudging me for emphasis.

280

"Then that's the temple," I answered, pointing to a building so large and grand it seemed a sculptured mountain. "Gods," I breathed.

"Gods for somebody, Gray Eyes. Remember, yours are as good as theirs." Hesketh's voice was mildly acid. The gaunt, grizzled artisan gave respect to little. "And there's our destination." He prodded the mare into a trot across a great open area, several acres of it, that showed signs of the fair to come. Some of the permanent buildings showed new coats of paint or wore banners, while the skeletons of temporary stalls and stores were being assembled. Here people showed more humor and industry, pausing to exchange greetings with my master.

"Against this wall," Hesketh said, halting us outside a tavern already patronized. I stepped down and moved to help him. He seemed frailer this day. "Like my horse and my wagon, I groan and tremble," he often said with rue. "Begin setting up," he ordered. "I'll be back soon." Straightening his creaking bones carefully, he went into the tavern.

I pulled the pieces of ramshackle framework and awning from the wagon-bed and put it together, with the help of wooden pegs and a mallet. It was old but serviceable, with that wall for support.

Stepping back to study my handiwork. I hit something solid that yelped. I turned and saw a paunchy, balding man favoring his stomach. "Watch where you're going, boy," he began. Fell silent, staring at my breasts. "Girl?"

"My apprentice, Gray Eyes." Hesketh was right behind the paunchy one looking rather amused. "Gray Eyes, this is Tabor the tavern-keeper. You'll come to know him well."

"A barbarian girl," the taverner mused, eyes generally fixed on my upper half. "I've heard these northerners are tall and well made, but when I saw this great thing in leather at work, I thought it was a lad." He spoke as if I were a prize dog he admired.

I looked down at him. Indeed, these townfolk were punier than my kind and not so fair of face. And given to rudeness? I picked the paunchy one up and set him aside, and resumed my work. Ignoring his indignation.

"She speaks the same tongue as we do," Hesketh told Tabor. "I wouldn't treat her as deaf or stupid."

"My apologies," Tabor offered, finally looking at my face. "You're a comely one, and I see why you are called Gray Eyes."

"Clever of you." Hesketh clapped a hand on Tabor's shoulder. "And to anticipate your other questions, yes, she is truly my apprentice, and no, she does not share my bed."

"I meant no harm." Tabor was sheepish.

"It was your own foot you stuck in your mouth and bit on." Hesketh chuckled. "Help me unpack, Gray Eyes."

"Did you bring it?" Tabor interrupted. "This year I may have enough coin to buy it."

"I brought it. Not that you or anyone else will ever get it from me." Hesketh spoke with a strut. "Gray Eyes!"

"I have it." I fetched my master's pride, wrapped in velvet.

Hesketh was a worker in horn and bone, making containers for unguents and combs and utensils and whatnot. And, in his prime, far more: a maker of forms and figures you'd swear needed finely grained wood or soft metals to be so cunningly crafted. But age had plundered his skills and strength until that was a matter for memory. What remained was the marbled horn.

Translucent, with a rippling stripe of black (hence its name), the horn came from a breed of antelope long vanished from the land. As a boy Hesketh had found one of the creatures dead of a fall and taken its horn. As a man, he'd given it the shape of its owner, carving the grace of startled flight.

He laid it on the stall counter for us to admire, and the ghost of handsome youth infused his sere face. It softened his temper to see it, and forced me to humility.

Too, the horn's siren song called others, some fairgoers who jostled about to admire. "Will you even set a price?" Tabor asked on behalf of himself and of everyone else.

Hesketh grinned his refusal, rewrapped his treasure, and shooed everyone away.

I took a step back and once again trod on someone. Turned, to behold a pleasant sight. A young man fully my height and more, with flaxen hair and light eyes like mine. His dress and the quarterstaff he carried showed him as one of the fair-wards. "Hello," he said.

"Hello," I answered. Then, "Is something wrong?" After all, he was one of those keepers of the law during the Ithkar Fair.

"If there was, he'd not be so polite about it," my master said. "I think he's come to welcome a pretty girl to the fair. New this year, lad?"

"Yes, sir. My name is Dann." He extended a hand to Hesketh, then to me.

"I am called Gray Eyes." I shook hands while wishing I wore something besides grimy trail clothes. And I asked, "Are you northern?"

"Sort of; my mother's people came from above the Galzar. I'm town bred, but I've visited there."

We took a few seconds to stare at one another, not too lustfully, and then Hesketh dropped a small purse into my palm. "You've work to do."

"Yes, master." Back to earth.

"Go to the temple and find whoever's collecting the second gift offering this year and pay him. Then stake out our place at the campgrounds. And find yourelf a seamstress and get yourself a dress or skirts so you won't look like some kind of wild woman. Take the horse and wagon with you." He had pulled out his large display box. "It's early yet, but some of my regular customers may come by." The horn was out of sight; once more, he was all bristle. "And don't forget what I told you of magic ways hereabouts."

"Yes, master." Oh, he had drilled that into me. Things magical in Ithkar were the province of the great wizards and their merchant patrons, and then only magic of the right-hand path. If one conjured wrongfully, a trial was the least payment for it. Spells might be cast for protection and little more.

"Maybe I can help," Dann said. "Show her where everything is and all." Hesketh cocked an eyebrow. "Haven't you got rounds to make?"

"The fair opens officially tomorrow, sir. Today the wards were told to familiarize ourselves with the grounds and be of help to folk come early."

The old artisan harrumphed. "Um. I'm glad I've lost interest in women. It saves much time and energy."

I should have bitten my tongue. Instead, I loosed it. "But master, you did not lose interest in me until I threw you twice from your own wagon."

He harrumphed again, while Dann choked on a laugh and I wished not for the first time I might curb my northern bluntness.

"Go on about your—my—business," Hesketh growled. "With no further comment. Keep whatever company you choose."

So he set to displaying his sample wares, and I to doing my errands, leading the sleepy mare. Walking with me, Dann was not derelict. His eyes made good search of the street and the people on it. "Where to, first?" he asked. "The temple?"

"The campgrounds. I want to tend to the horse."

He nodded agreement. Then his gaze fell on a beggar squatting next to a building just across from the tavern. Stride quickening, he went to the man, a scrawny creature with unkempt black hair held to his head by the blindfold he wore. "You'd be Twill?" Dann asked the beggar, tapping the man's bowl with his staff.

"Aye, master. Have you a coin for a hungry blind man?" He held the bowl up.

"I'm a fair-ward, Dann by name. And I was told yours, Twill. You will abide by the same rules this year as last. Stay a little hungry."

The man's mouth thinned from its servile smile. "Aye." He lowered the bowl.

Dann rejoined me, and answered my puzzled look. "He's not really blind. There're a few beggars at the fair who are really able-bodied. We have to watch them."

"Is that allowed?"

"Not officially. He should be hauled into the fair-courts and whipped and expelled from town."

"Why not, then?"

"Because he'd probably return and start waylaying honest citizens or take money from beggars who are truly crippled. The fair is so crowded, Gray Eyes, we can't be everywhere. Letting men like that beg, or gamble—if they're not too greedy—keeps them from worse wrongs. There'll be enough throat cutters to catch as it is." He eyed me. "You see the sense of it, don't you?"

"I see the sense of it, but not the justice."

"This is the town, Gray Eyes. Nothing goes in straight lines."

I was soon to discover how right he was. But for the moment, I spent a bright morning amiably enough. At the campgrounds I claimed a place and left the mare and wagon secured. The tax was paid to a man at the temple who was only moderately officious. And the seamstress I found measured my dimensions without comment on the size of barbarian women.

It was almost midday when we returned to Tabor's tavern. By then, Dann was holding my hand and promising to show me all the fair's marvels. I was wondering how he'd find time to chase me and an assortment of black-guards as well. I was also wondering about lunch.

Then Hesketh's stall came into view, and my good humor died. It was empty and bare, which made me think only the worst. My master had been steadily weakening of late.

"We'll ask Tabor," Dann said, pulling me after him into the tavern. Inside, we blinked against the dimness, seeing first only a barmaid serving one customer. Then the taverner stepped through a curtained doorway at the back of the room, saw us, and made a summoning gesture.

Hesketh lay sleeping on a cot in that room, which

looked to be where Tabor did his bookkeeping. "He had some kind of seizure," the tavern-keeper whispered. "He seemed drunk—I know he wasn't—and was propped against the wall outside. One of my customers told me."

I knelt next to the old man, felt his face, and listened to his breathing. The skin was cool, the breaths regular. This time, he'd likely be all right. "It was probably the sun," I told the others.

"Do you want a heal-all?" Dann asked.

"No." I stood up. "He's seen heal-alls. They all tell him his sickness is age." I looked at Tabor. "Thank you for helping him."

"He is my friend," the rotund man said.

Dann spoke tentatively. "Gray Eyes, I'm sorry but I must leave. Walking with you outside I could keep an eye on things, but I can't stay in here."

"See to your rounds," I said quietly. "And I'll see to my master."

The fair-ward squeezed my arm in sympathy, promised to return when he could, and left.

Suddenly, belatedly, I remembered. "Where is the display box?"

"Under the cot." Tabor raised it up and put it on the table.

I began rummaging through the box. Stopped, struck cold with apprehension, then rummaged further in a frenzy.

The taverner peered 'round my elbow. "What's wrong?"

I showed him the velvet that had swaddled the horn; now it held nothing. "It's not there." Fearful, I looked over my shoulder at Hesketh. Merciful gods, he still slept.

Tabor wrung the velvet with fat fingers, face such a ruin of sorrow I wasted no time suspecting him. "It was folded when I put it in there. And the carving is so small . . ."

He shook his head. "Gods! Hesketh was always showing it to people, but he was never careless."

"He was also ill. He knows little of what goes on around him when these fits come." Trying to sort my wits, I made another useless examination of the sample box and then shut it. "I will have to find the horn." Small words, large task.

"We'll tell the fair-wards," Tabor said quietly. "Though it may do little good."

"Why?" My voice jumped more than it should, stirring Hesketh briefly. I stepped out into the tavern's main room, Tabor following. "Why?" I asked again.

"They're good at some things—stopping fights, or catching a thief who's been seen and gone running, or arresting people accused of wrongful conjuring. But call them after the fact and they can do little. In a couple of days the fair will be bursting at the seams, and they'll have no time to investigate."

"The fair isn't bursting now!"

"Ithkar has a dozen places a thief might sell a carving like that. No; we can do little but hope a chance remark about the horn will reach a fair-ward's ears. Or someone's ears."

"Then I'll try myself to find it." These town-bred were soft in the head as well as the belly; it seemed. How did he know there was no trail without looking?

"How?"

"I have no plan yet. But I must find the horn. And because I must, I will."

Tabor shrugged. "Suit yourself. But this place isn't your mountainland. Things are complicated here. Go tell the fair-wards. Mayhap they'll catch a rumor to follow. I'll deal with Hesketh somehow—but after he wakes he'll find out what has happened." He was mournful with good reason; his was the harder task.

"At least wait until I return."

"And when will that be?"

"No later than sunset, whether I'm successful or not."

"Sunset," he agreed. "Oh, you do know about the laws against wrongful conjuring? If you do any during your . . . hunt, you'll risk a trial by the fair-court."

A small thing to worry on, compared to Hesketh's wrath. "I will be back," I said, and strode into the noon sunlight.

And stood there a moment, paralyzed with puzzling and mocked by my own boldness. Where did I go, whom did I talk to? Looking about the sprawl of fairground, still lightly populated by artisans and a few buyers, I saw one apparent fixture of the place. The not-so-blind beggar Twill. Himself a crooked piece of the evidently bent social fabric of Ithkar.

Feeling in my pockets—those travel leathers were damp with my own perspiration—I felt some of the coins Hesketh had given me. He had been generous, and because the seamstress would take payment after I received my new clothes, I had a goodly piece of change yet. I walked over to Twill, emptied the entire sum into his bowl, then hid in a nearby alley. Watching, and wagering on his curiosity and greed.

The beggar's fingers curled spiderlike around the bowl, feeling the coins. Then the blindfolded head turned slightly right and left; that cloth was perhaps porous enough to see through, and he wanted no witnesses. Finally one finger raised the edge of the cloth, so that a healthy eye might see his largesse.

"Is there enough money to work a miracle?" I asked, leaving my hiding place. "Can you now see?" I sank to one knee in front of him, enjoying his slack-jawed surprise.

He scuttled back, but not so quickly I couldn't retrieve what I'd dropped in the bowl. His hands started to contest mine, then dropped. "Beg pardon—my lady? I do not understand you. Why jest with a poor blind man?"

"The jest is yours, played on those who truly are blind. You can see, I know. Are not such things frowned on here in Ithkar? What is the penalty?"

For answer, he gibbered. "You were with that fair-ward today, weren't you? What do you want of me? I keep my side of the bargain. I beg little. Do you want payment? . . ." And so on, in a ramble of surprise and surliness.

That he stumbled over his own guilt made my conniving easier. So much the better. Conniving has an acrid taste. "I want information, that is all."

"What?"

"From here you have a good view of Tabor's tavern across the way, don't you?"

He blinked; I could see that through the cloth close-up. Which meant he in turn did have quite a view.

"You can see it, can't you?" I repeated.

He answered cautiously. "If I could, what might I have seen?"

"The old man in that stall. Any customers he had. And anyone thieving from him."

"Him? He wasn't there long. He looked sick, or maybe drunk. Someone took him inside. Took his wares inside, too."

"Before that, beggar. I'm after a thief."

"There were only two people who stopped by. The daughter of Elidor and her maid."

"Elidor?"

"He's one of the horse-traders who come to the fair every year. It was his daughter and the maid. A girl named Alla." Twill scratched his chin with a grimy finger. "After they left, I recall, Alla ran back for a moment, and then left in a hurry. She could have taken something. Your old man was sitting down and looking sick by then."

"Where might I find this Alla?"

Twill chuckled. "What do you mean to do with her?"

"Confront her."

The chuckle became a whoop. "You're a simple-minded one. She belongs to Elidor's household, and he is one of the richest men in these parts."

"And this Elidor is above Ithkar's law?"

"Not exactly. What you must do is talk nicely to the magistrate about your problem—and of course you'd have my word as foolproof evidence—and mayhap he'll invite Elidor to dinner and politely ask that his servant be sent before the court. And be sure to bring me there to give my foolproof evidence."

Well, why shouldn't Elidor treat the law lightly? It seemed everyone else in Ithkar did. I pondered a moment, and decided to do the same. I had some skill in magic to help me with my hunt; I would use it. "Where is this Alla?" I asked again. "And how might I know her?"

"She's at Elidor's tents, I suppose. He has a liking for gold, and that's what color they are. Alla—she's like a walking batch of sausages. With some shape, but too much of it. Her hair is very black." He was growing querulous. "Now, will you be off? People might hear us. Or do you mean to have me beaten for being a fake?" He sounded familiar with the experience.

I stood up, leaving one coin in his bowl. "For your information."

"You won't be able to just walk into Elidor's tents, fool. His guards will see you and toss you out!"

"They'll see less of me than you have," I promised, and left him to his chicanery. On the way to do my own.

It took longer than I wanted to reach Elidor's tents. I can never travel swiftly when I'm invisible.

I found a shadow and said the conjure words easily enough, but from then on, gods, what obstacles there were. The trouble is, it is all up to you not to get bumped into or stepped on, or do any bumping and stepping of your own. No one else will make way, obviously. As it was, I had a cartwheel and the ox pulling it both do their best to demolish my right foot.

Elidor's tents, athrong with evidently half the population of Ithkar, were little improvement. I threaded as best I could in and around men in long robes, stepping on one or two—whose owners turned around and almost elbowed me in the process—and enduring more foot stomping. Still, it was better than the street. There, I'd just missed dishwater and a chamber pot's contents coming from windows overhead.

Through a maze of silks I wandered, until the woman I sought did me the favor of crossing my path. Plump, giggling, and raven-haired, she was whispering with an elegant lady who moved with the confidence of wealth. Elidor's daughter, most likely.

"Have a good time, Alla," the confident one said. "I intend to do the same this eve."

"Yes, my lady," the maid replied, flouncing past me.

I followed the flounce back outside; she did at least clear a path. Then the ducking, dodging, and jostling resumed, while I followed her away from the fairgrounds and into a warren of narrow byways.

Breathless and bruised, I watched gratefully as she went up the back steps of what looked to be an inn on the far side of a market square. When she did not come out after several minutes, I crossed the square and went up the stairs.

A doorway opened into a dim hall lined with other doors. In general, it was quiet. Good. Otherwise, I'd raise a ruckus intruding on innocent people. Innocent of the horn's theft, at any rate.

I tiptoed down the hall, listening for giggles. Third door on the left, there the sound was in all its blessed silliness. A deeper undertone of male amusement answered it. I said the words to make myself visible, and knocked.

Alla opened it, eyes round with questioning. Behind her, a man stood hastily pulling his shirt on.

"Good day," I said to them both. "I wish to speak with Alla."

"Not my wife," the man muttered. "No. Who are you?!"

The two of them shrank together. "Maybe your wife sent her," Alla quavered.

So they had their secrets, too. Maybe that would make Alla babble as Twill had. "This will only take a moment."

"No!" Alla burrowed into the man's chest.

I lifted her away and into the hall. She rather whimpered. "Help me," she pleaded to the man.

He took an unenthusiastic step forward.

"You had best bolt the door after me," I said. "You don't know what I might do to you."

He shut himself in. Hastily.

"Did you see that?" Alla sputtered, fear turning to indignation. "He shut me out with no thought but his own safety." She hit the door with her fist. "You, you'd better keep me out, coward—"

I covered her mouth in midsputter. "Enough. I've some business with you. Quiet now, and listen." When she stilled, I dropped my hand. "You went with your mistress, the daugher of Elidor, to the fairgrounds this morning, didn't you?"

She whimpered once more, then nodded her head.

"Did the lady wish to buy there a piece of marbled horn carved in the shape of an antelope?"

Another nod, a shaky one.

"The man who owned it would not sell, I know. Did the Lady Elidor tell you to steal it?"

We were back to indignation, the maid's cheeks puffed as a chipmunk's. "Gods strike you down!" She remembered to keep her voice low. "A daughter of Elidor would not steal! I took it." Now she winced. "Oh, woe. It was yours? Oh, woe."

"Oh, be quiet. So you took it. Where is it, then?"

"I gave it to the lady. She had given me coin to buy it; told me to return and cajole the old man further."

"And you took it? With your lady's money as well?"

She swallowed. "You were sent by my lady?"

"No." These townfolk thought always in tangles, it seemed. "But I want the carving."

She shook her head convulsively. "I don't have it. I gave it to the lady." Her words were hurried.

I groaned. "Then she has the horn?"

"Oh, not anymore. She gave it to Calvar straightaway."

"Who is Calvar?"

"Her lover. He is one of my lord's horse-trainers."

"Then would I find him in the lady's company?"

"Oh, no." She leaned closer, as if exchanging a confidence. "Elidor would not approve of the lady's choice—a common horse-trainer." She giggled. "My lady wants only a little pleasure before she marries the man her father chooses."

"She is pledged to another?"

"Oh, no. She will bed no more with Calvar when that happens."

All one might want to know about Elidor's household and be afraid to ask, I was learning. "Where do I find Calvar? How will I know him?"

"Today he is seeing to preparing the pens for my lord's animals. Wherever that is on the fairgrounds, I guess. As to finding him—he's a handsome thing, with a great mass of curly hair. And a scar here." She touched her cheekbone. "From a horse's hoof. It's small but deep."

Back to the fairgrounds, then. I took a step back, my interest in Alla done with. "So I will find this Calvar."

"And will you tell my lady what I did, taking her coin and all?" Belatedly, she decided to be alarmed.

"I want only to find the horn."

She sighed with relief when I started back down the hallway. Behind me, though, I heard plump fists whacking the door, and now an argument raging from both sides of it as to her lover's manhood, or lack thereof. It appeared I had blighted the sausage's romance.

The maid spoke truth about Calvar. Early afternoon— did Hesketh sleep yet? I wondered—and I stood sneezing at the dust Elidor's animals and men raised. Striding through the commotion, the handsome curly-haired trainer did an efficient job.

He glanced at me in passing, and registered no pleasure. Understandable. With lank hair and reddened face and a layering of town grime, I was beginning to feel rather like a horse myself. I was also tired, hungry, and thirsty. It might be said my disposition was suffering as well.

Forcing patience, I waited until Calvar finished his portion of things and left the others. I followed him around a wall of baled hay, grateful for the temporary privacy it offered. When he stopped at a well serving part of the fairgrounds and started raising the bucket, I caught up with him. "Calvar, the horse-trainer?" I asked.

He set the bucket on the edge of the well and squinted at me. "Elidor's household isn't hiring now."

Well, sometimes northerners came south as trainers of horses and mules. "I've come on another matter, sir," I enlightened him.

He squinted again; the sun was to my back. "Oh, you're a girl?" And, I think, he snickered.

Oh, my disposition was definitely suffering. "You have in your possession a piece of marbled horn. It was a gift from the daughter of Elidor." I spoke through gritted teeth.

"I don't know what you mean," he said warily. "I barely know the lady. She has never given me anything." Perhaps he thought me his liege's spy or emissary, and a peculiar choice at that.

"She gave you the horn without knowing it was stolen. I mean to retrieve it."

"I have no horn of any kind, woman. And I have nothing more to say to you." He started to walk by me, and paid for his carelessness.

I grabbed his right wrist with one hand and the elbow joint with the other, twisting his arm against his back, then threw my weight behind the hold and forced him against the well. He hit with a thud that drove the air from his lungs. So much the better. He was too strong to hold for long, even though he moaned at the pain.

"Where is the horn?" I demanded.

"You're mad," he wheezed, and made a mighty effort to squirm away. "Barbarian cow!"

I changed my two-handed grip to one, and used the free hand to hold his belt and haul him partway over the rim of the well. "Tell me, or you'll go headfirst in there!" My disposition was positively vile.

"No, no. I'll tell you." That breathlessness was my ally; neither wind nor leverage was easily available to him. "Only let me down."

"Talk first."

"I don't have it anymore. I lost it gambling."

I leaned on him, collapsing with frustration. "Who has it now?"

"A boy named Laws. He works at a tavern on the fairgrounds. Tabor's. Do you know it?"

I let him up, wondering how much I resembled a dog chasing its tail. "You gambled the horn away?" Gods!

He worked his arm gingerly, not yet interested in retaliation, while leaning heavily against the well. "I thought to win a goodly purse with it, and have both the horn and coin to buy a gift for my lady. She is fond of expensive gifts."

It made sense, in a pretzeled way. "How would I know this boy Laws?"

"When I saw him today he wore a bright red shirt. He

wears a lot of red." Calvar regained some surliness. "And
if you say anything about this, I'll deny it—deny I know
the lady."

"I only want the horn," I reiterated, and turned away
from him. And heard him mutter once more about barbarian cows. Did I say he leaned heavily against the well? He
did, so much so it was easy to kick his feet out from under
him. He landed in a patch of muddy earth, and mired
himself badly.

"What's a barbarian who knows no better to do?" I
asked. Then went on my way, chuckling. Just a little.

I saw the boy Laws, red-shirted and lanky, running in
and out of Tabor's. The taverner had set a bench and table
outside, leaving the youth in charge of it.

Poor lad, he had shoulders rather narrow for the irate
mischief I meant to heap on him. I conjured myself invisible,
then moved to stand behind him. He had delivered a
tankard of ale to a customer and lingered for conversation.

"Laws," I whispered in his ear.

"What?" He started, and looked about him.

The customer peered upward. "What's the matter?"

"Uh, nothing." He settled down a bit.

"Laws, beware the carved horn," I whispered in the
other ear, and jumped away as he spun around.

"Did you hear that?" the boy asked.

The customer shook his head.

A third whispering, and the boy made another circle,
while casting hostile glances at baffled onlookers. "Magic,"
he decided out loud, but to no on in particular. "It's
magic."

"Boy, have you been sampling Tabor's brew?" one
asked.

"No. But it's . . . Someone's talking to me. I think."
He scratched his head, deciding whether or not to be
alarmed.

"Do not tamper with magic," I whispered, dodging
toward him and then away. "Beware of the carved horn."

Laws decided to be alarmed, and flapped his hands
about. I evaded the motion, and he dealt a glancing blow
to another customer, who did not appreciate it.

"I didn't touch you," Laws protested. "Ohhh." A little
wild-eyed, he went into the tavern and blurted an excuse
for leaving, came outside, and scurried away.

I followed him down an alley to a tiny room attached to
a warehouse. He hurried inside—evidently it was where he
lived—and tried slamming the door behind him. I narrowly avoided a broken nose for my trouble, letting it
sway on rusty hinges.

The youth did not notice at first, only burrowed under a
sleeping pallet and brought out a small sack. And from the
sack, he brought out the horn. He sat cross-legged on the
pallet and contemplated it a moment. As did I, though
with pleasure rather than befuddlement.

"Does it seem strange to hear a voice from thin air
giving you warning?" I asked.

He swallowed the horn in one fist. "Where are you?
Are you a wizard? It's not in my mind I'm hearing this."

His bold curiosity was admirable. Trouble was, I wanted
him more timid. "The horn was stolen, and passed through
many hands before yours. The owner wants it returned."

"Is it a wizard's?"

"I'd rather not say."

"Are you a wizard?"

"I'd rather not say. Laws, put the carving on the cot

and return to work. You want no dealings with it.'' I tried to imply menace.

''No.'' He thrust it inside his shirt, and punched at the air in front of him. ''I won it honestly. If it's magical, that makes it worth much.'' Reaching the edge of his daring, he retreated a little. ''I did win it without cheating. I haven't cheated since I was thrashed a threemonth past.'' An idea struck him. ''But I will sell it to you.''

Impertinent twit. ''Put the horn down, boy.''

''Be fair, wizard.''

Fair? And who'd been fair with me, in this trail of deceitful foolishness I'd followed? ''Put it down.''

''No.'' He ventured an adolescent smirk. ''I want payment.''

Payment? I upended him and sat on his prostrate form and wrested the horn away. It was not difficult; he hadn't half Calvar's strength.

''Let me up,'' he demanded.

I pocketed Hesketh's treasure, pausing a moment to caress its grace, and considered letting the squirmer up. But my game needed more playing. I did not want him encountering my master with the horn and opening that brash mouth. Besides, I was rather enjoying myself. ''Do you think so lightly of magicking you would set yourself against a demon?''

''What demon?'' he squeaked.

''The owner of the horn. You've seen him. Hesketh, the artisan.''

''That sick old man? He couldn't hurt anybody.''

''Not in that form. But in his true form . . . oh, my. It frightens me to think of it.''

''What form?'' His defiance wilted a bit.

"I'd rather not say—and I am his trusted servant. But it makes the gods shudder."

"Really?"

"As surely as I am invisible. It's not only your grand wizards who know magic in Ithkar. I was hard-pressed to persuade him to let me retrieve the horn without bloodshed."

"Bloodshed," Laws echoed weakly. "What might he do to me?"

"I'd rather not say."

He had one protest left. "How do I know all this is the truth?"

"Do you want to risk your life to verify it?"

The fanciful tale took root in his mind. "I meant no harm."

"And no harm will be returned. I will say this; when next you see Hesketh or anyone who is apprenticed to him, treat them only as they seem to be."

"I will. I promise."

I stood then, and hauled him up by one arm. "Now return to your work. And say nothing of this."

He left, on quite shaky legs.

When I returned to the tavern, late afternoon was stretching shadow everywhere, and Laws was back to serving customers outside.

Inside, I met with a sight enough to slough off much of the day's fatigue. Hesketh and Tabor sat at a table, eating bread and soup. Dann was with them.

Tabor looked up, expression uncertain. Dann smiled. Old Hesketh harrumphed, sounding as if he'd made good recovery. "You smell gamy, Gray Eyes. What have you been up to?" he asked.

"Doing your business, master. It took longer than I planned." I made a reassuring nod of my head to Tabor.

"I was asking Master Hesketh if I might escort you this evening," Dann said. "Are you hungry?"

"Famished," I answered. I'd have to be careful not to eat Dann out of a month's pay.

"It's all right with me," Hesketh interjected. "If she's back to open up tomorrow." He rose, accepting Tabor's arm for support. "Get my box and blanket, Gray Eyes. Show me where the wagon is."

"Yes, master." I hurried into the room where he had slept, snuck the horn into its velvet inside the box, and returned, carrying it and the blanket. I said nothing of his illness. He was better, and in his stubborn pride never wanted to speak of his frailty.

"Do you want me to meet you at the campsite?" Dann asked.

"Give me a while to clean up and change clothes," I answered. "I've only another leather shirt and breeches like these, though."

Dann had no objection. "I'll take my leave and make my own self respectable." He was out the door in a stride.

Master Hesketh and I left the tavern, while I offered another reassuring expression to Tabor. He stayed at the table, looking quite relieved.

On our way, we passed Laws, who stopped and studied us. And said nothing. I gave him my most gracious smile.

I thought of Dann, and of the marbled horn safe where it belonged. As I said, townfolk do things in the most complicated ways. As I also said—anticipating the evening—Ithkar does have its pleasures, too.

BIOGRAPHICAL NOTES

Having been born in Georgia, Mildred Downey Broxon has lived over most of the North and South American continents. She has worked as an industrial painter, special teacher, and psychiatric nurse, having degrees in both psychology and nursing. After her first story was published in 1972, she served two terms as vice-president of the Science-Fiction Writers of America. She is also a member of the Society for Creative Anachronism and the Mystery Story Writers of America. Her many interests reach from Irish mythology and history to gourmet cooking and world travel. The widow of Dr. William Broxon, she lives in the Ballard area of Seattle surrounded by books, cats, and seven typewriters.

The name Lin Carter has been associated with the fantasy field for a number of years. Not only has he been responsible for editing collections of little known or near forgotten works of an older day, in the volumes *Dragons, Elves, and Heroes* and *Golden Cities Far*, but he has also written such critical studies as *The Young Magicians*. He has created a hero of his own, Thonger of Lemuria, and has collaborated with Sprague de Camp on Conan tales. It is fitting that this master of fantasy by represented at Ithkar Fair; who has a better right to attend?

Marylois Dunn is new to the fantasy field, though she has written extensively in the genres of mysteries and books for younger readers. Living in Texas, she is a lover of the outdoors, a planter and harvester of herbs and miniature roses. She also has a taste for and practices photography and needle art. Her latest book is a collaboration with Ardath Mayhar.

George Alec Effinger says that he has been translated and published on every continent except Antarctica since he began writing in 1970. His hobby is collecting, but he insists that his life is relatively colorless, having included no bizarre jobs nor spectacular action. But ill health has not kept him from having at least eleven novels now "in the works."

Gregory Frost is a graduate of the well-known Clarion Writers' Workshop. His first novel was published by Ace in 1984, and he has written a number of short stories for such magazines as *Twilight Zone*, *Fantasy and Science Fiction*, and *Asimov's Science Fiction*. He now lives with his wife, Mara, in eastern Tennessee.

In "real life" Joseph Green is the associate editor of the Kennedy Space Center's employee newspaper—*Spaceport News*. Florida born, he roamed the country for two decades installing Bomarc and then Minutemen missile bases. Known primarily as a writer of "hard" science fiction, he is the author of five novels and some sixty-five short stories, novelettes, and science articles. He now makes his home on Merritt Island in Florida, where he often collaborates with his wife, Patrice. They share household life with two children, three cats, and one grandmother.

After growing up in the South, Linda Haldeman now lives in western Pennsylvania and teaches at Indiana University of Pennsylvania. She has published three novels and uses fairy tales and folklore as bases for the other worlds she writes about.

Shariann Lewitt's education has covered a wide field from an MFA in playwriting to actual "digs" as a practical archaeologist. Her first play was produced in New York when she was nineteen. Her first novel has just been issued by Ace, and she pleads guilty to also being an aviation buff, a balletomane, and a downhill skier.

R. A. Lafferty began to write in his forties, after having first established an electrical business. He states that he has done little exciting enough to generate a biography but says that his usual life as a Catholic, conservative but independent political believer, and short-story writer has been happier than that of most people he knows.

Brad Linaweaver, a free-lance journalist since 1975, broke into the science-fiction field in 1980 with a short story in

Fantastic. Some three years later, his story in *Amazing*, "Moon of Ice," was nominated for the Nebula and is now being expanded into a novel. He has taught creative writing and has stories coming up in other anthologies.

A. R. Major spent two years with the 101st Airborne Division, ETO, as a machine gunner and forty-two years as a Southern Baptist pastor, including three and a half years in Brazil as a missionary. His hobbies include collecting and reading science fiction, painting, fencing, and archery. He also writes for a local newspaper.

Mary H. Schaub is a college-trained mathematician who worked as a corporation bookkeeper until 1971. She has had stories published in *Analog* and *Galileo*, as well as in anthologies. Her reading ranges from the *Wall Street Journal* to historical and mystery novels, and she says that her own book collection weighs down the house against any blows that may be delivered by North Carolina hurricanes.

Lynn Ward lives with a roommate who is a self-confessed Trekkie and also three cats, one of whom thinks she owns Lynn. Lynn's hobbies are questioning authority and the martial arts. She works in a school district as a speech language pathologist "surrounded by mundanes." Her mentor is Ardath Mayhar, who told her about *Magic in Ithkar* in the first place. Her favorites are Ardath Mayhar, Ursula Le Guin, and James Tiptree, Jr. "The Marbled Horn" is her fourth sale, but her first big one—the others were to semipros. She's been active in SF fandom for eight years. Her first novel is now under consideration at a publishing house, and she is halfway through her second.

ANDRÉ NORTON

GORDON R. DICKSON

☐	53567-7	Hoka! (with Poul Anderson)	$2.75
	53568-5		Canada $3.25
☐	48537-9	Sleepwalker's World	$2.50
☐	48580-8	The Outposter	$2.95
☐	48525-5	Planet Run	$2.75
		with Keith Laumer	
☐	48556-5	The Pritcher Mass	$2.75
☐	48576-X	The Man From Earth	$2.95
☐	53562-6	The Last Master	$2.95
	53563-4		Canada $3.50

Buy them at your local bookstore or use this handy coupon:
Clip and mail this page with your order

TOR BOOKS—Reader Service Dept.
P.O. Box 690, Rockville Centre, N.Y. 11571

Please send me the book(s) I have checked above. I am enclosing
$_____ (please add $1.00 to cover postage and handling).
Send check or money order only—no cash or C.O.D.'s.

Mr./Mrs./Miss _____
Address _____
City _____ State/Zip _____
Please allow six weeks for delivery. Prices subject to change without
notice.

POUL ANDERSON
Winner of 7 Hugos and 3 Nebulas